JUST A LITTLE DANGER

MERRY FARMER

JUST A LITTLE DANGER

Copyright ©2020 by Merry Farmer

This book is licensed for your personal enjoyment only. This book may not be re-sold or given away to other people. If you would like to share this book with another person, please purchase an additional copy for each recipient. If you're reading this book and did not purchase it, or it was not purchased for your use only, then please return to your digital retailer and purchase your own copy. Thank you for respecting the hard work of this author.

This book is a work of fiction. Names, characters, places, and incidents are products of the author's imagination or are used fictitiously. Any resemblance to actual events or locales or persons, living or dead, is entirely coincidental.

Cover design by Erin Dameron-Hill (the miracle-worker)

ASIN: B08777DH4S

Paperback ISBN: 9798655358997

Click here for a complete list of other works by Merry Farmer.

If you'd like to be the first to learn about when the next books in the series come out and more, please sign up for my newsletter here: http://eepurl.com/RQ-KX

❦ Created with Vellum

CHAPTER 1

LONDON – MAY, 1890

*L*ondon in the summer was one of the most miserable places Metropolitan Police officer Patrick Wrexham could think to be, but it was where he, and countless others, were forced to stay while the loftier members of British society, the toffs and the nobs, buggered off to the country. There were still a few weeks of balmy weather to go before the heat and the stink set in, but as Patrick strode from Whitehall, across Trafalgar Square, and on to The City, he spotted more than a few carriages laden with baggage carrying relieved ladies away from the most miserable place on earth.

It was just his luck that the most miserable place on earth was his home, and had been for his whole life. That didn't mean that a single soul whom he passed on his journey knew who he was, however. His fellow pedestrians barely saw him, in spite of his crisp, clean uniform. Few men bothered to step out of his way, in spite of his burly build and above average height. Patrick stepped out of their way instead, wanting nothing more than to reach his destination as quickly as possible without drawing attention.

The sooner he reached the law offices of Dandie & Wirth, the better. For the last few weeks, Patrick had been involved with the indomitable team of David Wirth and Lionel Mercer as they investigated a child kidnapping and human trafficking ring. The very thought of the ring turned Patrick's stomach and had him clenching his jaw. It was horrific enough that anyone would kidnap children and sell them into slavery—both at home and abroad, if the information David and Lionel had been able to collect was right. It was worse that the kidnappers preyed on the poorest strata of society, children whom no one cared about and whose lives were miserable enough already. Patrick knew that kind of misery all too well. It had been a part of him for as long as he could remember.

He rested a hand instinctively on the small pouch attached to his belt, as if it contained a hoard of precious jewels. In fact, it held half a hard sausage and a heel of bread, but as far as Patrick was concerned, that was worth more than the crown jewels. He knew what it was like to be a starving child, so desperate for the tiniest morsel of food that he would have done anything, gone with anyone, just to ease the gnawing in his belly. He had no doubt that whoever was luring the most vulnerable children of London into a life of horror barely had to lift a finger to carry out their evil deeds. The callousness of the kidnappers made their deeds even blacker in Patrick's mind.

The worst part of all was that the more information uncovered about the kidnapping ring—by David and Lionel, but also by others, including Joe Logan, whose sister, Lily, was one of the children who had been taken— the more apparent it was that the ringleaders of the entire, sordid operation were noblemen. Not just any noblemen, but those with titles that set them far above even their peers.

In short, the men responsible for the destruction of young and innocent lives were untouchable. All the same, Patrick was determined to bring them to justice.

Whether it was the inner heat of his fury or the way his thoughts had him scowling like a dragon about to breathe fire, more than a few of his fellow pedestrians suddenly seemed to notice him and jump out of his way. A pair of well-born ladies even gasped and dashed quickly to the other side of the street as though he would eat them alive. Their reaction only depressed Patrick, dampening his fierce expression as he walked on. The ladies likely feared for their virtue in the face of a man of his size, but they had less than nothing to worry about. Patrick had never been interested in women of any sort a day in his life, aside from having them as friends. If growing up in the orphanage hadn't destroyed any possibility of him trusting another soul, he would have banded together with the gang of older girls who always seemed to get the better of the tyrants who ran the place. But no, he'd learned early on it was better to trust no one and to fend for himself.

He reached for his pouch of food once again, then jerked his hand away as soon as he realized what he'd done. Shame twisted his gut. He had to remind himself that he had a steady job making decent money, that he hadn't gone hungry for years, and that even if something catastrophic did happen to him, he could rely on The Brotherhood to help him out. Not that he had been able to bring himself to set foot inside The Chameleon Club—the central social location of most Brotherhood activity—more than a handful of times, let alone ask anyone for help. It was a miracle he'd let David Wirth convince him to join The Brotherhood in the first place. The organization was for men who loved other men. Patrick didn't consider himself capable of loving anyone.

He was saved from the downward spiral of his thoughts as he reached the plain, grey stone building that housed the law offices of Dandie & Wirth. The building itself represented confidence and competence, and it put Patrick at ease. Concentrating on vile kidnappers and corrupters of the innocent was far more palatable to him than dwelling on the darkness in his own soul.

The main room of the office was empty when he stepped in. Something about the place always set Patrick at ease, in spite of the intensity of the sort of work David and Lionel did. It was decorated in calming shades of lavender, with rich, warm wooden shelves lining three walls, a large mahogany desk directly opposite the door, and curtains that would have been more at home in a lady's boudoir than a law office. Two leather sofas sat facing each other in the center of the room over an oriental carpet. The room always smelled of tea and cakes, as well as some sort of spicy cologne that fired Patrick's blood, no matter how hard he tried to deny the carnal side of his nature.

"Hello?" he asked, glancing around.

A moment later, Lionel Mercer strode out of the back office. "Why, hello, Officer Wrexham." He greeted Patrick with a smile, thrusting out his hand as he approached.

Patrick cleared his throat, feeling himself flush, as he took Lionel's hand. The man was unnerving. He had a lithe, almost delicate build, but one handshake was enough to prove to anyone that he had more power in his little finger than even Patrick, with all his muscle, had in his entire body. Lionel was dressed like a fashion plate in a blue waistcoat that set off the vibrant blue of his eyes. His lips were soft and sensual, and almost always curved into a secret smile. Not a hair on his head was out of place, which made Patrick feel like a hulk by comparison.

"Tea?" Lionel asked, walking past Patrick to the stove in the corner of the room.

Patrick cleared his throat, swiped his hat from his head, and asked, "Is David in?" He cursed his voice for cracking and rushed on with, "He'll want to hear what I've uncovered."

David came out of his office. "What have you uncovered?" Patrick noted that he was flushed and had a somewhat distracted air about him. It was enough to make him wonder what he and Lionel had been doing in the office moments before, but seeing as that was none of his business, he pushed the thought out of his mind.

Patrick shook David's hand once he approached. It was far less unnerving than greeting Lionel, which shifted him back to business.

"I've had reports that Chisolm is back in England," he said. "Though I haven't been able to locate exactly where he is yet."

"That's more than we knew about the man yesterday." David smiled encouragingly. "By any chance have Joe Logan and Alistair Bevan returned as well?" he asked Lionel.

"Not yet," Lionel answered, bringing Patrick a steaming cup of tea. "It seems there were some difficulties along the border between France and Spain."

Patrick's brow inched up as he took the offered tea. He had forgotten Lord Farnham and his valet had left for a holiday in Spain when Farnham's father, Lord Winslow, who was reportedly quite ill, had left with his wife and other son for their country estate.

"If they can't get home that way, they need to find another," David said. "The sooner we talk to Joe about his sister, the sooner we'll be able to unravel another part of this mystery."

"About the man with the lion?" Patrick asked.

As part of their mission to a cotton mill in Leicestershire, Stephen Siddel and Lord Hillsboro had stumbled across Lily Logan. The poor girl had been sold into prostitution, but she was present at the mill when it was raided and a great many children were rescued. Lily had disappeared again before she could be freed, but not before conveying the cryptic message that "the man with the lion" was responsible for the entire trafficking ring. She'd been confident that her brother would know whom she was talking about. Unfortunately, the rest of them didn't.

"Precisely." David nodded. "I can't help but think that finding the man with the lion, whoever or whatever that is, is the key to unraveling this whole thing."

"And nobody else has a clue who the man with the lion is?" Patrick asked, his heart sinking. Every new revelation in the investigation brought them one step closer to solving the whole thing while pushing them two steps back.

"Nobody," Lionel answered, brow furrowed in frustration.

"That's not true."

They all snapped to face the door as none other than Everett Jewel, the famous actor, swept into the room, making an entrance as grand as any he might make on the London stage. Patrick's heart dropped into a whirlpool of butterflies in his stomach, and his cock jumped as though it would stand up to give the glorious man a standing ovation. The reaction was so sudden and so visceral that he nearly dropped his tea. He did the only thing he could think of to hide his sudden attack of nerves and the flush he was certain painted his face by taking a long drink from his cup, even though it was so hot it scalded his tongue. The pain might help him control his body's reaction to Jewel, but probably not.

"I know who the man with the lion is," Jewel said, marching to stand in the center of the room, his back straight and his eyes ablaze with intrigue.

He wore a suit every bit as fashionable as Lionel's and every bit as eccentric, except where Lionel wore muted, pastel tones that blended with his naturally pale coloring, Jewel wore a maroon jacket and vivid green tie that practically screamed for attention. Jewel's eyes were outlined with kohl, as though he'd forgotten to remove his stage make-up, that accentuated eyes so blue they were nearly violet. They were a stunning contrast to his black hair and would almost have made him seem feminine, if not for his carefully trimmed beard and moustache.

Rather than breezing on to reveal who the man with the lion was, Jewel turned to Patrick. His eyes narrowed mischievously, and he broke into a grin that showed off his surprisingly straight and white teeth. "Hello," he practically purred, inching closer to Patrick and extending a hand. "I don't believe we've met. Everett Jewel. And you are?"

Patrick's mouth dropped open, but not a sound came out. He knew good and well who Jewel was. He'd spent far more than he wanted to admit on tickets to the theater to watch Jewel perform night after night. He'd skulked in the back of the crowd at The Cock and Bear pub—where Jewel often went after shows to continue entertaining a certain type of crowd with ribald songs and other theatrics after shows—more times than he could count. His face heated even more at the inconvenient memory of how many nights he'd lain awake in bed, stroking himself like a madman, while imagining what Jewel must look like naked.

Lionel's derisive snort spared Patrick from the embarrassment of attempting to form words to reply to his idol. "Is it impossible for you to walk into a room without demanding every man drop to their knees and suck your cock?"

"Lionel!" David glowered at him.

Jewel merely turned his saucy grin on Lionel. "Wishful thinking, eh, Lionel?" He sauntered closer to Lionel, arched one eyebrow, and grabbed the bulge in his trousers. "I'm always ready to go when you are." Lionel sniffed and turned away, but before he could say anything, Jewel continued with, "Oh, that's right. You're out of the game at the moment." Jewel glanced back to Patrick as though they were the best of friends. "More like sour grapes because he couldn't get what he wanted, if you ask me."

"I could have, and I *have* had, any man I want,"

Lionel snapped, far less composed than Patrick had ever seen the enigmatic man.

"Except me," Jewel answered with a shrug. He shifted to stand by Patrick's side. "He's still bitter about that," he said with off-handed arrogance.

"You always were a delusional ass." Lionel crossed his arms and tilted his chin up, but his pale cheeks were flushed scarlet. "And you are forgetting our very real history."

David cleared his throat, sending a withering look to both Jewel and Lionel. "There's no time for the two of you to play Who Has the Bigger Dick, and no one cares anyhow."

"We both know who would win in any case," Jewel commented to Patrick in a low, teasing voice.

Patrick nearly choked on his tea. His trousers were uncommonly tight.

David held up a hand to both Jewel and Lionel, as though they'd both made a ribald comment and needed to be stopped. "Children are being snatched from the streets and sold into slavery, but by all means, if the two of you believe your pitiful rivalry is more important…."

Lionel lowered his chin by a fraction, a stony look of contrition hardening his features. "Fine. If you believe you know who the man with the lion is, then by all means, enlighten us."

Jewel shifted his weight, glanced to Patrick, then said, "Isn't it obvious? It's Barnaby Adler."

Lionel's expression hardly changed.

David rubbed his chin. "We've considered Adler," he said. "We know Adler is involved. His name was on several of the papers we retrieved from Chisolm's house last month."

"It couldn't be him," Lionel said, jaw tight. "He's a tradesman at best. Men like Chisolm and Eastleigh would never stoop low enough to take orders from him."

"Adler has a tattoo of a lion on his chest," Jewel said, his cocky, teasing demeanor turning dead serious. "And I know as well as anyone just what he's capable of when it comes to stealing children and twisting innocence."

The tension between the other three men grew so palpable that it put Patrick off the rest of his tea. Lionel seemed suddenly unwilling to look at Jewel, whereas David glanced to him with a look that could only be described as pity. A thousand possibilities about what had inspired those reactions tightened Patrick's gut, but he didn't dare to voice a single one of them.

"I'm sorry." Jewel turned to Patrick, his seriousness evaporating into showmanship and flirtation once more. "I was rudely interrupted before learning your name. And I would very much like to know you. Intimately." He gazed coyly at Patrick, raising a hand to trace the insignia of his uniform over his thunderously beating heart.

"I–" Patrick's mouth fell open, but words eluded him.

"Everett, this is Officer Patrick Wrexham of the

Metropolitan Police," David introduced them. "He's been helping us with our investigation."

"A policeman," Jewel said, sucking in a breath as though aroused, and as though he hadn't been staring at Patrick's uniform the whole time. "I always did have a soft spot in my heart for a man in uniform. And a hard spot elsewhere." His gaze dropped to below Patrick's waist.

It was Patrick's bad luck that the evidence of the way Jewel aroused him was there for all to see.

Again, Lionel inadvertently saved him by snapping, "Come off it, Jewel. Wrexham is here to help with the investigation, not to suck your cock. You should be treating him with respect instead of flirting with him in this obscene way. Can't you see how uncomfortable he is?"

On second thought, perhaps Lionel hadn't saved him. Patrick would rather have sunk through the floor than been the center of attention.

David cleared his throat, visibly frustrated. "Adler is a possibility," he said, ignoring the interlude in an attempt to force the others to the matter at hand. Patrick gave him his full attention, praying it would take him out of the limelight. "We won't know the man with the lion's true identity until Joe Logan returns from Spain, though. Even then, Joe might not know what his sister was talking about. So for the time being, since we know Adler is involved anyhow, I believe it's vital we investigate him."

"Fine," Lionel said. "Wrexham can use his contacts at Scotland Yard to have the man followed."

"I know where he is," Jewel insisted, standing straighter. "Or, at least, I know where to find him."

"Then Everett will ferret out Adler," David said with an impatient nod.

"I do not want that man involved in our investigation." Lionel crossed his arms even tighter, narrowing his eyes at Jewel. "He only wants to be a part of this whole thing so that he can be the center of everyone's attention and take credit for it all in the end."

"That's a lie," Jewel said with a level of drama that even Patrick found to be too much. That bravado lessened, and Jewel's shoulders dropped, as he said, "You know why I have a vested interest in bringing anyone who would do something so vile to innocent children to justice."

Patrick expected Lionel to fire back with a snide comment. Surprisingly, the enigmatic man kept his lips pressed shut. He glanced out the window, as if recusing himself from the rest of the argument, perhaps because he knew he wouldn't win.

David let out an impatient breath and rubbed his forehead. "Wrexham and Everett can work together on this investigation."

It felt as though lightning shot through Patrick's veins. He jerked straighter, glancing sideways at Jewel. "I'm not certain that's a good idea."

"Why not?" Jewel asked, a combination of hurt and teasing in his glittering eyes. "Don't you like me?"

"I—"

"Kindly stick to the matter at hand and save your tomfoolery for later, Everett," David said, raising his voice. "I made the suggestion because the two of you make the perfect team. Wrexham is a police officer with connections at Scotland Yard. Not only does Everett have contacts none of the rest of us have, he is well-known and recognizable. His fame could open doors that would otherwise remain shut. Meanwhile, no one ever seems to notice Wrexham, even when he's standing right in front of their nose."

Patrick flinched inwardly at the all-too accurate description of himself. No one noticed him, and no one wanted him, whereas Jewel….

"He's too loud," Lionel said in a flat voice. "He'll bungle the whole thing up by signing autographs and posing for amateur photographers, thus allowing Adler, and everyone else involved, to get away scot-free."

"I will not," Jewel said, sniffing in offense.

"Wrexham will keep him in line," David said, growing visibly exhausted by their rivalry with each passing second.

"Yes," Jewel echoed in an entirely different tone of voice. "Officer Wrexham will most certainly keep me in line."

Patrick grew so hot that he feared sweat stains would

be visible under his arms and around his collar. "I'll do my best, sir." He nodded to David.

"It's settled, then," David said. "Wrexham and Everett will work together to track down Adler. At least until Joe and Alistair are able to return home. And with any luck, we'll have this whole thing solved within weeks."

CHAPTER 2

*E*verett felt as though he'd been handed a sticky, gooey treat that would leave him licking sweetness off his lips and fingers once he was done consuming it as he and Officer Patrick Wrexham left Dandie & Wirth's. Wrexham seemed to want to walk a step or two behind him as they started down the street, but Everett wasn't having any of that.

"Never skulk in the shadows, darling," he said, looping his arm through Wrexham's to stroll on as though they were two school chums. "You have as much of a right to see and be seen as the next man."

"I...do?" Wrexham mumbled.

Everett glanced to him with a grin, excitement pulsing through him. The shy ones were always the very devil once you got them in bed. He couldn't decide which he'd enjoy more, bending the muscular officer over a chair and taking him to the hilt or letting the man bugger him senseless. With any luck, he'd get a chance to do both before the next day dawned.

"I suppose lurking in the shadows comes in handy in your line of work," he said in a tone that would have been more suited to whispering sins in the deep of night.

Wrexham was charmingly flustered. He cleared his throat and pulled his arm out of Everett's but continued walking at his side as they turned a corner. "My duty is to uphold the law. I've found it easier to do that by keeping a low profile."

He was lying. Or at least he was making up stories to tell himself. Everett knew people. He knew their mannerisms and their secrets. He'd reached the heights of fame on the stage that he enjoyed by careful observation and imitation of human nature. Patrick Wrexham was as fascinating a specimen of manhood to study as any he'd ever come across. He'd known it from the moment he saw the man in David and Lionel's office.

"There's nothing wrong with your profile, sweeting," he told Wrexham in a low purr.

Wrexham's face went bright red, and if Everett wasn't mistaken, his gait became uncomfortable. Sure enough, the man's trousers bore all the signs that Everett's flirting was hitting its mark. Seeing that made Everett as randy as if they were at a Parisian cabaret.

"I'm committed to this investigation," Wrexham said, clearing his throat. "My superiors at Scotland Yard have given me leave to work with Dandie & Wirth."

"How very clever of them." Everett inched closer to him, brushing his hand along Wrexham's sleeve.

Wrexham eyed him anxiously and widened the distance between them. "The trouble with investigating noblemen is that the law protects them to a frustrating degree," he went on. "Even though Lord Chisolm's house was raided and evidence connecting him, his son, and Lord Eastleigh to the trafficking ring was discovered, no one in Scotland Yard is willing to take action."

"Yes," Everett said with a frown. "Fame, fortune, and title can cover all manner of sins." As he knew better than most. He would likely be in jail or worse if not for his fame. Accusations had certainly been made against him, but they were easy to circumvent with a quick exchange of cash and the promise of box seats to London's most sought-after theatrics. The world had never been a fair place, but sometimes that worked in one's favor.

Wrexham studied him with a pink-faced, sideways look. As soon as Everett caught him staring, he snapped his eyes forward.

"It's all right, darling," Everett teased him. "You can look all you want. I'll let you see much more, if you play your cards right."

Wrexham nearly missed a step. He coughed to cover his stumble, his face going redder than Everett thought was possible. Everett's heart swelled in his chest. The man was perfectly lovely in every way, and so much fun to play with.

"I believe David Wirth is right about Mr. Joe Logan

knowing the identity of the man with the lion," Wrexham said, his voice hoarse. He cleared his throat, then went on with, "But I think we're wise to search for this Adler person, as you suggested, for questioning at the very least."

Everett wanted to continue teasing the flustered officer, but even the mention of Adler destroyed any mirth he felt. "Adler is a snake of the lowest order," he said, feeling suddenly hollow inside. They turned another corner, but rather than continuing on the way Wrexham seemed intent to go, Everett tugged his sleeve to lead him in a different direction, toward Drury Lane. "He preys on the weak and the defenseless," he went on. The old, raw part of him that perpetually felt like an eight-year-old boy flared up, threatening to take over everything he'd worked so hard to become.

"Who is he, exactly?" Wrexham asked, staring at Everett again, but now with a curious frown. "I mean, I assume he's a procurer of some sort."

Everett huffed a humorless laugh at the characterization. "Some sort, yes." He rolled his shoulders, uncomfortable with losing the upper hand, within himself as much as in his discussion with Wrexham. "He's been snatching children off the street and selling them to the highest bidder for decades. He doesn't have to bother with snatching them most of the time. You'd be surprised at how easily desperate and unscrupulous parents will hand over their beloved offspring for a few coins and a loaf of bread."

Wrexham reached quickly for the small satchel attached to his belt. He moved his hand away again as fast as he'd reached for it, embarrassment painting his face. Everett found the whole, split-second action puzzling, but he was too consumed by his own pain to linger on it.

"I want Adler brought down, one way or another," he said. "Men like that deserve to rot in hell for what they do."

"Agreed," Wrexham said in a deadly voice.

Everett's brow shot up, and a smile spread slowly across his lips. His dear, delicious officer meant that, and not as lip service or a way to get into Everett's trousers. It sent a different sort of thrill than he was used to coursing through his blood. Perhaps he and the stolid policeman had more in common than he'd first suspected.

"I know where to start our search for Adler," he went on.

Before he could continue, a pair of well-dressed ladies with far too many ostrich feathers in their hats rushed toward him from the other side of the street. They narrowly avoided being flattened by a carriage in their rush to reach him.

"Good heavens, you're Everett Jewel," one of them squealed, stars in her eyes.

Everett instantly stood straighter and treated them to his broadest smile. "Why yes, you've found me out," he said, arching one eyebrow as though he'd planned the irritating interruption.

Out of the corner of his eye, he noticed Patrick step back, practically blending into the side of the building next to them. The admiring ladies didn't appear to notice him in the least.

"Might we have your autograph, Mr. Jewel," the second lady said breathlessly. She reached into her reticule with shaking hands, fumbling with the contents.

"I must have a pencil somewhere," the first lady said, giggling as she searched through her handbag as well.

Everett drew a pencil from the inside pocket of his jacket. "Ladies, you are in luck. I always come prepared." He peeked at Wrexham, strangely concerned with what the man might think of him for carrying around a pencil explicitly for signing autographs. But Wrexham's face was a blank mask.

"Oh, yes, lovely," the first lady continued to giggle. She drew a slip of paper from her handbag, passing it to him. "Would you?"

"It would be my pleasure," Everett said as though she'd asked him to perform cunnilingus. He scrawled his name on what appeared to be a haberdasher's bill as he cradled it in the palm of his hand. "And you, my sweet?" he asked the other lady.

"I...I don't have anything." She looked as though she might burst into tears.

"Give me your hand, darling." When the lady extended her trembling hand, he turned it over and signed his name across her white kid glove. "There you are."

The woman gasped, then burst into tears of joy, cradling her hand close. "Thank you, oh thank you."

"Now if you'll excuse me, my dears." He tucked his pencil back into his pocket and touched the brim of his hat to them.

The two ladies rushed on, glancing back over their shoulders at him several times before turning a corner. Several others along the street looked as though they might rush in to ask for his autograph as well. Everett certainly wasn't in the mood to cause a public scene, for a change. His smile dropped, and he turned to Wrexham. Something about the man's stolid stance and steady presence made him feel safe, as though the man wouldn't allow a soul to so much as lift a finger against him.

No, that wasn't right. Everett was perfectly capable of taking care of himself. More than most people knew. He'd beat the stuffing out of men who thought they could attack him for being who he was. And he refused to lower himself to the level of someone who needed something as pedestrian as help or comfort. It was arousal. That was what he felt. Wrexham was a handsome police officer with a pugilist's build. He wanted to fuck him, nothing more. He absolutely did not find the man's presence comforting. Men like him had no use for comfort, only lust and satisfaction.

"I'm surprised you didn't leap into the limelight back there," he told Wrexham as they walked on.

"Me?" Wrexham blinked in surprise. "Why would I do that?"

"Doesn't everyone love attention?" Everett shrugged.

"No."

It was Everett's turn to register surprise. "Come now." His shock melted into a sly grin. "We all want attention. We all want adoration."

Wrexham kept his mouth shut, as if he wanted to tell Everett he was high on opium but didn't dare disrespect him.

"Lionel Mercer would have eaten his heart out to snag the attention if he'd been with me," Everett said with a shrug.

"Were you lovers?" Wrexham asked quietly.

The question was so blunt that Everett laughed loud enough to draw half the eyes on the street. "Briefly," he said, though it was partially a lie. "He wishes it were more."

Everett swayed closer to Wrexham as they walked on, telling himself he was just teasing the stoic man and not desperate to feel his body close to his own. Wrexham stepped away, widening the gap between them, which made Everett frown.

"Come now," he said. "There's no use in denying you want me." He added a coy grin to his blatant overtures.

Wrexham's face went red all over again. "You may not be concerned about the Labouchere Amendment, but I am," he mumbled under his breath.

Everett snorted. "That useless piece of legislation?" They paused at the corner and checked both ways before crossing the street. "It's a useless piece of shit designed to meddle in our lives for no other reason than spite. You know they only employ it when one of our sort sets a foot out of line in other ways."

Wrexham glanced around with something close to terror in his eyes, as if everyone might hear and know and start throwing stones at them.

"You're not ashamed of who you are, are you?" Everett asked with a teasing grin.

"I'd rather stay on this side of the law," Wrexham mumbled.

"Of course you would, darling." Everett winked as they reached the opposite side of the street and continued on toward the theater where his show was being staged. "I love a bit of law myself," he went on. "Perhaps I'll have you restrain me and punish me for my sins."

Wrexham's only reaction was to harden his jaw and shift to put more distance between the two of them. Which seemed utterly odd, considering how turned on he could tell the man was.

"Or perhaps you'd like to have the shoe on the other foot, for a change?" he asked. "It must be so taxing to be the man in a position of authority all the time. I could play copper to your miscreant, if you'd like."

Wrexham cleared his throat. "I don't know what you're talking about."

The man most certainly did, but the more Everett pushed, the timider Wrexham grew. It was as scintillating as it was frustrating. Everett couldn't remember the last time his advances had been turned down so summarily. He tried inching closer to Wrexham, but that ended with Wrexham moving away so suddenly that he nearly fell off the curb into the street. Everett wanted to laugh, and to demand why Wrexham was being so difficult.

"We're here," he said as they turned into an alley and headed toward the stage door at the back of the theater. Several of the stage crew and a few of his fellow actors stood around in the growing twilight, smoking cigarettes and laughing as they took a final rest before the night's performance.

"Why are we here?" Wrexham asked as Everett marched right past the crew with waves and short helloes.

As soon as they were in the relatively dim hallway backstage, heading toward the dressing rooms, Everett glanced over his shoulder at Wrexham with a gentle laugh. "Darling, it's a Thursday night. I have a performance."

"You do?" Wrexham seemed surprised.

Everett shook his head, pushing open the door to his dressing room as they reached it. "I can't simply drop everything to chase after Adler," he said. "I have an adoring public with an insatiable appetite. They need feeding, love."

He gestured for Wrexham to enter his dressing room, and once he did, Everett shut the door behind him. Wrexham shuffled into a corner to stand at attention, which Everett found adorable. Everett tossed his hat onto his dressing table, unbuttoned his jacket, and began shedding his street clothes, all while staring Wrexham straight in the eyes.

Wrexham cleared his throat, his back going straighter, and clasped his hands in front of what Everett was certain was his growing erection. He would have looked like any other police officer set to watch over a public event, but for the pink in his cheeks and the way he deliberately avoided staring at Everett as he undressed.

Except that he couldn't help but stare once Everett pulled his shirt off over his head and unfastened his trousers. Wrexham could pretend and deny all he wanted, but the man was smitten. Everett knew adoration when he saw it, and he loved it. He bent to remove his shoes, then shucked his trousers. He was sorely tempted to remove his drawers and fondle himself for Wrexham to see. A little show before the show wouldn't do any harm. And if he were lucky, perhaps Wrexham would drop to his knees to suck him off.

That delightful thought was cut short by a knock on the door. The door opened, and the theater's stage manager popped his head into the room.

"Just thought I'd let you know that Miss Terry is ill this evening, Mr. Jewel, and her understudy, Olivia, will be going on in her stead tonight," the young man said without blinking an eye.

"Thank you, Foster." As Foster started to duck out again, Everett said, "Oh, and Foster?"

"Yes, sir." The young man opened the door all the way in spite of Everett's state of undress. A couple of stagehands passed by in the hall, glancing into the room before walking on as though they saw Everett in his all together every day.

Everett turned to Wrexham, whose eyes had gone wide to match his pink face. "I'd like you to meet Officer Wrexham," he said. "Scotland Yard has kindly loaned him to me as a bodyguard."

Wrexham shifted slightly, staring hard at Everett.

"Sir." Foster nodded to Wrexham.

"Officer Wrexham is to be treated like one of the family," Everett said. "Let everyone know, will you? He has my leave to watch the show from the wings, if he'd like."

"Yes, sir." Foster nodded to Everett, then to Wrexham, then backed out, shutting the door behind him.

"There," Everett said with a smile. "That takes care of that. Not a soul will question your presence by my side at all times."

"Won't they?" Wrexham raised one eyebrow.

Everett hadn't seen him look half as clever as he did in that moment. So the man knew what others might be tempted to assume by catching him loitering in the dressing room of a man with a particular reputation after all, did he? His assessment of Wrexham changed once again. Perhaps he would be more than just a delightful toy to have his way with.

But, of course, that was ridiculous. Everett didn't

form attachments. Even with men who shared his determination to bring down evil of the likes that Adler perpetuated. He had affairs, dalliances, and good times, that was all. He didn't deserve anything else.

The silence between them dragged on as Everett's thoughts tunneled back to the dark recesses of his mind. He was grateful beyond telling when Wrexham's gaze slipped south to his drawers, which, truth be told, didn't hide much. It was so much easier to fall back on the physical. He gratefully shook off his moment of danger.

"Would you like a little taste?" he asked with a sultry smile, reaching for the drawstring of his drawers. "As long as you're quick, we've got enough time before curtain for you to get your fill."

"No," Wrexham croaked. He cleared his throat and snapped his back straight in true policeman style.

Everett was genuinely disappointed. And disheartened. Something about Wrexham upset his apple cart, but he couldn't for the life of him lay a finger on what it was. Yes, he wanted the man. That feeling was as normal as the stink that pervaded London in the summer. What wasn't normal was the way his heart seemed to beat harder in the man's presence. A man he knew nothing about.

He pushed himself into motion, striding toward the rack where his costumes hung.

"It's just the usual performance tonight," he said, taking his Act One costume from its hanger. "I meant it when I said you could watch from the wings. Afterwards, we'll skip the carousing at the pub and dive straight into the investigation."

"After your performance?" Wrexham asked, avoiding looking at Everett as he dressed.

"Yes." Everett slipped into his costume trousers and shirt. Only then did Wrexham glance his way again.

"So you know where Adler is?" Wrexham asked.

"Not precisely," Everett admitted. "But I know someone who will most certainly know exactly where he is. And he wouldn't dare to hold back on me."

CHAPTER 3

Patrick had never watched a theatrical performance from the wings before. There was more activity and more that held his attention backstage than there was in view of the audience. Stagehands rushed here and there, moving scenery and placing props where actors entering the stage could grab them. Women with costumes hovered near the stage, ready to help with quick-changes. The actors themselves hurried to make their entrances, stoic and focused as they skulked in the shadows, but glowing and alive the moment they stepped into the light on stage.

The theater where Jewel was performing had the very latest electrical stage lights in place, which dazzled Patrick with their modernity. He could only imagine that Jewel and the other actors were utterly blind on stage, the lights were so bright. There was no possible way they would be able to see the audience past the first few rows.

Even from the wings, Patrick had a hard time seeing them.

Patrick stuck to the shadows, pressing his back against the wall on one side of the stage so that he wouldn't be in the way. His spot gave him a surprisingly good view of the center of the stage, where Jewel spent most of the play. It gave him a perfect view of Jewel.

The man truly was beautiful. Patrick could deny it all he wanted, but his body and soul responded to everything about Everett Jewel. The way he moved was captivating. His voice was as rich and smooth as treacle. He had a presence about him that expanded through the theater, giving Patrick the feeling that Jewel was whispering his lines directly into his ear instead of speaking them for a full theater to hear.

He couldn't shake the memory of Jewel stripping down to his drawers and offering to remove those as well. It had taken every ounce of concentration Patrick had not to drop to his knees and pleasure Jewel when he'd made the suggestion, even though he'd never done such a thing before or had it done to himself in return. If the stagehand hadn't come along on with his message, Patrick could only imagine what would have happened.

But no, he couldn't let anything like that happen, not in the theater, not anywhere. The only reason he was with Jewel at all was because David Wirth was relying on him to work with Jewel to bring down the leaders of the trafficking ring. And even if there were time for other things, Patrick couldn't allow it. The very thought made his pulse race with lust, shame, and fear.

The final, roaring applause of the audience shook him out of his thoughts—thoughts that had gripped Patrick with so much tension that his back and jaw ached as he forced himself to breathe and shake it out. Jewel took his bow, then gave in to the audience pressure and sang a quick song, even though the play wasn't a musical. Once that was done, Jewel motioned for the stage manager to bring the curtain down, and Jewel strode into the wings.

"That's done," he said to Patrick, gesturing for him to follow as he strode through the backstage area and on to the corridor with the dressing rooms. "Now we can get down to real business." He glanced over his shoulder, raking Patrick from head to toe with a saucy grin, as though the business he spoke of was of the carnal variety.

Before they made it to his dressing room, a young stagehand rushed to intercept Jewel, handing him a bouquet of roses. "From Lady Darnell," he said, eyes wide. "She said to tell you you'll be richly rewarded if you spend the night with her."

Patrick's eyes went wide. "She's a married duchess," he murmured before he could stop himself.

"She's a darling, but tell her I'm otherwise engaged tonight," Jewel told the stagehand. Though he kept the roses, carrying them into his dressing room as the young lad ran off.

Once Patrick and Jewel were alone with the dressing

room door closed, Patrick cleared his throat, took up a post near the door, and stood at attention to keep his wits about him. "You don't actually take ladies like that up on their invitations, do you? I mean, I thought you were—I thought you preferred—" Heat flared through him, and he couldn't finish his impertinent question.

Jewel laughed as he began undressing, tossing the pieces of his costume onto a chair in the corner of the room. "I've been singing for my supper far longer than anyone knows," he said, a deep note of bitterness in his voice, in spite of his coy grin. "Women, men, it doesn't matter when your life and livelihood is at stake. I perform whatever I need to perform when I need to perform it. The part I play doesn't have a thing to do with who I really am."

The way Jewel turned away from him as he murmured his last line filled Patrick with unexpected sorrow. "And who are you, really?" he asked, surprised at how gently his question came out.

Jewel paused in the middle of shrugging out of his shirt, his back to Patrick. His shoulders were hunched, and for a heartbeat he was still. The strong muscles of Jewel's back distracted Patrick for a moment, but his uncomfortable feelings of lust were dampened when he noticed Jewel staring at himself in his dressing table mirror, a lost look in his eyes.

"I have no idea," Jewel said, so quietly that Patrick wasn't sure he heard him. Jewel took in a deep breath, straightened, and continued undressing, his rogue's smile back on this face. "That's not true. I'm Everett Jewel, darling of the stage and the most desired man in London." He tossed his shirt aside and unfastened his trousers, stepping out of them and turning back to Patrick. "I know you want me," he teased, dropping his trousers in a pile and approaching Patrick like a lion stalking his prey. "I can see it in your eyes, no matter how much you try to hide it."

Bitter self-consciousness threatened to drown Patrick. He should deny his feelings. He was used to denying them, used to stuffing them so deep inside of himself that even he forgot he was just as much a sexual creature as any other man that had walked the earth. But those feelings were inconvenient. More than that, they were dangerous. They could end his life in a thousand different ways.

Jewel strode near enough for Patrick to smell the salt of his skin mingled with greasepaint and cologne. His mouth was so close that all Patrick would have to do was lean in and steal a kiss.

Instead, he cleared his throat and stiffened his body to attention. "The investigation," he said. "You say you know where to find Adler?"

A flash of disappointment filled Jewel's eyes, and he took a step back. "I know where to find someone who surely knows where Adler is." He crossed to the rack where his street clothes hung and put on his trousers before heading to the dressing table to remove his make-up. "God only knows where Adler is and what he's up to now."

Jewel didn't say anything else as he scrubbed stage make-up from his face, washed with some sort of creamy cleanser, dabbed his face and neck dry, then proceeded to outline his eyes with kohl all over again. Patrick watched, mesmerized, unable to decide whether he was shocked that a man would decorate his face like a strumpet or aroused by it. Either way, the effect brought out Jewel's eyes to a degree that would stop even the stodgiest man in his tracks on sight.

When that was done, Jewel finished dressing, then headed for the door, motioning for Patrick to come with him.

"I'm skipping the stage door tonight," he called out to one of the stagehands as they headed down the corridor. "Tell my adoring public not to be too disappointed. Imply that I have a private engagement if you have to."

"Yes, sir," the stagehand said, then jogged off in the opposite direction.

"The poor dears will be devastated," Jewel told Patrick with a grin as they made their way to a small, nondescript door that let out into a side alley at the far end of the theater.

The strange thing was, in spite of the clear arrogance of Jewel's statement, Patrick sensed the man really did care about disappointing whoever might have been lingering around, waiting to catch a glimpse of him. It only added to Patrick's sense that Jewel had hidden depths, and it made him want the man more.

Jewel did nothing to hide his face as they walked away from the theater, but something about him changed. People passed the two of them in close quarters as they strode purposefully on, but no one recognized Jewel. Or, if they did, it was only in passing and without stopping him. Patrick could see at once it was because, unlike earlier in the day, Jewel didn't want to be recognized. Patrick had used the tactic himself so many times that it had become second nature. Disappearing in plain sight was a skill that had saved his life more times than he could count growing up. It seemed as though Jewel knew the art as well.

"Where are we going?" Patrick asked after they'd walked eastward in silence for at least fifteen minutes.

"Home," Jewel said with a shrug. His grin had slowly disappeared as they marched through the city, leaving the fashionable and bright area around Drury Lane behind and entering neighborhoods Patrick had only ever visited when he was called to investigate some horrible crime.

A thousand questions popped into Patrick's mind, but he left all of them unasked, choosing to get his answers through observation instead. He wasn't as surprised as he thought he'd be to hear a dazzling and celebrated actor hint that he was from one of the worst parts of London. The theater wasn't exactly the most savory profession, even though performers were adored and sought after.

Patrick couldn't hide his shock when Jewel marched into a building so dilapidated it looked as though it might collapse into a pile of matchsticks at any second. The place stank of soot, urine, and burned cooking. A dog barked somewhere, but the rat that scurried across the hall didn't seem to care. Upstairs, a baby cried, but whether anyone attended to it was unclear.

"Roger," Jewel shouted, storming through the hall and into the dingiest, most depressing sitting room Patrick had ever seen. "There you are, you filthy cunt."

The sitting room contained a few pieces of broken, mismatched furniture. A woman who looked ancient, but who Patrick suspected was younger even than him, sat in the chair closest to the fire, swaying and shaking as she attempted to sew something by the light of its dull flames. A filthy young lad of about eight slept like the dead on the floor beside her. A portly man with a pock-marked face and dirty, mismatched clothes sat in the other chair, a nearly empty bottle in one hand.

"Get up, you useless, old prick." Jewel marched across the room, grabbing a handful of the man's shirt and wrenching him to his feet. "Where is Adler?"

The man snorted and struggled as he stood, clearly soused. "Get off me," he drawled, swaying as he found his balance. "I don't know."

"You do," Jewel insisted. "You always know." He shook the man, then turned to give the woman a smile. "Hello, Bessie. Are you well?"

"Well, well," the shaking woman, Bessie, said with a toothless smile.

Still holding the man with one hand, Jewel reached into his pocket, took out a gold coin, and tossed it to the woman. "Get yourself something decent to eat, love. And for the kids too."

Patrick jerked a hand instinctively to his pouch of bread and sausage. His heart told him to give what he had to the miserable woman and anyone else in the house, who obviously needed it more than him. Fear kept him frozen, though, and the resulting stinginess made him hate himself.

Jewel turned back to the man, shaking him once more. "Where is Adler?" he repeated.

The man recovered enough to push Jewel away and to stand taller. "Get your hands off me, you putrid sodomite," he slurred.

"I am what you made me, Father," Jewel growled.

Patrick's brow shot up. It came as no surprise to him that a man in filthy, ill-fitting clothes, who stank of piss and gin, would think he was better than Jewel, who was clean, well-groomed, and wealthy, simply because of whom he fancied. What shocked him was the name Jewel had called him. "Mr. Jewel?" He blinked at the man.

"Never!" The man sniffed and swayed, eyes bleary. "It's Caldwell to you."

"You thought I'd keep this cunt's name when I began my career?" Jewel asked Patrick, offended.

Patrick shook his head and muttered something that didn't form into words.

Jewel turned back to his father. "I'll ask you once more, you conniving piece of shit. Where is Adler?"

"I don't know," his father shouted, then lost his balance and plopped back into his chair.

The boy on the floor stirred, but never fully woke.

"He don't know," Bessie mumbled. "Try Dora."

Jewel's face pinched in disgust at the suggestion. He let out a sigh, rubbed a hand over his face, then motioned for Patrick to follow him out of the room.

They left the house without a word. The dog was still barking out back, and the baby was wailing louder than ever. Patrick's teeth were on edge, as though he should do something to ease the suffering of people in the house but couldn't imagine what.

"Are they your family?" he asked once they were back on the street.

"Not really, no," Jewel said through a tight jaw. "Not since my dearest papa sold me to Adler when I was eight years old."

Patrick swallowed the bile that rose up his throat at the thought. "Eight years old?" he asked, hoarse.

Jewel glanced morosely at him. "I was the weakest of my brothers and prettier than my sisters. That cunt was out of gin and too much of a drunkard to hold a job. All it took was for a passing merchant to lick his lips while staring at me to give Father ideas. He'd heard of the ways Adler brokered certain sorts of deals and completed the transaction before I knew what was what. I couldn't refuse."

Patrick's stomach twisted. He didn't need to be told how the story continued from there. He knew too well. He'd seen it happen more times than he could count growing up to the boys and girls who never learned to blend into the furniture.

They barged into another, crumbling building at the end of the street without Jewel saying another word. Instead of announcing his presence and shouting loud enough to bring down the rafters, Jewel merely mounted the stairs to the first floor and pushed open the door to the left.

"Aunt Dora," he greeted the shriveled woman sitting in a rickety chair, glancing out the window.

The woman turned her head to greet Jewel with a vacant grin. The few teeth she had were blackened, and a horrible smell emanated from her that made Patrick recoil. She wore a cloak patched with a riot of rags that had once been colorful, but were now as faded as she was.

"Everett," she said in a papery voice, trying to push herself out of her chair. "There's a good boy. I've got some lovely sweets for you, lad."

Something about the way she spoke prickled the hair on the back of Patrick's neck. It wasn't just that the woman had clearly lost her senses. She spoke as one might if they were attempting to lure a child with toffee.

"Don't get up, Aunt Dora." There were equal parts

disgust and pity in Jewel's voice. He reached into his jacket pocket and tossed the woman a coin, as he had with Bessie. "I just want to know where Adler is."

"Adler," she echoed, nodding. "Adler. Adler. Adler."

"Where is he?" Jewel asked, patient but stony.

"Oh, Adler is here and there," Aunt Dora said, almost singing, settling back into her chair. "He came to see me the other day. Wanted me to bring him some more little lovelies for his school."

Patrick's breath hitched in his throat. He peeked at Jewel, half tempted to arrest the woman. But there was just enough compassion in Jewel's sour expression to hold him back.

"Where is he?" Jewel repeated.

"Taken a place down in Batcliff Cross," Aunt Dora said. She cocked her head to the side, then nodded. "Yes. Yes, that's the place. Said he'd have a nice, juicy steak for me if I brought him some little treats there. I do love a bit of meat now and then."

Patrick's skin crawled. Mostly because he was certain the woman was talking about beef and not cock. She was thin as a rail and had the hungry look about her that Patrick knew too well. Which increased his own compassion for her. Hunger made humans into monsters.

"Buy yourself a steak and kidney pie with that," Jewel said, nodding to the coin that had landed on her lap.

Aunt Dora glanced down, seeing the coin for the first time. "Oh? Where did this come from?"

Jewel didn't wait around to answer her. He backed

out of the room and headed down the stairs. Patrick followed. He remained silent as Jewel charged through the seedy, stinking streets, as though he couldn't get away fast enough.

Only when they reached a nicer part of town, close to Drury Lane again, did Jewel return to something close to his old self. He rolled his shoulders and took in a deep breath as the scent of expensive perfume worn by ladies who had attended the theater that night and sweet and savory treats from the pubs and late-night cafes filled the air around them.

"Now you know my secret," he told Patrick with a sly, sideways look. "Several of them, actually. Whatever shall I do to swear you to secrecy?" His flirtatiousness was back, but it had a harsh edge to it.

"I won't tell anyone," Patrick said in a soft voice. More than anything, he wanted to reach out to the man, to tell him he understood, and that his background wasn't much better. He wanted to embrace Jewel and tell him everything would be all right. He'd never felt anything half as tender before, and it terrified him.

He snapped his gaze straight forward, his face heating. He could feel Jewel watching him as well, and when he risked a glimpse, his gut quivered and his cock stiffened at the hungry, excited way Jewel stared at him.

"One last stop," Jewel said, promise in his voice.

Patrick said nothing as they walked on, even though he was desperate to know where they were going. The teeming, nighttime streets of the theater district gave way to the fringes of some of London's most fashionable residential neighborhoods. Jewel's spirits improved even more. Eventually, he walked right up to the door of a stylish terraced apartment and ushered Patrick inside.

"Here we are," he said with a saucy smile, leading Patrick up two flights of stairs.

He took out a key and unlocked a door, letting Patrick into the finest flat he'd ever seen. It was three times the size of the dismal houses they'd visited in East London, and was furnished with beautiful, new furniture, hung with impressive artwork, and dressed with perfect curtains and carpets. Everything was immaculately clean.

Patrick paused in the main room, glancing around in wonder and feeling utterly out of place. Jewel walked on, crossing into what Patrick could see at a glance was a beautifully furnished bedroom. He removed his jacket with an impish grin as he stepped into the bedroom.

"Well, come on," he said, turning back to Patrick. "We can't suck each other's cocks all night and fuck until we're dry if we don't start now."

Patrick's throat squeezed tight. His gut clenched at the same time as his cock stiffened in response. Want like nothing he'd ever known coursed through him. He wanted to touch and be touched, to kiss and suck and lose himself in all the ways he'd fantasied about. Hell, Everett Jewel, *the* Everett Jewel, the man he'd envisioned while masturbating until he thought he'd go blind, had brought him home and was propositioning him.

"Wrexham?" Jewel paused halfway through tugging

his shirt out of his trousers. He stepped back through the doorway into the main room. "Patrick?" he asked, approaching slowly and seductively.

Patrick was frozen to his spot. He couldn't even breathe. Panic overwhelmed him more and more as Jewel sidled up to him.

"Something wrong, love?" Jewel asked, fondling the Metropolitan Police insignia on his jacket, over his pounding heart. He glanced coyly up into Patrick's eyes. "You do want to fuck, don't you?"

The edges of Patrick's vision went black. Yes, he wanted to fuck so badly he could hardly think. But he didn't know how.

"Cat got your tongue?" Jewel teased his fingers up to Patrick's lips. "I'll get it back."

He leaned in. His lips brushed against Patrick's. His tongue teased the tight seam holding Patrick's mouth shut. Jewel's scent filled his nostrils.

Patrick gasped and leapt back, heart beating so furiously he was certain he would pass out.

"I can't," he choked. "I...I can't."

Jewel's expression flashed from surprise to disappointment to hurt that was both genuine and deep. "But you want to," he said. There was something tragic and vulnerable in his voice, almost like pleading.

"I can't," Patrick repeated.

He turned and lunged for the door, throwing it open and fleeing into the hall.

"Please stay," Jewel called after him.

Patrick's throat closed up, but he rushed on. He wasn't sure if he shut the door behind him in his flight. All he knew was that he had to get out of the building and away from Jewel before he did something he couldn't take back.

CHAPTER 4

By morning, after a restless night's sleep, Patrick ached with regret so fiercely that he felt as though he'd been in a brawl and come out the worse for it. His head throbbed as he fixed coffee on the tiny stove in the corner of his cramped but respectable one-room flat. His back twinged with pain as he washed and dressed in a fresh uniform. Worst of all, his heart felt shrunken and hollow with guilt. That guilt only increased as he played the scene in Jewel's apartment over and over again.

Jewel had begged him to stay. He now recognized the note of desperation in the man's final words as he'd run away, like a coward. Jewel had been right as well. Patrick *had* wanted him. More than ever before after their trip into East London. It was one thing to see Jewel as an erotic and adored star of the stage, shining with charisma as he dazzled the high and the low night after night. The man's vanity was well-earned, and Patrick didn't blame him one bit for being an arrogant peacock. But Patrick had seen a different side of him, a darker side, and knew there was even more darkness behind that. Jewel's hints and half-confessions had stirred a sort of sorrow deep within him. Or, if not sorrow, then a visceral sense that there were worlds of pain and hardship underneath the beautiful and desirable exterior Jewel presented to the world. The tiny glimpse behind the curtain of the man's inner life Patrick had had the night before only made him want to know Jewel more.

Patrick grimaced at himself in disgust in the mirror as he combed his hair and shaved. He could have had everything he'd ever dreamed of but had never dared to pursue...if he hadn't been such a coward. He could have known Jewel, emotionally and Biblically. And what was he so afraid of? It wasn't as though the mark of the beast would appear on his forehead the moment he let himself experience pleasure with another man, especially one he adored.

He finished shaving, scrubbed his face, and finished dressing, fastening his belt last. By habit, he checked the pouch attached to his belt, inspecting the food he kept there. The sausage was fine, but the bread was going stale. He took that out and set it on the stove to toast before crossing to the locked chest on the room's single, small table, where he kept his food. He fetched the key from its hiding spot under the mattress of his narrow bed, then unlocked the box.

Anxiety welled in his gut as he surveyed the contents of the chest. He hadn't had time to visit the grocer in days, but instinct attempted to convince him someone had snuck in and stolen his food. Old, raw memories of his stomach gnawing so fiercely with hunger that it kept him awake at night, groaning, rushed in on him.

He took a deep breath and pushed those memories aside. "You will not starve," he told himself, shutting the lid of his chest and closing his eyes. "You are a grown man with employment and income. You can purchase provisions freely. Your days of fighting for food to survive are over."

He took another breath, forcing himself to believe his words. The scent of toast and coffee calmed him. He locked his chest, replaced the key under his mattress, then moved to the stove to gobble down his breakfast. It satisfied his hunger, but not much else.

No wonder he'd run from Jewel. Sex required intimacy, and intimacy was a liability. The second he let anyone in, especially a man as desirable and wanted as Jewel, they'd see how broken he was and cast him aside. Just like every prospective parent who'd visited the orphanage and shoved him out of the way to look at the prettier boys.

He finished his coffee, regretting the way it only added to the acid burn in his gut, before heading out the door. His problems were trivial compared to the horrors that the children Lord Chisolm and his cronies continued to steal were being forced to endure. A good and moral man wouldn't give a single thought to his own pain when evil like that existed in the world.

He reminded himself of that fact over and over as he headed through London, on foot and by omnibus, to the edge of Hyde Park. He hadn't made specific arrangements to meet up with Jewel again to continue the investigation. Any man who wasn't an utter coward would return to Jewel's flat so that they could continue their pursuit of Barnaby Adler together. But since the very thought of setting foot in Jewel's flat again filled Patrick with a mix of terror and arousal, he headed to The Chameleon Club instead. For men like them, all roads led to The Brotherhood eventually. It was reasonable to believe that Jewel would come looking for him there. He might already be at the club.

In spite of having been a member of The Brotherhood for years, Patrick still felt utterly out of place at The Chameleon Club. Modeled on every other upper-class gentlemen's club in London, The Chameleon Club was the height of sophistication and elegance. So much so that he had only entered its hallowed halls twice before, years ago. Its marble hallways were decorated with exquisite artwork and fresh flowers. Rules of strict propriety were in place that prevented the sort of activity men like them could find at a molly house, which gave the club more of a feeling of tranquility and education than lasciviousness.

Men from all strata of society were welcome into The Brotherhood and the club with open arms, at least in theory, but that didn't make Patrick feel as though he belonged. He felt like a hog that had been let loose in Buckingham Palace as he walked into the vast dining room, which was the usual center of activity at the club in the morning. Over a dozen, round tables were set up throughout the room, though only about half of the tables were occupied, and even then, not at full capacity, as Patrick shuffled through the room, hat in hand, shoulders slightly hunched, as though someone would realize he didn't belong at any moment and have him thrown out.

The scent of bacon, ham, and coffee wafted from a series of long buffet tables at one side of the room, drawing Patrick in that direction like sirens calling him toward jagged rocks that could kill him. The amount of food spread across the table nearly brought him to tears. Sights like that had haunted his dreams as a child.

Before he could stop himself, he reached for a sweet roll from a plate towering with treats and tucked it discreetly into his pouch. He glanced around, and when it was apparent no one had seen the action, he snuck another one. From there, he inched down the table toward a platter of bacon.

"You can use a plate, you know."

Patrick's blood froze in his veins and the hair on the back of his neck stood up as Lionel Mercer stepped up to the table behind him. He reached for a perfect, porcelain plate from one of the piles placed artistically on the table and handed it to Patrick.

"Your membership dues cover the cost of meals,"

Lionel went on with a smile filled with so much compassion it brought Patrick to shame. Lionel Mercer was famous—or infamous—for knowing everything about everyone in London, which meant it was likely he knew full well what sort of demons caused Patrick to steal and hoard food.

"I know," Patrick mumbled, taking the plate without looking directly at Lionel. "Old habits die hard."

Lionel hummed in complete understanding and thumped Patrick's shoulder. For a man of such delicate and refined appearance, Lionel had a heavy hand, and his grip was powerful as he squeezed Patrick's shoulder before letting go. "How fares the investigation?" he asked, a bitter twist to his smile. "Jewel lead you on a wild goose chase yet?"

Patrick heated at the mention of Jewel and at Lionel's salty tone. "We found someone who claims to know where Adler is hiding," he said, loath to reveal too much. As irrational as it was, Patrick writhed with jealousy at the idea that Lionel and Jewel were lovers at some point, even if only for a short time, as Jewel had implied the night before.

Lionel huffed a laugh. "Well, we'll just see whether that lead pans out or not."

Patrick finished filling his plate and turned to Lionel with a frown. "You don't believe Jewel knows his business?"

Lionel picked at a piece of lint on his perfectly

tailored sleeve. "I believe Everett thinks a little too highly of himself and his abilities."

"So you think he's lying." It was madness to turn defensive against Lionel Mercer, but the urge to defend Jewel was too strong to resist.

Lionel's benign smile melted into something a little too knowing. "Darling, let me give you a bit of advice," he said, resting his hand on Patrick's shoulder and leading him to the nearest table. A slender, brown-haired, blue-eyed man who had once been introduced to Patrick as Niall Cristofori, the playwright, was the only one sitting there, reading *The Times*. "Everett Jewel changes lovers as frequently as he changes his drawers and with just as little consideration. Don't allow yourself to be drawn down that primrose path."

Patrick's stomach tightened, but he couldn't find the words to object to Lionel's statement fast enough. What was more, Cristofori glanced up from his paper, but rather than staring at either Patrick or Lionel, he glanced past the two of them with wide eyes, as though seeing a runaway carriage about to crash.

The crash came a second later as Jewel barked, "Get your hands off of my officer, Mercer."

Everett was exhausted and irritable even before he arrived at The Chameleon Club. Watching Wrexham run away from him the night before had ripped his heart out in ways he could never have anticipated. He thought he'd been irresistible. He wasn't naïve enough to mistake the fact that Wrexham had been hard for him half of the night. Even the jaunt to his bloody father's house hadn't dulled Wrexham's ardor, though Everett had noted a shift in the emotion in Wrexham's eyes once he'd seen the misery that was his past. He never should have taken Wrexham home with him. Either that or he should have confessed all to the quiet, handsome man, pouring his heart out and shedding tears to win him over.

But no, he couldn't have been false with Wrexham if he'd tried, which was a startling change from the way he usually conducted himself. The simple fact of the matter was that he'd bared his soul to Wrexham, whether he was fully aware of it at the time or not, and he'd wanted to bare even more. But Wrexham rejected him, and at exactly the moment that he needed someone by his side, in his bed. Wrexham had run out, leaving Everett with the choice of going to bed alone and facing the nightmares he knew full well would torture him or forcing himself to stay awake all night so that he could avoid them.

He'd chosen to stay awake, and the moment he stepped into the dining room at The Chameleon Club, he knew that he, and everyone else in the room, in all likelihood, would pay for it.

"Get away from him," he snapped at Lionel, marching toward where Patrick had just set a ridiculously full plate on the table where Cristofori sat. The way Lionel touched Wrexham made him see red.

Wrexham jerked away from Lionel, wells of regret in his eyes. In his already fragile state, that hang-dog expression made Everett want to simultaneously weep and shout for him to grow a backbone and demand an explanation for why he'd run out the night before.

"Wrexham is not *your* officer," Lionel sniffed, pulling himself up to his full, imperious height, like the arrogant prick he was. "He's not *your* anything. Not if I have anything to do about it."

Everett clenched his jaw and balled his hand into a fist. Between exhaustion, hurt, and the pounding headache behind his eyes, all he wanted to do was punch the smug smirk off of Lionel's face. It was high time the man got over his disappointment that things had fizzled between the two of them all those years ago. Why the prick continued to hold onto something that was never meant to be was beyond him.

"You were the one who insisted the two of us work together on this investigation," he said, forcing himself to shake his hand out.

"It was David, not me." Lionel's pale face flushed scarlet.

"Yes, and where is your delightful *partner* this morning?" Everett asked, full of innuendo, one eyebrow arched.

"David is not—" Lionel huffed through his nose. "We are not—" He crossed his arms, his face going redder, if that were possible. "He's seeing to arrangements to get Alistair and Joe home as quickly as possible," he finished, jaw clenched. "So we can locate the man with the lion."

"I've already located the man with the lion." Everett crossed his arms in imitation of Lionel, trying to make himself taller. Lionel had a good two inches on him, even with the thick-heeled shoes Everett wore, but he could create the illusion of height.

"And, of course, you just assume you are right." Lionel rolled his eyes.

"What's this about a man with a lion?" Cristofori rose from his seat and walked around the table to join them. He exchanged a wary look with Wrexham, as if the two of them knew it was their responsibility to prevent any more fur from flying.

Wrexham shifted uneasily—and adorably—checking briefly with Lionel and then Everett, who nodded, before turning to Cristofori. "We have reason to believe that the leader of the child kidnapping ring we've been seeking to bring to justice is a man with a lion, possibly a lion tattoo."

"Barnaby Adler—a man who we already know is involved in the ring—has a tattoo of a lion on his chest," Everett added. "And I know where to find him."

"I'll believe that when I see it," Lionel muttered.

Cristofori glanced between Everett and Lionel with a frown. In spite of the fact that he and Everett were friends and in the process of collaborating on a future play, Everett had the disappointing feeling that Cristofori was about to side with Lionel. "What makes you think Adler is the man?" he asked.

Everett narrowed his eyes. There was something guarded in the way Cristofori asked the question, as though he knew something but didn't want to speak up.

"Who else could it be?" he asked.

Lionel shook his head. "Men like Chisolm and Eastleigh would never stoop to take orders from a mere tradesman."

"I don't know. I've seen sons of the gentry stoop surprisingly low myself." It was a cheap shot at Lionel, but Everett couldn't resist. Lionel thought far too much of himself. Though he was certain Lionel thought the same about him.

Lionel's eyes flared with ire to the point where they practically glowed with it. "I have been insulted enough for one morning," he said with barely concealed rage. "I have important work to do. Work that does not involve chasing wild geese. Good day." He nodded to Cristofori, then to Wrexham. "Good luck managing this arsehole."

He stormed off before anyone else could steal the last word from him.

Everett wanted to groan and rub his eyes, both over Lionel's pointless theatrics and to ease the throbbing that threatened to split his head open. "Does the club have any headache powder?" he asked Cristofori.

"I'll get you some." Cristofori patted his arm, then walked off.

That left Everett alone with Wrexham. He sent the

man an apologetic look, then sank into the chair beside the place Wrexham had taken for himself. As Wrexham sat, Everett plucked a piece of bacon from his plate in an attempt to calm his upset stomach. Wrexham's brow furrowed, and for a moment Everett believed his adorable officer might just punch him in the face.

"How were you possibly planning to eat that much food in one sitting?" Everett asked, letting his exhaustion seep into his voice. "A horse couldn't eat that much in one go."

"I—"

"If you're not careful, you'll plump up, and then I'll have to roll you down the street as we search for Adler," Everett went on.

Wrexham stared at him with a look that defied description. No one had ever looked at Everett that way before. It was equal parts indignation and bewilderment, as if the very idea of eating to the point of growing fat had never occurred to Wrexham. Everett answered Wrexham's look by taking a spare fork from the place beside him at the table and digging into one of the three fried eggs on Wrexham's plate.

"Share and share alike," Everett said with his mouth full.

Wrexham watched him, tension rippling from his muscular body. Everett pretended to ignore it, though he could hardly taste the food for wondering what Wrexham was thinking. Slowly, Wrexham reached for his own fork and tucked into his meal, but that didn't stop Everett from eating off the same plate. Or from noticing that Wrexham's hand shook as he lifted a forkful of ham to his shapely mouth.

They finished half the plate in silence before Wrexham asked, "If you hate Lionel Mercer so much, why are you helping with his investigation?"

"I don't hate him," Everett said, continuing to eat without meeting Wrexham's eyes. "I actually like him, if you can believe it. If I didn't, I wouldn't bother tweaking his nose."

Wrexham paused, his fork suspended in mid-air. "You two were lovers."

Everett shrugged, regretting ever mentioning it. "Ages ago. It didn't last. We're both colossal pricks." At last, he glanced to Wrexham, completely unsurprised to find a measure of envy in the man's eyes. "One arrogant bastard in a relationship is quite enough. Two, and it becomes a war, not a love story."

"Does Lionel know that?" Wrexham resumed eating.

Everett put his fork down with a sigh. There were only a few sausages left on the plate at any rate. "I have no idea what Lionel Mercer knows. I suspect that the bee he has up his bum right now has nothing to do with me and everything to do with David."

Wrexham nodded slowly, as if considering that possibility.

Cristofori returned to the table with a glass of fizzing water. "Sorry. That took longer than I anticipated." He handed the glass to Everett.

Food and Wrexham's company had reduced Everett's headache so much that the quick shot of medicine almost wasn't needed, but he downed the glass in a few gulps.

"Niall, you are a king among men," he said with a smile. He plunked the glass on the table, then stood, grabbing Wrexham's sleeve to tug him to stand as well. "And now, we have a criminal mastermind to catch."

Wrexham fumbled to his feet, eyeing the remaining sausage on the plate as though it were a lover's cock that he was loath to leave behind. He hesitated, flinched toward it, hesitated again, then snatched the link up, moving it quickly to the small satchel attached to his belt. As he opened it, Everett caught sight of at least two rolls tucked inside.

He laughed before he could stop himself and clapped a hand on Wrexham's shoulder. "Good Lord, man. It's not as though you're going to starve before luncheon."

Wrexham looked at him with such offense that it was almost feral, as if he'd yanked his trousers down and exposed his most shameful secret to the entire room. He hid the sausage in his satchel then fastened the cover before turning to march away from the table.

"I'm sorry." Everett jogged after him, the same sort of panic he'd felt the night before when Wrexham ran out on him nipping at his heels. "I don't know what I said, but I didn't mean it. It's just this headache, and I didn't sleep last night, and Lionel gets on my last nerve."

It wasn't until they were halfway across the room that Everett realized he was chasing after Wrexham. He couldn't remember the last time he'd chased a man. He couldn't remember wanting to.

Wrexham stopped in the doorway, turning to Everett with an expression every bit as weary as Everett felt. "It has nothing to do with you," he mumbled.

For the life of him, Everett couldn't comprehend why that simple statement wounded him so deeply.

"Come on," he said, pushing forward and brushing Wrexham's hand as he did. "Let's go find Adler."

CHAPTER 5

*P*atrick was certain from the moment he and Jewel alighted from their hired carriage and glanced around the bustling rush of Batcliff Cross docks that they'd reached a dead end. He'd visited the second-rate dockyard several times in the last few weeks, including with Stephen Siddel a fortnight before. That final trip had revealed the scant evidence Siddel needed to prompt a trip north, to a mill in Leicestershire. Siddel and Lord Hillsboro had discovered dozens of children who had been forced into slavery at the mill and rescued them, but instinctively, Patrick felt that had been luck, and that Batcliff Cross had nothing more to offer.

"He must be lurking around here somewhere." Jewel planted his hands on his hips and scanned the area as though he were a pirate captain glancing out over a sea full of possibilities. In spite of the wan cast to his face and the dark circles under his eyes that had nothing to do with the kohl painting them, his expression was full of fervent hope. It was a stark contrast to Patrick's sense of foreboding. "We just have to find someone willing to ferret him out."

Jewel strode forward as though he owned the place, radiating purpose. Patrick followed, eyeing him warily. It wasn't just the futility of the search for Adler—or the difficulties of the investigation in general—that gnawed at him. Jewel had caught him at his absolute worst at the club. The man he adored, and would have slept with, if he weren't such a coward, had laughed at him for stealing a sausage. Patrick was old friends with humiliation, but Jewel teasing him had been a new low. The man must think he was pathetic and common.

"Don't trail behind me like that, man," Jewel called over his shoulder, slowing his steps until Patrick caught up and walked by his side. "I don't need a shadow, I need a—"

Patrick blinked, his brow twitching up as he waited for Jewel to say what he needed. He didn't. Instead, Jewel pressed his lips tightly together and strode on in silence, his brow knitting. Patrick narrowed his eyes as he studied the man. Was he annoyed or merely tired? Was the flush that suddenly painted his face from exertion, or was he embarrassed to have Patrick with him? The more Patrick watched him, trying to read the man's mood, the more puzzled he was.

"You there," Jewel called out in a booming voice to a middle-aged man with a ledger in one hand. The man stood in the doorway of one of the warehouses near the waterfront, issuing orders to several younger dockworkers. "I have a question for you."

Patrick winced at Jewel's brash approach, especially when the man glanced his way in irritation. The man was clearly a manager, but that didn't mean he would take well to being interrupted, particularly by someone dressed in a dark red jacket more suited to Drury Lane than London's waterfront. It didn't help that the manager's expression darkened at the sight of Patrick's uniform.

"I've already paid my dues this month," the manager said, puffing himself up as Jewel approached, and gesturing for his workers to go about their business. "I won't let Holcomb squeeze another shilling out of me."

Patrick filed the name away, wondering if any of his colleagues in Scotland Yard might be able to use it in a racketeering investigation.

Jewel wasn't so subtle. "What are you talking about, man?" He smiled and extended a hand as though meeting the Prime Minister. "I only have a question for you."

The manager stared suspiciously at Jewel's hand without taking it. He peeked at Patrick, then cleared his throat and stood straighter. "What question?" he asked Jewel.

"I'm looking for a man by the name of Barnaby Adler," Jewel said, turning on his charm. "I've been told he's staying somewhere in this area."

"Never heard of him." The manager turned away, stepping into the warehouse door.

"Are you certain?" Jewel hurried after him, his charming façade fading. "I have it on good authority he's here somewhere."

The manager shrugged. "Maybe he is, maybe he isn't. I don't have time to keep track of every Tom, Dick, or Harry who waltzes in and out of the place."

Without so much as a good day, he disappeared into the warehouse.

"Hang on." Jewel started after him, but Patrick grabbed his sleeve, stopping him from entering the warehouse.

"He isn't going to tell you anything," Patrick said.

Jewel scowled at Patrick's hand on his sleeve. Patrick pulled away, which seemed to puncture whatever ire Jewel was holding onto. For a split-second, Jewel looked downright lost without Patrick's hand on his arm.

A moment later, Jewel shook himself and stepped away from the warehouse. "How do you know he wouldn't tell me anything? I'd hardly begun to ask."

"He doesn't know." Patrick squared his shoulders, his years on the police force feeding his certainty. "He didn't have that look about him."

Jewel looked as though he would argue. Instead, he let out a breath and rubbed a hand over his face. "All right. Who does know, then?"

It would have been a ridiculous question, but for the fact that Jewel met his eyes as if he had complete faith that Patrick would know, or at least know how to find out.

It was an odd sort of endorsement that nudged Patrick's confidence in a useful direction.

"Never ask the managers," he said, gesturing for Jewel to continue down the dock with him. "They have no incentive to reveal anything. Never ask the diligent workers either. They're likely in their manager's pockets."

"Who can we ask?" Jewel lowered his voice, a light of conspiracy in his eyes.

Patrick glanced around, taking in the various strata of workers and hangers-on in the area. It was clear who was gainfully employed and who was there for less than savory activity. Under normal circumstances, he would have been able to pick out the kind of sly loafer who would be willing to spill all manner of information if it meant a few coins or the coppers looking the other way at some point in the future by the way they stared at him. The trouble with having Jewel by his side was that everyone stared at them.

"Oy! I know you." A woman who was probably far younger than her haggard appearance suggested pushed forward from the edge of an alley. She wore her skirt tucked up on one side, and her blouse was cut low enough to give away her profession. She approached Jewel with a rapt smile. "You're that actor."

As if by rote, Jewel stopped to flash a beaming smile at the woman, in spite of what she was. "Madam, I'm flattered to be recognized." He strode toward her, taking her hand and raising it to his lips as though she were a duchess.

The whore giggled and blushed. "Blimey!"

Several other women of similar profession took notice and left their spots to come closer, eyes bright with recognition.

"I saw you in that musical review a couple years back," one of them with ginger hair said. "You were lovely."

"Thank you, my dear." Jewel lit up at the praise. He moved from whore to whore, kissing their hands and treating them to lewd winks that had them all blushing like schoolgirls.

The more he fawned over them, the more attention he got—from passersby on the dock as well as from the whores. It was enough to send Patrick retreating to the shadows by the side of the building, as eager to observe where Jewel was going with his flattery as he was loath to have any attention drawn to himself.

"Ooh, I wish I had that broadside with me," one of the older whores sighed as she clung to Jewel's hand. "Nicked it from that theater where you did that Shakespeare play last year," she admitted boldly. "I'd have you sign it, and then it'd be worth a pretty penny."

"I wish you did have it." Jewel smiled back at her. "I'd sign it in a heartbeat."

The whores cooed and laughed over his generosity.

"My darlings," Jewel went on, "I was wondering if you could do me a favor."

"I'll do you any favor you want, love," the ginger whore said, rubbing his arm suggestively.

"No thanks, love. I like men."

Patrick nearly choked at Jewel's blunt statement, delivered so casually. He snapped straight, jerking his head this way and that to see if anyone had overheard. His pulse shot up so hard that it left him sweating and breathless.

The whores merely hummed and grinned, surprised, but as if they couldn't have cared less. "Me too, sweetheart," the older one said.

Everybody laughed, even Jewel. Patrick could only stand there, gaping. It didn't matter that they were at the docks, surrounded by the dregs of society. Any admission as bold as the one Jewel had just made could get men like them arrested and tossed in a cell to be forgotten. Jewel was either ballsy or an idiot.

"I'm looking for Barnaby Adler," Jewel went on, leaning closer to the whores, as though they all shared in a conspiracy.

"Uff. What do you want a snake like him for?" the first whore asked.

"If it's your cock you want sucked, it's that sweet soul, Garrett, you want," the older whore said.

"Oh, yes, Garrett." The others all seemed to agree. They smiled and nodded to each other.

"He's got such a lovely arse," the ginger whore said fondly.

"No thanks, darling," Jewel told her with a grin. "I never pay for cock. Too many bad memories, if you know what I mean."

The whores answered him with another round of sympathetic coos and looks of adoration and sympathy. And knowing. Patrick's gut knotted at the exchange—so seemingly gentle and friendly, but barely hiding a truth so dark it made him sick. His life had been bad enough, but the more time he spent with Jewel, the more he could see what lay beneath the layers of greasepaint and kohl.

Jewel reached into his pocket, taking out a large coin. "Give that to your Garrett for me." He handed the coin to the oldest whore. "Tell him that if he wants out of the game, come to the Concord Theater and tell a Mr. Rice that Everett Jewel said to hire him as a sweeper."

"Will do, love," the older whore said, then patted Jewel on the cheek. "I knew you was a good 'un."

Jewel rewarded her with a smile. "Now, about Adler," he went on.

"That bastard ain't here anymore," the ginger whore said, her face pinching with hate. "Not since his lot raided the *Nightingale*." She gestured to Patrick with her thumb.

Patrick swallowed hard, shocked that the whores even knew he was there. Uneasiness slithered down his spine over being called out. He stood at attention, tugging nervously at the hem of his jacket.

Jewel met Patrick's eyes for a moment of reassurance before facing the whores again. "So Adler isn't here?"

"No, love. Sorry," the first whore said. "Not for weeks."

Jewel was visibly disappointed. Patrick's alarm at

being noticed melted into sympathy that squeezed around his heart. That burst of emotion sent a wave of anxiety through him. He had known all along they wouldn't find Adler at the docks, but Jewel had been so full of hope that Patrick had held onto that hope as though it were his own.

"If we hear word of where Adler's at, we'll find a way to let you know," the older whore said.

"Of course we will." The ginger one continued to stroke Jewel's arm, but with sisterly affection instead of seduction.

"Thank you, loves. You are queens among women." Jewel took a moment to say goodbye to each of them as grandiosely as he had greeted them. Once he was done, he nodded to Patrick, and they walked on.

"I can't say I'm surprised Adler isn't here," Patrick confessed as they made their way back to one of the streets where they could hail a cab.

Jewel's shoulders slumped. "Aunt Dora might be addlepated, but she isn't usually wrong."

"She wasn't wrong," Patrick reassured him. "Those ladies said he was here until the raid on the *Nightingale*. That was less than a month ago."

Jewel sent him a weak smile, as though he were trying to be grateful for the support.

"Adler is a known criminal," Patrick went on. He checked with Jewel to make certain his guess was correct. When Jewel nodded silently, Patrick went on. "It stands to reason that Scotland Yard has some sort of record of his activity. That could include his whereabouts. All we need to do is check the files to see if anyone knows—"

Beside him, Jewel suddenly froze, his eyes wide. Every last drop of color drained from his face. Patrick's heart stopped in his chest. He searched in front of them for whatever had caused such a drastic change in Jewel's demeanor.

A shiny, black carriage was parked at the edge of the street, several dozen yards ahead of them. Even through the chaotic crowd on the dock, Patrick could clearly make out none other than Lord Chisolm stepping onto the curb from the carriage.

Jewel doubled over, making a choking noise that had the hair on the back of Patrick's neck standing up and his teeth on edge. Patrick acted without thinking, sliding an arm around Jewel's back and practically lifting him off his feet as he rushed Jewel into the alley between the warehouses beside them. Jewel vomited up half his breakfast before Patrick got him out of the street. He shook like a leaf as Patrick pressed his back against the alley wall in an attempt to steady him.

"Easy, now," Patrick said in a low, calming voice. "Breathe."

Jewel nodded, then thumped his head back against the wall. His eyes rolled up to the narrow strip of sky visible above the warehouse roofs, and he gasped for breath. Patrick clamped his arms, continuing to hold him against the wall for a moment before stepping away, intending to check which direction Chisolm had gone.

Jewel made a strangled noise as Patrick let go of him—a sound so lost and terrified that Patrick gripped his arms once more.

"I'm just going to check which way he went," he said, all seriousness.

Jewel met his eyes, kohl smudged from sudden tears. For a moment, they stood stock still. Patrick held Jewel's gaze with a steadiness he didn't know he had. The balance had flipped between them. Jewel was counting on him to be strong. Patrick knew it with every fiber of his being, and he wasn't about to let him down.

Finally, Jewel nodded and relaxed by a fraction. Patrick took a cautious step back, only letting go of Jewel's arms when he was confident Jewel could handle it. He shifted to the side, stepping out of the alley just enough to look for Chisolm. The black carriage was gone, and Chisolm was nowhere in sight.

"He's gone." Patrick returned to Jewel's side. "His carriage isn't there anymore, and there's no sign of him." He didn't dare say Chisolm's name. Whatever had set Jewel off, it was too raw to commit the sacrilege of speaking Chisolm's name.

Jewel nodded tightly, shifting to stand straighter. He gulped in deep breaths, as though forcing himself back to calm. Gradually, those gulps turned into smaller gasps, then deep, regular breathing. Jewel wiped his mouth with his sleeve, grimaced, and began to pace in circles, as if shaking off the remnants of his horror.

Patrick had a fair guess what that horror was. The

puzzle wasn't that hard to put together. The things Jewel had said about his father the night before, the way he'd spoken so freely with the whores, and now his reaction at the sight of Lord Chisolm. All of it added up to a story that Patrick didn't want to hear. It broke his heart enough without needing Jewel to spell everything out.

"I'm sorry," Jewel whispered at last, barely glancing to Patrick before snapping his eyes away. "I wasn't prepared. I can manage when I'm prepared. It's just the exhaustion and the surprise and...." His face pinched as though he might weep, but he sucked in a breath, opening his eyes wide for a moment, before blinking and rolling his shoulders. "I'm sorry."

Patrick watched him, feeling as though he'd been punched in the heart. The man in front of him, struggling to pull himself together, was not the dazzling angel he thought he knew. This Jewel was far more precious. Patrick's soul throbbed within him as he battled to find words to capture the way he felt about the Jewel he saw now.

"I've embarrassed you." Jewel stopped his pacing a few feet in front of Patrick. He lifted his gaze slowly to meet Patrick's. "I am sorry."

"You've nothing to be sorry about." Patrick wished he could think of something less useless to say.

Jewel's mouth quirked into a feeble smirk, and he let out a half laugh. "I have so many things to be sorry about." He glanced to the end of the alley as if ready to move on, but terrified Chisolm might be out there after all.

"We'll go this way." Patrick started past him, striding toward the far end of the alley.

Jewel fell into step beside him. Neither of them said a word, but Jewel reached for Patrick's hand, holding it tight until they reached the other side.

CHAPTER 6

*E*verett detested the sticky, dirty feeling of humiliation. He knew the feeling all too well, but had thought it was in his past. He'd embraced arrogance, wore cockiness like a badge of honor, and thrilled at the idea of playing the prima donna whenever possible. Because it had taken him decades to fight his way beyond the degradation of humiliation he'd been thrust into as a boy.

Now, twenty years later, one unexpected glimpse of the esteemed Clarence Eccles, Lord Chisolm, and Everett was a humiliated mess all over again.

Which was why he had to behave like a perfect arse the moment he and Wrexham stepped down from the hack they'd hired at Batcliff Cross when it let them out near the main entrance to Scotland Yard. He needed to get his moxy back, and arrogance was a sure-fire way to do that.

"I've never been to Scotland Yard before," he announced in an overly loud voice, sidling up too close to Wrexham's side as they made their way to the front stairs. "An entire building filled with men in police uniforms?" He gave a dramatic shiver. "I don't know how I'll be able to control myself."

Wrexham jerked his head toward him, face flushing and eyes wide with alarm at first before narrowing with caution. "Keep your voice down," he said. "Just because you're a celebrity doesn't mean the Labouchere Amendment doesn't apply to you."

"Why, Wrexham, I've never heard you say anything quite so fancy as that. Labouchere Amendment," he repeated with over-exaggerated elegance, as if speaking the name of the blasted law aloud would rob it of its power.

"You have to behave." Wrexham's jaw hardened as he stepped ahead to hold the grand front door open for Everett. "Remember, I work here," he said through clenched teeth.

There was more than just anger and frustration in Wrexham's expression. His dark eyes still held far too much pity for Everett's liking. Pity that turned Everett's stomach when he thought about how it had been earned. He would so much rather have Wrexham furious with him than pitying him. If he were honest with himself, he preferred adoration from his handsome and manly copper. But it was too late for that. He'd spilled his cards all over the table, and Wrexham would never look at him the same way again.

"Of course, I will behave, love." He patted Wrexham's cheek as he crossed through, into the vast and busy lobby of the Scotland Yard building.

Wrexham followed, his jaw tighter than ever, his face red, and his emotions completely indecipherable. "This way," he said, marching ahead of Everett with long, crisp steps.

As soon as Wrexham was in front of him, Everett's cheeky smile vanished. He was cruel to play with Wrexham. The man had done absolutely nothing to deserve that sort of treatment. In fact, more than anyone Everett could think of in recent days, Wrexham had treated him with openness and friendship. Hell, the man had literally held him together when the sight of Chisolm threatened to unman him. The strength in Wrexham's eyes as well as his body as he'd kept Everett pinned to the wall while the horrors of his past had their way with him was the only thing that had kept him from descending into madness. He would have pulled himself out of that morass eventually, but it had been nice to have someone there to shoulder the burden with him.

He wanted more of it. He wanted Wrexham with him at all times, ready to catch him when he fell. It was an entirely new thing to Everett to want a man for something more than his arse.

"Why the devil are so many people rushing about the

place like it's market day?" he asked, catching up to Wrexham's side and plastering on a mischievous grin.

"We're moving," Wrexham said, turning into a side hallway and striding on to a wide set of stairs. As they started up, he went on with, "This building is too small for the current needs of the Metropolitan Police. The whole operation is being moved from here in Whitehall to a new complex on Victoria Embankment."

"Good Lord." Everett smirked at a passing clerk with a crate full of ledgers and paperwork. The young clerk must have recognized him. He stumbled down a step, nearly dropping his box. "Careful, darling," Everett called down to the clerk as he and Wrexham moved around the bend in the stairs. "It would be a shame to fall and land on an arse as pretty as yours."

The clerk gaped up at him.

"Stop it," Wrexham muttered, sending Everett a fierce look. "You can't tempt fate in the middle of police headquarters."

"Of course, I can, darling." Everett winked. He also kept his mouth shut as they strode out into a first-floor hallway, continuing along until they reached an office that was as bustling as the lobby below.

"Is Norton in his office?" Wrexham asked another, harried-looking clerk just inside the office door.

"You'll have to wait," the clerk said without glancing up from the papers he was compiling.

"It's urgent," Wrexham went on. "And it won't take long."

"You'll have to wait," the clerk repeated, snapping his head up to glare at Wrexham, as though he'd asked the man to dive to the bottom of the Thames to retrieve the keys to the city for him. As soon as the clerk saw Everett, he blinked, his eyes going wide.

Wrexham huffed a breath and paced away from the desk, deeper into the office. It bothered Everett that the clerk had dismissed Wrexham so roundly, so he refused to even acknowledge the clerk in turn, even though the man clearly knew who he was.

"Hopefully we won't have to wait long," Wrexham mumbled when Everett joined him in the center of the office.

"Which one are we waiting for?" Everett asked, glancing to each of the three doors at the far side of the office. They all clearly led to smaller offices which were likely occupied by the department supervisors.

"That one." Wrexham nodded to the door at the far end.

They waited. For far too long. Everett crossed his arms and narrowed his eyes, studying the inner workings of whatever division of the police force Wrexham was attached to. He'd never stopped to ask what sort of police officer Wrexham was. Clearly, he'd risen up in the ranks from common street copper to investigator of some sort. Everett didn't have the first clue how the hierarchy of the Metropolitan Police worked. Wrexham still wore a uniform as he worked, but he wasn't out patrolling streets.

Norton's door opened in the middle of Everett's speculative thoughts, and a middle-aged, balding man stepped out, holding a folder and frowning. As soon as he glanced up, Wrexham moved toward him.

"Commander Norton," he began as Everett followed him. "If I could have a quick word, sir."

Norton pulled his eyes up from his papers to glance at Wrexham with a look of such obvious contempt that Everett felt as though he'd been slapped. "What do you want, Wrexham?" the man grumbled.

"It's about the investigation into the child trafficking ring, sir," Wrexham said, his back ramrod straight, his tone respectful. He played the part of the dutiful officer addressing his superior expertly.

Norton's lip curled in distaste. It was as far from the sort of respect Wrexham deserved for observing proper protocol as it would have been had Everett's audience flung shit on the stage instead of roses.

"It'll have to wait." Norton glanced down at his papers, marching directly past Wrexham to the desk of another officer. "Are these really the dimensions of my new office?" he asked the man. "I thought I'd have more room."

"Let me take a look, sir," the junior officer said, glancing uneasily past Norton to Everett.

Wrexham followed Norton, like a dog intent on getting the bone he deserved. "If you please, sir. All I need is whatever we have on record as the last known address of one Barnaby Adler."

Not only did Norton not give Wrexham the information he needed, the bastard pretended as though Wrexham hadn't spoken at all, as if he weren't there. "I want you to get down to Victoria Embankment at once and tell Younge that I won't stand for an office this size. I want one of those ones on the second floor at the very least."

Wrexham cleared his throat. "If you please, sir. Is there someone who might be able to look up Adler's last known address for me?"

At last, Norton glanced over his shoulder at Wrexham. Everett knew enough of the world and other men to know when someone had guessed what sort of man he was dealing with. He would have staked his fortune on Norton knowing full well Wrexham was a pouf, in spite of his manly and muscular appearance, and that he was in the habit of dismissing Wrexham because of it.

"I don't have time for your wild goose chases, Wrexham." Norton straightened, walking toward his office without a backward glance. "You'll have to—"

"I beg your pardon," Everett said in his most bombastic stage voice.

Everyone and everything in the office stopped, and all eyes, including Norton's, snapped to him. At least half of the men in the room knew who he was, and those who didn't could guess he was out of the ordinary.

"Officer Wrexham asked you a question," Everett went on, striding toward Norton with his shoulders thrown back and his head held high. He caught a brief glimpse of his reflection in the glass of a framed painting. His eyes looked downright ferocious with the way his kohl had smudged during his episode after spotting Chisolm, like some macabre, gothic painting. "Are you going to answer it?"

Norton flinched as Everett came to within a few feet of him. It was clear he knew who Everett was, and likely *what* he was, judging by the confused mix of awe and repulsion in his expression. Several awkward beats passed before Norton said, "He'll get what he needs when someone has time to get it for him."

"Someone will have time to get it for him now," Everett insisted, pivoting to address the entire room. It was no different than delivering a dramatic monologue to a full theater. "Do you not realize the importance of the work Officer Wrexham is doing, sir? Children are being kidnapped and sold into slavery. They are being forced to perform unspeakable and humiliating acts for men so wicked that Satan shudders at the thought of them. Officer Wrexham has devoted his time to foiling those men and bringing them to justice. He is saving the lives and souls of innocent babes...and you do not have the time to find one single name and address for him?"

By the time he reached the end of his speech, he was shouting so loud that people passing in the hallway stopped to watch the performance. Norton evidently saw the scene as undermining his authority.

"There are dozens of highly important investigations

going on right now," he growled, attempting to regain the upper hand.

The man was a fool if he thought Everett would share the spotlight so easily. "Are you saying that the mighty Metropolitan Police cannot give their full attention to more than one investigation at a time? That their reach is so short that one, noble officer cannot be given the simple information he needs in order to bring the most atrocious sort of evil to justice?"

"I...I'm not saying...I didn't say that," Norton stammered.

Everett glanced around the office. He had everyone's full attention, though Wrexham looked as though he would either flay him alive or drop to his knees and swallow Everett's cock in thanks. That image pushed him on.

"What do you think would happen to the authority of the police if word got out that its leaders cannot enable their men on the street to do their duty? How would you expect to maintain order in this city, or gain a single shred of respect, if common criminals knew there wasn't a lick of organization or discipline in the lot of you?"

"Now see here." Norton took a step toward Everett.

"How do you think that would play, man?" Everett went on. "Is that what you want? To be the laughingstock of London?"

"What the devil is going on here?"

Everett jumped slightly at the deep voice of authority. He turned to the door as a handsome man in his middle years wearing a finely-tailored suit stepped into the room.

"Lord Clerkenwell." Wrexham snapped to attention, saluting the man. As did everyone else in the room, including Norton.

Everett burst into a wide smile. It wasn't every day that the shoe was suddenly on the other foot as he came to face a man whose celebrity status loomed even larger than his own. He'd wanted to meet Jack Craig, Lord Clerkenwell, Assistant Commissioner of the Metropolitan Police ever since hearing the story of how the man had risen from being the son of a Clerkenwell whore to one of the highest-ranking officers within the police force. The man's reputation was second to none, partially for his incorruptible character on the job and partially for the way his father-in-law, the indomitable Lord Malcolm Campbell, had forced Her Majesty to grant him a title after he'd gotten Lady Bianca Marlowe with child so that the two could marry. It was a story so juicy that Everett longed for Gilbert and Sullivan to make it into an operetta so that he could play the lead role.

"My lord." Everett rushed forward, showing all the deference he could to a man he considered one of his personal heroes. "Allow me to explain."

Lord Clerkenwell arched one eyebrow and crossed his arm. "Everett Jewel, I presume?"

"It's a pleasure to meet you, my lord." Everett thrust out a hand, unable to wipe the grin from his face. When

Clerkenwell shook it, it was all Everett could do not to laugh with glee. "My lord," he went on, "Officer Wrexham here is in the midst of a vital investigation into a child trafficking ring." He gestured to Wrexham—who looked as though he wanted to sink into the floor.

"Yes, I know." Clerkenwell nodded respectfully to Wrexham. That earned the man even more merit in Everett's eyes.

"But it seems Mister Norton here," Everett deliberately refused to refer to Norton by his rank, "refuses to supply Wrexham with the simplest of information."

"Is that so?" Clerkenwell fixed a hard stare on Norton.

"M-my lord," Norton began defensively.

"What information?" Clerkenwell cut him off, turning to Wrexham.

"The last known address of Barnaby Adler, my lord," Wrexham said with a nod.

Something clicked in Clerkenwell's eyes. "Oddly enough, I was just discussing Adler this morning." He glanced to Everett, frowned at Norton, then turned back to Wrexham. "I'll have one of my assistants get you his last London address, but it appears he's hiding out with a traveling carnival which is currently summering in Brighton."

"Brighton, my lord?" Wrexham's brow inched up.

"Brighton," Everett repeated. "Lovely place. I once performed at the Royal Pavilion, when—" He snapped his mouth shut when both Wrexham and Clerkenwell stared at him. There was a time to take the stage and a time to bow out gracefully.

Clerkenwell glanced back to Wrexham. "You're assisting Dandie & Wirth in this investigation, correct?"

"Correct, my lord," Wrexham answered.

Clerkenwell nodded. "I'm transferring you to my division so that you can continue your work with them uninterrupted. If you need anything else, my man, Smiley, will assist you. I assume you'll be heading to Brighton in search of Adler?"

Wrexham blinked, clearly bowled over by how fast the tables had turned. "If you think it appropriate, my lord."

"I do." Clerkenwell nodded, glanced to Everett, then on to Norton with a satisfied look. "Carry on."

Clerkenwell left the office as quickly as he'd arrived. Everett couldn't contain his excitement over the turn of events. He always had loved a good *Deus ex Machina* when it came to solving impasses, on stage and in life.

"Well," he said, turning his smug grin on Norton. "It appears that settles that." He strode to Wrexham's side, following him as Wrexham headed for the hall, his expression tight and unreadable. When they reached the door, Everett spun to face the baffled men. "Carry on, gentlemen," he said, then bowed with a flourish worthy of the most enthusiastic standing ovation.

"You could have landed both of us in extraordinarily hot water," Wrexham muttered as they made their way across the building to what Everett assumed was Lord Clerkenwell's office.

Everett shrugged. "As the Bard said, all's well that ends well."

Wrexham shot him a wary sideways glance, then shook his head. There was a spark in his eyes, though, and he couldn't do anything to hide the flush that painted his cheeks. Wrexham might pretend to be a duty-bound stick-in-the-mud, but Everett could see he'd enjoyed the performance. And who wouldn't enjoy watching their arse of a superior being taken down several notches? Wrexham would thank him later.

Everett let himself daydream about all the ways Wrexham could thank him as they fetched Adler's last known London address from Lord Clerkenwell's office, then caught a cab to take them on to whatever destination Wrexham had next in mind. Fantasizing about what Wrexham's hands would feel like on his body, whether his lips would be soft or demanding, and what his prick would taste like was more than enough to banish the last, lingering bits of misery and weakness that seeing Chisolm had caused. He leaned back in his carriage seat, closing his eyes with a smile, and imagining how perfect it would feel to sink his cock deep into Wrexham's arse and how loudly they would both cry out when they came. He didn't even try to hide his body's reaction to his daydreams, even though he caught Wrexham gaping at the bulge in his trousers every time he peeked his eyes open.

"We're here," Wrexham announced at last, his voice hoarse, as the carriage stopped.

Everett popped his eyes open, as if suddenly waking from a delightful slumber. "Excellent. Where are we?"

They climbed out of the carriage onto one of the most dismally ordinary streets Everett had ever seen. Every building was exactly the same shade of dull grey without so much as a window box of flowers or a painted door to distinguish one house from another.

Wrexham cleared his throat after paying the driver—something Everett cursed himself for not jumping to do first. "My flat," he muttered.

Everett's brow shot up. "Heavens." He burst into a wicked smile. Apparently, he was about to get his thanks after all.

Wrexham eyed him warily, then marched forward and into the drab building. "I figure it's best if I leave for Brighton immediately."

"If *you* leave for Brighton?" The idea of being parted from Wrexham sent snakes writhing through Everett's gut. "What about me?"

Wrexham glanced over his shoulder at Everett in surprise as they reached a door on the first floor. "Don't you have performances?"

"Yes, but I also have an understudy," he said. He leaned against the wall beside Wrexham's door, his mouth curving into a seductive smile. "So the two of us are free for a romantic holiday by the sea."

Wrexham's face grew even redder, and fire danced in

his eyes. He cleared his throat and dragged his gaze to where he was attempting to fit his key in the door. There was something shatteringly erotic in his attempts to poke the long, stiff key into the waiting lock. Everett's already tight trousers grew unbearable.

"What a lovely home you have," he said in a low, seductive voice as he stepped into the depressingly bland, one-room flat. "It simply oozes charm." Everett had seen broom closets with more character.

Wrexham cleared his throat, marching straight to the wardrobe and opening it. He took down a small suitcase from the top shelf, carrying it to the narrow, lumpy bed. Everett's mouth tugged into a smirk at the sight of the bed. He needed far more room than that to maneuver, but if it was what had to work with, he'd make do.

"I'm sorry." Wrexham jerked straight. "Could I offer you some tea?" He hesitated, something guarded and feral glowing in his eyes. "Something to eat?" He barely managed to push the words out.

"I'm in the mood for a big, thick sausage," Everett said, leaning jauntily against the side of Wrexham's wardrobe.

Wrexham hesitated, then nodded and crossed to a strongbox that sat on a small table near the room's tiny stove. Everett didn't have the slightest idea what the man was doing. Did he have some sort of devilish devices hidden away in the strongbox that would help their congress along? He generally preferred fucking *au naturel*, but he wasn't opposed to playing with toys now and then.

He knew he'd committed a cardinal sin by laughing out loud as Wrexham opened the locked chest to reveal an elaborate stash of food. "Darling, is your cooking so precious that you fear thieves will break in and steal your buns?"

Wrexham flinched, eyes wide with shame as he glanced to Everett. He slammed the lid of his food chest shut. Everett caught his hands shaking before he pulled them behind his back. He stepped cautiously toward Wrexham, watching as the man worked up the nerve to speak.

"When I was a boy," he started, but gave up. He swallowed, eyes downcast. "Growing up, in the orphanage, there was never enough." He was barely audible. His shoulders hunched. "We had to fight for everything—beds, clothing...food." Slowly, he raised his eyes to meet Everett's. "Do you know what it's like to starve as a child while watching others gorge themselves at the head table?"

Nausea clawed at Everett's insides. "No," he admitted quietly. He'd never had to go hungry, as long as he'd swallowed what had been thrust in his mouth first.

"You don't ever forget the feeling," Wrexham whispered.

"No, you don't," Everett agreed with equal agony.

Neither of them moved. At least, outwardly. Inside, Everett pulsed so desperately that it was a wonder he didn't shatter into a thousand pieces. He needed Wrexham, needed to explain everything to him, needed to beg his forgiveness, needed to demand to know why they'd been forced to suffer so much. He needed to feel the man's body entwined with his, needed his heat and his sighs of pleasure. He needed someone to weep and scream with who would understand.

He surged forward, reaching for Wrexham to draw him into a passionate embrace. Every inch of his body ached for the man, inside and out.

His hands had barely brushed Wrexham's face when Wrexham jerked away from him, holding his arms up as though Everett had come at him with a knife. Only he was the one who felt the sting of the blade sinking into his heart.

"I know you want—"

"I can't," Wrexham cut him off before Everett could finish his plea.

Everett ground his teeth and balled his hands into impotent fists. The heat between them was enough to ignite the dismal drapes covering Wrexham's windows. Wrexham's trousers were tented to the point where a blind man could have seen his arousal. So why, in God's name, was the man rejecting what they were both gagging for?

Everett stepped toward him, hand outstretched. "If I could just—"

"I think you should leave." Wrexham turned away from him, wincing as though in pain.

Pain that Everett felt deep in his gut. He opened his mouth, but no words came out. He, the man who could and had talked his way out of any situation, was at a complete loss. He held his ground at first, refusing to let Wrexham reject him so coldly. The trouble was, there was nothing cold about the rejection at all. It was all fire and passion that burned so hot he could see Wrexham being consumed alive.

"I'll go," he said in a strangled voice, taking a step back. "I don't want to go, but I will."

Wrexham glanced miserably at him. "Thank you."

"We'll meet at Victoria Station tomorrow and head to Brighton together," Everett went on, moving away and hating every inch between them. "I'll purchase tickets for whatever train leaves closest to nine."

Wrexham nodded, shoulders dropping as though he were forcing his body to unclench.

"Don't worry about—" Everett ended with a helpless shrug. There was so much to worry about that it would do no good to deny it. He turned and marched to the door. "I'll see you tomorrow, then," he said with false cheer before rushing out to the hall.

Once the door was shut behind him, he sagged against the wall, burying his face in his hands. For years, he'd managed to keep Pandora's Box shut tight, but all it'd taken was one soul as wounded as his to wrench it open again.

CHAPTER 7

*V*ictoria Station was crowded when Everett strolled in after yet another fitful night's sleep. He'd dressed in a plain, dark grey suit and scrubbed his face of all lingering cosmetics, and for a change, he blended in with the rest of the dull clerks and tradesmen going about their morning business. Few people gave him a second look, and no one stopped to gape. It felt as unnatural as the sun rising in the north, but the heaviness that had settled over him with Wrexham's dismissal the day before and the rawness of his wounds from that interaction made him reluctant to be seen, for a change.

He purchased two first-class tickets to Brighton at the ticket window without the clerk even meeting his eyes. The man behind him shunted him out of the way in his haste to make his purchase. Everett glared at the short, beefy man for a moment before taking his tickets in one hand, his suitcase in the other, and marching out to the center of the station to wait for Wrexham. The lack of attention was unnerving, and it made him wonder what sort of life he would have had if his father hadn't viewed him as a shiny object, worthy of sale. Would he have ended up just like any other grey-faced, hollow-eyed laborer, like his brother Frank? Or would he have turned to drink, like his father, or landed in prison, dead before the age of twenty, like his brother Morris?

Or would he have taken the exact same path he'd been forced down, only by his own choosing? Some men were born to drag themselves through the dirt of life, toiling without looking up at the sun, and some were destined for greatness, even if they had to suck a few cocks or bend over and take it up the arse to get there.

"I almost didn't recognize you."

Everett came close to leaping out of his skin at Wrexham's softly-spoken words. He shoved his thoughts aside, as though they were filthy pictures he'd been looking at when he wasn't supposed to, and spun to face him. Immediately, his heart dropped to his groin. Wrexham was dressed in plain clothes, which were extraordinarily plain indeed. But he'd scrubbed himself up nicely, was clean-shaven, and wore his sandy hair combed rakishly to the side instead of in the abominable fashion of being parted down the middle that Everett couldn't stand.

It took several seconds for Everett to realize he was staring and holding his breath. He didn't help the situation by blurting, "You look lovely," when sense finally returned to him.

Wrexham blushed and glanced sheepishly down, his eyelashes brushing his cheek. Everett's cock stiffened in response. He cursed himself for behaving like a green lad with his first fancy.

"I bought tickets." Everett thrust the two tickets awkwardly at Wrexham, feeling like an utter fool. It was a terrible idea not to dress up and paint his face for the trip. Without his costume, he was unrecognizable, true, but he was also utterly out of his depth.

Wrexham took the tickets, studying them for a moment. "Nine fifteen," he said. "We'd better head to the platform." He turned and started away from Everett, then paused as though he'd been struck by lightning, facing Everett again. "First-class?" His brow flew up.

"Of course." Everett put on a coy grin, sauntering up to Wrexham's side. He was tempted to take the man's arm and escort him on as though he were a debutante on his way to his coming-out ball, but without his theatrical persona, he wasn't sure he could pull it off. "Why have money if you can't travel in style?"

The train had just begun boarding when they reached the platform. Wrexham remained painfully silent as they waited for a drab but diligent maid to sweep out the compartment that they had tickets for. Wrexham stood at attention, but his face remained a fetching shade of pink, and he continually stole glances in Everett's direction. Every time Everett caught him staring and smiled, Wrexham would snap his eyes away.

It was intolerable. There was no earthly way the two of them would survive the journey to Brighton—let alone their mission once they got there—unless the impasse between them could be breeched. And the only way for that to happen was if Everett swallowed his pride and did the one thing his years of theatrical training had taught him could diffuse any tense situation.

"Here we are," he said with a grin once the maid finished tidying their compartment. "All ship-shape, just for us."

He stepped over the gap into the train and pretended to catch his foot on the carpet. With studied elegance, he flung himself comically across one of the seats, then tumbled to the floor, deliberately making himself look like as much of an arse as possible.

"Are you all right?" Wrexham leapt into the compartment after him, tossing his suitcase on one of the seats and reaching to help Everett up.

"I'm fine, just fine." Everett grabbed hold of Wrexham's arm—feeling a quick thrill at how strong and solid his muscles were—and stumbled to his feet. "Oh, dear. How very clumsy of me," he said with a teasing grin.

Wrexham eyed him warily before letting go and reaching for his suitcase to store it in the compartment above his seat.

Everett did the same, but as he lifted the case, he subtly undid the clasps so that once he hoisted it over his head, the lid sprung open and a cascade of clothes, toiletries, and sundries spilled out, covering him and his seat. He made sure that a pair of his drawers landed on his head.

"Good heavens," he exclaimed, feigning shock.

Wrexham twisted to frown at Everett over his shoulder. The second he saw Everett's predicament, his brow flew up and his mouth twitched, as though he were trying not to laugh.

"I'm certain I'm wearing these on the wrong end," Everett said, adjusting his drawers so that they sat, like a kerchief, on his head. "Though I have, on occasion, been called a nob head."

Wrexham snorted, turning away as though he didn't want to offend Everett by laughing. The sound was like the music of the angels, as far as Everett was concerned, as was the glint in Wrexham's eyes when he finished securing his suitcase and turned to help Everett.

"You mustn't be so clumsy," he said, picking up Everett's socks and the leather case that contained his cosmetics from the floor.

"It wasn't on purpose," Everett said, even though it absolutely was.

Wrexham peeked up at him from his bent-over position. The spark in his eyes told Everett that he was reasonably certain the stunt was deliberate. "Did you need to pack so much?" he asked, tucking the socks and case into Everett's suitcase, which he'd moved to the seat as he stuffed his things back in.

"One never knows what sort of event he'll be called on to attend in Brighton," Everett answered with mock imperiousness. "Why, last time I was there, I was asked to perform at the Royal Pavilion."

"So you said at Scotland Yard." Wrexham set to work folding Everett's jumbled clothing with a grace and care that left Everett overheated, but without meeting his eyes.

Everett leaned back against the wall of the compartment. "Prince Albert and his particular friends were in residence." He crossed his arms and studied the set of Wrexham's shoulders and the deliberate way he nestled each article of Everett's clothing in the suitcase. "Which was unusual to begin with, since the royal family despises the Pavilion. The whole place is in bad need of repairs."

Wrexham hummed to show he was listening, his expression growing sober.

That wasn't at all what Everett was going for, so he put on a smile and fixed Wrexham with a rakish look. "I performed the Dance of the Seven Veils."

Wrexham started, snapping his head toward him. "You...what?"

"Oh yes." Everett's grin widened. "It's the only time I've performed in drag."

"In what?" Wrexham stopped what he was doing, his brow knit in confusion.

"Drag," Everett said. "It's a theatrical term. 'Dressed Resembling A Girl'. At least, that's one theory about what it means. Personally, it's not my style, though I have several friends who make a fine living impersonating women. It was a special request of His Royal Highness, you see. Bertie is quite a bounder. Drives his dear mama to distraction, and they say that's what killed his father. But he does know how to have a good time."

Wrexham's jaw hung open through the entire explanation, only closing when he said, "So I've heard." He turned back to packing.

"Anyhow, Prince Bertie and his coterie are known for loving the ladies," Everett went on. "And since there weren't any ladies on hand that evening, I was elected to do the honors. It was the performance of my life, if I do say so myself. I shaved every inch of hair from my body and dressed in silk before dancing my way into the hearts of England's finest gentlemen. Half of them were so drunk they didn't even realize I was a man."

"They didn't?" Wrexham stopped his work to blink at Everett.

Everett shrugged. "Not until I flung off the last veil to reveal my massive, fully erect prick." He grinned. "With a pretty pink bow and bells tied around the base."

Wrexham burst into a snorting laugh. He clamped a hand to his mouth, his face bright red and his eyes glittering with amusement.

"That was only the half of it," Everett breezed on, inwardly dancing on air to have made Wrexham laugh, though outwardly he maintained his air of arrogant indifference. "You should have heard the way those bells jingled as a certain royal duke sucked me off. In spite of his claims to be as moral and upright as a bishop."

Wrexham snorted so hard he lapsed into coughing.

"The bishop quite enjoyed me as well that night, if I recall correctly," Everett went on, lying through his teeth, but as giddy as a loon over the way Wrexham laughed in spite of himself. "My arse still hasn't recovered," he added, pretending to gingerly rub his backside.

"You're lying." Wrexham said, feeling sure of himself.

"I am not," Everett insisted with false offense. Wrexham finished with the packing, so Everett stepped in, standing flush against the man, and closed his suitcase. Their hands brushed before Wrexham pulled away.

"You're definitely lying," Wrexham said as Everett stowed his suitcase above his seat.

"You wound me." Everett clasped a hand to his heart as he twisted and sank into his seat.

Wrexham shook his head, grinning. "I can tell when you're lying."

Everett sat straighter. "Really? How?"

For a moment, Wrexham studied him, giving Everett the feeling that Wrexham was undressing him in his mind. That left him bristling with energy and unable to sit still.

"It's in your eyes," Wrexham said at last. "You look far too...clever when you're lying."

Everett dropped his jaw in mock offense. His heart raced and his trousers grew tighter by the moment. "I am clever, though."

"You are." Wrexham nodded. "And you know it."

Everett didn't know whether to be pleased or alarmed by the observation.

"Which is why you have that look when you're lying," Wrexham went on.

"It wasn't all a lie." Everett couldn't help but grin and flirt by tapping his foot against Wrexham's as they sat facing each other.

Wrexham didn't move his foot. It was a major victory, as far as Everett was concerned. He did, however, narrow his eyes and study Everett.

"The bit about the bishop was a lie," Wrexham said, lowering his voice. He peeked out the compartment door as if checking to see who might be listening in. "The bells and the duke weren't."

Of all the ridiculous things, Everett suddenly filled with embarrassment over that particular past indiscretion. It hadn't been half as fun as he made it out to be. "He was a clumsy old bastard," he said, still feigning jollity. "But I thoroughly enjoyed myself."

"No, you didn't." Wrexham's face went dead serious. So serious that sorrow filled his lovely, deep eyes.

Everett squirmed in his seat. The point of his story hadn't been to make him feel like an insect specimen pinned to a cork board. It had been to make Wrexham laugh. An uncomfortable heat infused him, and if it weren't for the train conductor coming along to check their tickets and close the compartment door, Everett would have considered bolting.

Minutes later, a whistle sounded, and the train jerked forward, pulling out of the station on its way south.

"The Royal Pavilion was a lark." Everett shifted the way he sat to drape dramatically over his seat. "But it was nothing to the private party that was held the night The Savoy hotel opened."

The rest of the journey to Brighton passed in a flurry of lurid stories—half of them true, half of them complete fabrications—as miles of sunny countryside sped past. Everett succeeded in making Wrexham laugh, probably more than the man had laughed in his life. Wrexham amused himself by guessing which of Everett's stories were lies and which were the truth. Unnervingly, he was right the majority of the time. As someone who had not only made a life on the stage, but had survived darker times than most mortals would ever want to imagine by lying to save his skin, Everett prided himself on his ability to bend the truth to suit his needs. Wrexham saw right through him, which left him rippling with lust.

"I've taken the liberty of telegraphing ahead to reserve us a hotel room," he said once they reached Brighton and walked out of the noisy station onto an equally noisy street.

Wrexham missed a step. Everett had to reach out and steady him, which he didn't mind at all.

"*A* hotel room?" Wrexham asked. "For both of us?"

Everett sent him a flat, sideways look as if to say, "Don't be silly". Aloud, he said, "It has two beds."

Wrexham was silent the rest of the way to the hotel—

which was down the hill from the train station, along the waterfront. Checking in was simple. Not a soul in the place gave them so much as a second glance. There was nothing curious about two men sharing a hotel room in the slightest, as far as Everett was concerned. And even if someone had suspected activity of a sordid nature, it was bloody Brighton. Anything that might or might not transpire between him and Wrexham would be innocent by comparison to half of what went on in the naughty holiday town.

All the same, Everett knew in an instant from the wariness in Wrexham's eyes as they deposited their suitcases in the spacious room with an outstanding view of the sea on the very top floor of the hotel that any fantasies he had of him and Wrexham tumbling into each other's arms and fucking the night away would remain just that, fantasies.

"It's a bit luxurious for an investigation," Wrexham said, crossing to peer out the window.

"Of course, it's luxurious." Everett shrugged. "I wouldn't stay anywhere less divine."

Wrexham craned his neck one way, then the other, looking at the expanse of the beach. "It must cost a fortune."

"I have money. I might as well spend it," Everett said.

Wrexham glanced warily back at him.

"Right," he said, his grin becoming impish. "Let's get to it."

Wrexham blanched. It would have been adorable, if

it hadn't underscored the unbreakably tense barrier between them.

"Let's go find this carnival and Adler with it," Everett said with a teasing look that told Wrexham he knew exactly what images his first statement had conjured in Wrexham's mind.

He headed to the door. When he reached it, he glanced over his shoulder, winking at Wrexham.

The carnival was easy to find. Brighton had hundreds of attractions for summer holiday-makers to enjoy, but a carnival was not something the extravagant town saw every day. The sprawling sea of tents, booths, and games was set up in a field on the east side of town. It was already crawling with people by the time Everett and Wrexham purchased their tickets and joined the flow of the crowd pulsing through the place.

"I didn't realize there would be so many people," Wrexham said, tucking his hands nervously into his pockets as he and Everett glanced around.

Everett nodded to a woman who gaped at him, as though she knew exactly who he was, then turned to Wrexham. The man had an uncanny ability to shrink in on himself to the point where he practically disappeared in front of Everett's eyes.

"It's a carnival," he said with a shrug. "Of course, there are going to be people. That's the point of the things."

Wrexham sent him a look that was almost sassy. "Yes, I know that. I'm concerned about finding Adler."

A wide grin spread across Everett's face. "I'd no idea you could be so tetchy, Wrexham."

"I'm not tetchy," Wrexham argued. "I'm just...." He failed to come up with anything to describe himself. "We need to find Adler and get to the bottom of this investigation."

"Yes, I do love getting to the bottom of things." Everett couldn't help himself. Not with Wrexham looking as relaxed as Everett had ever seen him. Which wasn't much.

"You're an arse, Jewel." The corner of Wrexham's mouth twitched.

Everett was certain every bit of his overexcited feelings for the man were on display for the entire carnival to see. "I don't think I've ever heard you call me by my name before," he said in a quiet, caressing voice. "Though I do wish you'd call me Everett."

Wrexham's brow ticked up, and his lips pressed firmly shut. He did, however, inch closer to Everett as they walked on. Everett greeted the tiny gesture as though Wrexham had thrown his arms around him and kissed him for all the world to see. He strutted on as though he were the cock of the walk.

"Wrexham, look!" He stopped suddenly, grabbing Wrexham's arm and pointing across the way to a tall stand with a platform at the bottom and a bell at the top. A barker stood beside the contraption with a huge mallet.

"Test your strength, laddies," the barker shouted.

"Impress your little lady by ringing the bell and winning a prize. Step right up!"

"Now I'll be able to prove to you just how virile a man I am," Everett said with a teasing grin, dodging through the current of the crowd to approach the game. Wrexham hurried along behind him. "How much for one try?" he asked the barker.

"Just a penny, good sir, just a penny."

Everett reached into his pocket to pay the man, then took the mallet from him.

"Get ready to swoon in wonder, Wrexham," he said, adjusting his grip on the mallet.

Wrexham crossed his arms and sent Everett a wry look of doubt. Everett took it as both flirtation and as a challenge. Fortunately for him, Wrexham didn't have the first clue how strong he actually was. The man had only seen him on stage and swanning about London, like the degenerate dandy he was. His gut fluttered with giddiness and an almost silly need to impress Wrexham as he stepped up to the game.

"Would you care to wager on the outcome?" Everett asked as he settled into a low stance.

Several people—including the woman Everett was sure recognized him—stopped what they were doing to watch.

"No," Wrexham said with a simple smile.

"Suit yourself." Everett shrugged, then made a dramatic show of preparing to swing the mallet.

The moment he knew he had an audience, he dove

into his antics with a showman's flare. Finally, he swung the mallet and smacked it hard on the platform. The ringer flew up the tower, making it almost to the bell, but falling short by less than a foot. The watching crowd groaned in disappointment on Everett's behalf as he exaggerated his dismay.

"Ladies and gentlemen," he said, appealing to the crowd. "I am desperately sorry not to have lived up to expectations for you. I don't usually have a problem getting it up."

The crowd roared with laughter. Ladies blushed and clapped hands to their mouths. One woman covered her young son's ears.

"Shall I go again?" Everett asked. "I'm usually good for more than one pop."

Again, the crowd laughed. But instead of letting him take another swing, the barker marched forward to retrieve the mallet.

"We have another paying customer," the man said as Everett started to protest.

The barker handed the mallet to Wrexham, who held out a shiny penny. Without a word, Wrexham strode forward to take Everett's place. He hefted the mallet in his hands, testing its weight, then stepped back from the platform and set the mallet, head down, against his leg so that he could remove his jacket. With a serious look, he handed his jacket to Everett to hold, then rolled up his shirt-sleeves, exposing thick forearms.

A hot flush poured through Everett. He didn't bother

to hide his admiration for Wrexham's form—though he did hold the man's jacket at the level of his waist, since there were children in the crowd—as Wrexham rolled his shoulders and lifted the mallet once more. For a man who loathed attention, Wrexham had the crowd rapt with attention.

With a final frown of concentration, Wrexham stepped up to the platform. He swung the mallet, hitting the platform so hard that the ringer soared up, ringing the bell loudly. The crowd burst into shouts and cheers. Everett's knees went weak. His mind instantly filled with all the things Wrexham could do with his monumental strength that would leave him moaning and undone. He'd never wanted to be flat on his back, splayed and helpless to another man's whims, more in his life.

As a final insult added to delicious injury, after handing the mallet back to the barker, Wrexham extended a hand to Everett, reaching for his jacket. As Everett handed it over, like a subservient doll, Wrexham winked at him, his lips curved in a devilish grin. If Everett didn't get the man alone and naked soon, he didn't know what he'd do with himself.

CHAPTER 8

He was having fun. At least, Patrick thought that was what he was doing. The sensation was so unfamiliar to him that it seemed wrong.

"Can you believe I've only ever been to one carnival in my life?" Jewel asked as they made their way up a row of booths selling every sort of food imaginable. No, Everett. He'd asked to be called Everett, and, curse his weakened heart, Patrick couldn't think of the man as anything but now.

"Only one?" Patrick asked, picking at a corner of the fried cod nestled between chips in the paper cone he carried.

"It's ridiculous for an entertainer such as myself to only have gone to one carnival in his life, I know," Everett said with a laugh, biting into a chip. Of all the savory treats they could have purchased from the numerous food stalls, they'd settled on the pedestrian choice of fish and chips. And yet, it seemed only fitting. Such simple fare was the sort of things that friends shared when they were frittering away an afternoon together.

And he and Everett were friends, strange as it was.

Stranger still, Patrick knew there was something deeper than friendship roiling right under the surface—something that unnerved and intrigued him.

"Carnivals were far too rich for my father's blood when I was a boy," Everett went on with a shrug as the two of them reached the end of the row of booths. "And after that, the sort of entertainments I was privy to were of a much more sophisticated sort."

They leaned against a thick post that had been driven into the soft ground to support the temporary fence that enclosed the carnival. Their hips and shoulders touched, raising Patrick's awareness of Everett's body to a wild degree, and yet, there was something comforting about the two of them sharing the space.

Patrick eyed Everett warily, his face heating at the thought of what sort of sophisticated entertainment a young Everett had been exposed to.

As if he could read his thoughts, Everett let out a wry laugh. "It wasn't what you're thinking." He paused to eat another chip before going on. "I mean, yes, that sort of entertainment abounded, and I was at the center of it more often than not. But the…shall we call them caretakers I found myself with were titled and refined. Or so they liked to consider themselves. I was exposed to opera and Shakespeare at the same time that I was exposed to buggery."

The casual way Everett told the story sent a chill down Patrick's spine, putting him off his fish and chips. He kept eating in spite of his sour stomach, though. There was no way to know when he would see another meal.

"Of course, I fell in love with the theater, as you might imagine," Everett continued, staring dreamily off into space. "The costumes, the make-up, the magic of the whole thing. I knew I wanted to be a part of that world, and I had the good fortune—if you could call it that—of having a keeper who encouraged my interest."

Again, Patrick's stomach clenched at the implications behind Everett's story.

Everett shrugged. "It would be a lie to say my whole life has been nothing but sin and misery. I was given an opportunity to excel in a profession most people are either abhorred by or forbidden from entering. And you know I love it." He glanced sideways at Patrick, nudging him with his elbow.

"You're a fine actor." Patrick smiled. "I've seen you perform at least two dozen times."

Everett's brow shot up in surprise. "Have you?"

Patrick nodded, feeling unaccountably sheepish for the admission.

"Good Lord, Wrexham. You've been a follower all this time and I never knew it?" Everett's eyes glittered at the idea.

Patrick merely shrugged.

"Why did you never wait for me at the stage door, then?" Everett stood straight, turning to face him. He tossed the remnants of his fish and chips over the makeshift fence and into the grass. That motion made Patrick feel even sicker than Everett's stories. Wasting food was a cardinal sin.

He stared mournfully at the discarded food for a moment before dragging his eyes up to meet Everett's. "I admire you," he said, unsure how to explain the complexity of his feelings. "To stand at the stage door with dozens of others would have meant I was the same as them, just another admirer in a crowd whose names you didn't know and whose faces you would forget." He shielded the intensity of his longing for Everett by staring at his chips. "It would have killed my soul to have you think of me as just another follower."

Everett's brow lifted, but the heat in his eyes was more regret than surprise, as if he'd only just realized how expendable every admirer who had ever waited for him with baited breath had been to him. "I could never feel that indifferent to you," he said in a soft voice.

"Couldn't you?" Patrick met Everett's eyes, then focused on his supper. The sudden urge to have both hands free so that he could reach for and caress Everett was overwhelming. Not that he would have dared to do something so bold, especially not in public.

Everett studied him, his brow furrowing and confusion taking the place of regret in his eyes. "Can you really not believe that you are fascinating and desirable?"

Patrick closed his hand around the top of the cone holding his fish and chips, crushing it to form a pouch. "Please don't make fun of me," he murmured, turning away so that he could stuff the remnants of his supper into the pocket of his jacket.

"I'm not making fun of you," Everett laughed. When Patrick whipped to face him with a scowl, Everett's expression grew dead serious. "I'm not making fun of you," he repeated, fire in his eyes.

Every fiber of Patrick's body vibrated with need, but it was too much to believe that a star that burned as bright as Everett Jewel could ever think of him as more than a toy to be used and discarded. Even if evidence to the contrary stood right in front of him, gazing at him with flashes of desperation in his beautiful eyes.

Patrick cleared his throat. "We're here to search for Adler," he said, straightening and tugging on the hem of his jacket. "We'd best get to it."

He walked off before Everett could say anything else that might tease or tempt him.

Everett caught up, falling into step beside him. They walked the perimeter of the carnival in silence, pretending to scan the booths, games, rides, and tents for any sign of Adler when what they were really doing was looking in every direction possible, except at each other.

The tension remained high as they turned into a row of carnival games. The noise of bells and laughter, blocks falling, children laughing, and applause crowded around them diffusing the emotion between them. Patrick found himself paying more attention to the smiling men and women enjoying their time than the twisting passions in his gut. Even so, he could feel Everett watching him as though trying to work out his thoughts.

"You're Everett Jewel, you are." A young woman and two of her friends stepped into their path, startling Patrick out of his thoughts.

"Why, ladies, you've discovered me," Everett greeted them with a flourish. "How very clever you are."

In an instant, Everett was on stage again. The transformation was distinct. He stood taller, smiled more broadly, and winked at the girls. Immediately, half the people milling around them recognized the importance of the man they'd ignored just moments before.

"Sing us a song, please," one of the girls said, clasping her hands to her chest. "I saw you in *Adonis* a few years back."

"Did you, darling?" Everett's teeth flashed along with his smile, unusually straight and white. It made Patrick self-conscious of his own crooked smile.

"You were divine," the girl sighed.

"How very kind of you to say, love." Everett took her hand, raising it to his lips. "For that, I'll bow to pressure and regale you with song."

He burst into a popular number by Arthur Sullivan that had been repurposed for the burlesque show, *Adonis*. Patrick grinned and stepped back, letting Everett shine. And shine he did. As he belted out the song in a loud, harmonious tenor, everyone within twenty yards dropped what they were doing to crowd around. The more of them flooded in, the farther back Patrick moved.

He didn't know how Everett did it. Being the center of so much attention was Patrick's idea of hell. But Everett lapped up the adoring glances and the fierce applause when his song was over, launching into another, much to the delight of the crowd. He was in his element, shining and virile. He exuded the sort of magnetism that had Patrick's heart thumping against his ribs. He wasn't the only one enthralled either, which put him at ease. No one could single him out for watching Everett with the hunger of a man who hadn't had a solid meal in weeks when at least a dozen other men were staring at him the same way, whether they had the same inclinations that Patrick did or not.

He sent a curious glance across the growing crowd, wondering if it was so very wrong of him to want Everett the way he did when everyone else in the crowd wanted him just as much. Those thoughts were quickly eclipsed when he spotted a middle-aged man in a long coat hovering near the back of the crowd. Rather than watching Everett adoringly, the man narrowed his eyes and hunched his shoulders.

Patrick's instincts flared to life, and he watched the man as though he would attack. He'd never seen Barnaby Adler before, but if someone had told him the suspicious man was him, he would have believed them. Even if he wasn't, the stranger obviously had ill-intent. He might not have been anything special in any other area, but Patrick could pick out a criminal from fifty paces in every circumstance.

He started toward the suspicious man just as Everett finished his second song. The crowd applauded, begging for another.

"No, no, I couldn't possibly," Everett told them, looking as though he would break into another song at any moment. Instead, Patrick noticed out of the corner of his eye that Everett turned toward the spot where he had last stood. His face fell. "Where's my copper?" he asked, seemingly making a joke, but with serious concern in his eyes.

Everett spotted Patrick in the thick of the crowd just as the suspicious man realized he'd been targeted. Whether it was Adler or not, the man flinched when he saw Patrick coming toward him. He thrust his hands in his pockets, turned his collar up, and disappeared into the crowd.

"Wrexham," Everett said as he pushed his way through his admirers, heading toward Patrick. "How are you supposed to guard my body if you don't stay near me?"

As tempted as Patrick was to wince, he recognized Everett's statement for what it was. By claiming him as what amounted to an employee, he was making the most innocent and iron-clad excuse for the two of them to be wandering a carnival in Brighton together.

The ruse was so perfect that Patrick didn't bother addressing it when Everett reached his side. "Is that Adler?" he asked, nodding to the retreating man.

Everett stood taller and squinted, then let out a breath. "I have no idea. Adler or not, whoever it is just got away."

"We should follow him."

Everett nodded, and the two of them marched after the man. Several of Everett's followers attempted to come along, but when Everett failed to acknowledge them at all, they gave up the chase and resorted to lingering at a distance.

Whoever the man with the coat was, he had disappeared entirely by the time Patrick and Everett neared the carnival's entrance.

"I think we're done for the day," Everett said what Patrick was thinking, rubbing a hand over his face. "It's getting late at any rate," he went on.

It was as if Everett's words were a cue for Patrick to realize how exhausted he was. Searching the carnival was tiring enough, but after two nearly sleepless nights and the journey to Brighton, he was ready to drop.

"If we leave, Adler could get away," he reasoned aloud.

"If that was Adler, which we have no proof of, how would he know we are after him?" Everett reasoned. "We have a history, true, but he has no reason to think I'm here for any reason other than amusement. And it's unlikely he knows who you are."

"True." Patrick glanced around the carnival again, as though Adler would leap out from behind the nearest tent and turn himself in.

"He'll be here tomorrow." Everett moved forward, grabbing Patrick's elbow and escorting him on. "Besides, I've grown rather tired of crowds. It's time we were alone."

His words sent a shiver down Patrick's spine. Nothing in Everett's face suggested he'd meant the words to be flirtatious. That was almost as unnerving as if Everett had stroked a hand down his arm or wiggled his eyebrows suggestively.

They left the carnival, heading back to the hotel through crowded streets. Everett made a few amusing observations about some of the people they passed or about the sea, but Patrick hardly heard them and only responded with a grunt here and there. He was too aware of what waited for them back at the hotel to make casual conversation. The more they walked, the broader Everett smiled and the closer he swayed to Patrick. The light in his eyes overtook any lingering signs of exhaustion, especially when he stole quick peeks at Patrick. If the two of them were secluded in a hotel room together for the night, there was no telling what might happen.

The worst of it was, Patrick wanted it to happen. The truth shocked him. It also terrified him. By the time they climbed the steps of the hotel porch and made their way up the staircase that took them to the top floor and their room, Patrick was trembling with pent-up desire and daunting fear. He knew what he wanted, and he knew he was afraid of it. What he didn't know was whether he would be able to act on it or whether he would run.

"God," Everett groaned once they were behind closed doors. He removed his hat and tossed it haphazardly toward one of the room's chairs. It missed and fell to the floor, but Everett ignored it. He unbuttoned his jacket and threw that aside as well. "I love an audience," he said, loosening his tie and turning to face Patrick, "but sometimes it's all a bit much."

He stopped when he noticed Patrick with his back pressed up against the door. Patrick hadn't been aware of shrinking to the position, but he was frozen there now, watching Everett, his heart pounding as he waited to see what would happen.

Everett grinned at the sight of him and slowly pulled his tie off of his collar, dropping it dramatically. "Oh, dear," he said, stalking closer. "It appears I somehow managed to corner you, Officer Wrexham."

Patrick flattened his palms against the door, telling himself to breathe without managing to draw breath.

"Whatever shall I do with you now?" Everett sidled closer, closing the space between them with agonizing slowness. He moved like a cat on the prowl until he reached the door and planted his hands firmly over Patrick's shoulders. "What an interesting predicament we find ourselves in," he hummed, his body leaning into Patrick's without quite touching him. He brought his lips to within a breath of Patrick's. "You've told me twice before that you can't," he said. "But from where I'm standing, what you can't do now is get away."

Panic whipped through Patrick, but lust pulsed right along with it. He didn't dare to move, lest his body come into intimate contact with Everett's, and yet his cock was so hard it was painful. Everett's scent filled him, sweetness and spice with just a hint of fish and chips. It was nonsensically erotic, and Patrick groaned as if Everett had slid a hand along his trousers to stroke him.

He squeezed his eyes shut, fully expecting Everett to take wicked advantage and kiss him senseless. Nothing happened, no matter how hard Patrick braced himself. Everett stood where he was, not quite touching him but effectively blocking him from moving. Lust and tension sizzled in the air to the point where Patrick was certain he would explode out of his skin.

As last, when the still frisson between them was too much for Patrick to bear, he opened his eyes.

Everett stared straight into his soul, unblinking. "Would you care to tell me how you can be gagging for a fuck so desperately that the heat of it puts the sun to shame while so doggedly denying what we both want?" he asked in a low whisper.

"I—" Patrick's throat closed over the single syllable. Anything he said would be humiliating for both of them. But he couldn't hold back anymore. Not after the day they'd spent together and not after the things Everett had laid bare about his past. "I've never done it before," he blurted before he lost his nerve.

Everett blinked. "Not at all?"

Patrick shook his head tightly, the heat flooding him almost unbearable.

"Not even a little slap and tickle?" The corner of Everett's mouth twitched, but it wasn't amusement.

Again, Patrick shook his head.

"With anyone?" A note of incredulity crept into his voice. "Not even with a woman?"

"No," Patrick croaked. "I haven't even been kissed."

Everett's jaw dropped. He inched back, keeping his hands on the door behind Patrick, still preventing him from escaping. "You've never even been kissed?"

Patrick shook his head.

"Bloody hell, man." Affection and disbelief and sadness jumbled together in Everett's expression, as though he didn't know which emotion to settle on. He continued to stare at Patrick, finally saying, "We're taking care of that right now."

Before Patrick could react, Everett surged into him, slanting his mouth over his. Patrick knew it was coming, but he gasped in shock and stiffened so hard every part of him ached as Everett caressed his mouth with his own. He nipped at Patrick's lower lip and brushed his tongue along the seam before sliding his tongue against Patrick's. The sensation was so overpoweringly good that Patrick moaned in response, digging his fingernails into the door behind him. Everett answered his moan with one of his own, pressing his body against Patrick's. He used his lips and teeth and tongue to explore every inch of Patrick's mouth, rendering him helpless.

It was so potent that the tell-tale signs of impending orgasm gathered in Patrick's groin. That much pleasure alarmed him, and he gasped, pushing Everett away. As soon as he had enough space between them, he dashed to the side, pressing the back of his hand to his mouth.

"I don't understand." Everett spun to face him. His frustration was palpable. "You want this."

"I know." Patrick gasped for breath. "I know, but—" He didn't know how to go on. His hands trembled visibly. He didn't know where to hold them or what to do with them.

"This cannot go on," Everett said, oddly serious, walking slowly toward him. "God knows I would never, ever force anyone to do anything they don't want to do, but you cannot continue to live like this. Especially when you want it so badly I'm afraid you'll do yourself harm."

Patrick's eyes went wide. He would never hurt himself...but deep in his heart, he knew Everett was right. He couldn't go on the way he had anymore.

Everett's expression turned thoughtful, and he began to pace. The action seemed utterly at odds with the carnal energy in the room that made it hard to breathe. Patrick was helpless to do anything but watch him ponder the situation.

"You get yourself off, though, don't you?" Everett asked suddenly as he turned in his pacing.

Patrick's face went red hot. He nodded, beyond embarrassed by the admission.

It made no sense to him that Everett appeared relieved. "That's what we'll do, then." He stopped his pacing to bend over and pull his shoes off. "Go on," he said when Patrick just stood there. "Get your clothes off."

Patrick's jaw dropped as he watched Everett peel off his clothes. Everett's bewilderment had turned to action, and the saucy glimmer was back in his eyes. Patrick's thoughts scattered like dust in a storm as Everett straightened and pulled his shirt off over his head, then undid his trousers and stepped out of them and his drawers. His chest constricted at the sight of Everett's naked body, his cock proud and erect. Every bit of him was beautiful, from his broad shoulders and surprisingly strong arms to his trim waist and shapely hips. But it was his perfect cock, the hair around it trimmed neatly, that had Patrick's knees threatening to give out.

"Go on." Everett nodded to him, eyes dancing with arousal and mischief. "Take it all off. Unless you'd like me to take it off for you."

That was enough to jolt Patrick into action. With shaking hands, he unbuttoned his jacket and shrugged out of his suspenders. He was so vividly aware of Everett watching him undress that he fumbled with the buttons of his shirt and barely managed to get his shoes off without falling over. He had forgotten to breathe by the time he made it to the fastenings of his trousers, and his head swam. The only way he was able to get his shirt off and even think of shucking his trousers was because Everett turned away for a moment to peel back the bedclothes on the bed farthest from the window.

As Patrick pushed his trousers and drawers down—without the slightest idea where he found the courage to do it—Everett slid onto the bed, sitting with his back against the headboard. He sat with his hips open and his knees dropped to the side, which provided Patrick with a stunning view of his prick and balls, and more than a hint of his arsehole. The sight was so erotic that Patrick froze as his trousers dropped to his ankles and his cock jumped up.

"Fuck me," Everett gasped, eyes going wide, as he gazed at Patrick's sizeable cock. "If I'd've known that was waiting for me...." He didn't finish his observation. Instead, he grabbed hold of himself, stroking from his balls to his tip.

A sweat broke out all over Patrick's body. He couldn't drag his eyes away from the way Everett played with himself. It was erotic beyond any fantasy he'd indulged in about the man. His hand twitched for his own prick, but he forced his hand into a fist.

"Oh, no," Everett said, deadly serious. "That's exactly what I have in mind. We're going to do this together, since you aren't ready for anything more. You sit at that end." He pointed to the foot of the bed. "We're going to watch each other and enjoy ourselves. And believe me, neither of us are going to last long."

He was dead right about that. The strange thing was,

what Everett was asking didn't feel like too much. Patrick stepped out of his trousers, kicking them to the side, and rushed to the foot of the bed. What they were doing was sheer madness, but it was also the most tender and endearing thing anyone had ever done for him.

There was no board at the foot of the bed, so Patrick was forced to lean back and brace himself with one hand while stroking himself with the other. He mirrored Everett's position, sitting with his legs wide open and giving Everett a full view.

"Good God," Everett hissed as he handled himself faster. "You've got the most amazing cock I've ever seen."

Patrick sucked in a breath at the wild compliment. Or perhaps at the glorious pleasure that he gave himself. He spit on his hand so that he could rub harder, which elicited a groan of delight from Everett.

"I'd do the same," Everett panted, "but I don't think I'm going to last long enough for it to matter. Fuck." He fondled the head of his penis before returning to stroking, his eyes boring in on the way Patrick slid his hand furiously up and down his length. "Fuck, I want you in my mouth. I want to suck you dry and then suck you some more."

Visions of Everett doing just that mingled with the actual sight of the man's body, sweaty and glowing, the tip of his cock shining with pre-cum, and his face contorted with pleasure.

"I want you in me," Everett panted. "I want you so far

up my arse, pounding me until I scream. I want your big cock filling me and stretching me until I—"

Patrick came apart with a deep groan, milky white erupting from him and spilling across his belly and hand. Everett hissed the most blasphemous curse Patrick had ever heard and jerked his hips as cum burst from him as well. Patrick's eyes went wide at how powerfully he came and how far he shot. The mad thought that Everett could put someone's eye out flashed through his mind, and Patrick dissolved into wild, loose laughter.

He let himself go and slumped back, barely able to brace himself on both elbows.

Everett sagged against the pillows, laughing as well. "Come here," he panted, gesturing for Patrick to join him. "Tell me you're not afraid of me now."

A new energy pulsed through Patrick, and even though his body was limp and sated, his soul felt as though it could fly to the heavens and back. "I was never afraid of you," he said, dragging himself to the other end of the bed and slipping between the sheets with Everett. His fear wasn't entirely gone, but it felt good to tangle his overheated body with Everett's. They were both too spent for the moment for Patrick to feel as though he were in any danger.

"What were you afraid of, then?" Everett asked, nestling against the pillows with him. "What are you still afraid of?"

Patrick shrugged, his eyes growing heavy. He

couldn't find a name for his fear, and with Everett's arms closing around him, he didn't care.

Everett didn't press the issue. He let out a long, contented sigh, throwing one leg over Patrick's thigh. A tiny voice at the back of Patrick's mind warned him to pull away from Everett and climb into his own bed, but he didn't have the energy to listen to it. Strangely enough, he didn't have the slightest interest in listening to that voice for the first time in his life.

CHAPTER 9

Deep in the night, with the world quiet around them and the sound of soft waves on the beach just audible through the closed window, Patrick was awakened by a strangled cry. In an instant, he was fully alert, sitting bolt-upright and searching for a weapon. His racing heart pounded hard against his ribs as he realized first, that he wasn't alone in bed, and second, that the terrified cry that had yanked him out of sleep came from Everett.

Everett writhed and kicked in his sleep, fighting against some unseen force and tangling himself in the bedclothes as he did. The bed was narrow enough that Everett kicked and battered Patrick while also attempting to cling to him. Everett's eyes were tightly shut, but his face was pinched in panic.

"Everett." Patrick twisted to his side, resting a hand

on Everett's shoulder and shaking him. "Everett, wake up. You're having a nightmare."

"No, no! Get off of me!" Everett gasped in his sleep. "No!" His cries turned pitiful, like those of a young boy.

Every detail of the past that Everett had shared in the last few days curled around Patrick, like vines intent on choking the life out of him. He could guess what nightmares lashed at Everett, and it killed him.

"Everett," he repeated in as soothing a voice as he could manage, clamping an arm over Everett's torso to hold him in place and praying for him to wake up.

"Let me go. I don't want to." Everett continued to writhe and gasp, though his strength was fading. "Don't make me."

"It's only me, love," Patrick whispered. He lay on his side, attempting to cradle Everett against him in spite of his struggles. He brushed Everett's dark, tousled hair back from his face. "It's only me. You're safe, love. No one can hurt you here."

Everett continued to make sounds that never formed into words. The fight went out of him, and he snuggled against Patrick's body, curling as if he would close into a fetal position. That was impossible with Patrick's bulk taking up half the bed, so Everett wrapped around him as though he were the only lifeboat in a stormy sea. He nestled his sweaty forehead into the pillow beside Patrick's head. Within seconds, the tension drained from his body as his nightmare gave way to a deep sleep.

Patrick's heart continued to race. It was too dark to

see more than the outline of Everett's face, but he stared at it all the same. The moment passed with lightning speed, but the fear it had provoked in Patrick lingered on. It felt like hours before he could get back to sleep.

When he woke again, bright sunlight streamed in through the windows, which had been opened. The bed beside him was empty. Everett was already up, washed, and dressed. He was busy at the far end of the room, laying out Patrick's clothes and folding both of their things from the day before.

As soon as Patrick rolled over and propped himself on his elbows, Everett turned to him with a broad, carefree smile. "Awake at last," he said, shaking out Patrick's jacket from the day before. "I hope you don't mind, but I threw out those horrible fish and chips you had stashed away in your pocket. The smell of them turned my stomach and put me off my morning tea."

Patrick jerked to sit, his jaw dropping open in protest. He only just managed to stop himself from complaining at the loss of perfectly good food. He could only hope Everett hadn't found the bread and sausage in his usual pouch and thrown that out as well.

That concern was pushed out of his mind by the memory of the night before. Heat rushed through him for a moment as he recalled the intimacy they had shared and how good it had felt, but it was the memory of Everett's nightmare that propelled him out of bed.

"Are you all right?" he asked, swinging his legs over the side of the bed and standing.

Everett abandoned his folding to rake Patrick's naked body with a wickedly appreciative look. "You're even more beautiful in the morning sunlight than you were last night," he said, breathlessly.

Self-consciousness swirled through Patrick, and he glanced down at himself. He was already half erect from sleep, but if Everett didn't stop looking at him the way he was, he'd be obscene in no time.

Everett tossed his jacket aside and strolled slowly toward him. "Are you certain you don't want to forego searching for Adler to engage in a different sort of investigation?" he asked, one eyebrow raised rakishly. "I'm very good with my hands, you know, and even better with my mouth."

Aching temptation filled Patrick. A large part of him wanted to let Everett drop to his knees and do whatever the hell he liked to him. But he recognized the salacious offer for what it was, a diversion.

"You had a nightmare last night," he said, locking eyes with Everett.

Everett's clever grin faltered, and the teasing in his eyes dimmed. "No, I didn't." He turned away, marching back to the bureau where he'd been organizing clothes.

Patrick narrowed his eyes and took a step forward. "You did. You might not remember it, but you did."

"I never have nightmares," Everett said, a little too fast. "I'm far too elegant for that."

He was lying. Patrick could see it in the set of his shoulders and the tightness of his mouth. And as much of a fool as it made him, being lied to about something so intimate hurt.

"You had a nightmare," he said with a frown, changing directions to head to the washstand for a quick scrub.

"What could I possibly have a nightmare about?" Everett asked with an unconvincing laugh, still facing away from Patrick. "My life is charmed. I'm the darling of Drury Lane. Everyone I meet either wants to be me or be with me."

Patrick's shoulders bunched with tension as he rubbed a wet washcloth over his body, wiping away whatever remained of the intimacies the two of them had shared the night before. He couldn't remove the ache in his heart, though. Everett knew damn well what the things they'd done last night meant to him, even though they hadn't touched each other while doing it. He'd let Everett into a part of his life that absolutely no one had ever come close to before, and now the man was denying him the same honor. It made him feel as cheap as if he'd offered his arse for Everett to fuck without caring, then paid him and sent him away.

"Everything is fine, darling," Everett said in what Patrick assumed was meant to be a conciliatory voice as he brought Patrick's drawers to him at the washstand. "You are lovely and beautiful, and I'm quite certain that, given time and care, we'll be fucking like rabbits, and you'll enjoy every minute of it without a shred of fear."

He traced a hand down Patrick's back to fondle his

arse. Patrick tensed so hard he thought his bones might crack, both because the touch felt unbelievably good and because Everett was a rat bastard for suggesting that Patrick could shed his fears when he wouldn't even deign to share his own. Was that all he was to the man after all? An amorous follower whose heart and soul he could crack open before tossing him aside to move on to the next challenge?

He jerked away from Everett, grabbing a towel from the washstand to dry himself off and snatching his drawers from Everett's hand. He said nothing as he dressed and shaved. He could barely look at Everett, so deep was his heartache. Everett watched him for a while, desperation in his eyes, before giving up and moving to the unused bed. He mussed the sheets to make it look as though the bed had been slept in when really, that was a lie. Patrick's heart sank as he watched, wondering how much of Everett was a lie and how much wasn't.

He was utterly out of his depth. And that wasn't a position Everett was used to being in. There were certain things he believed steadfastly about himself —that he was strong, inside and out, that he had left his past behind, that he was no longer a victim, and that he didn't need anyone or anything to prop him up in life.

All of those beliefs had been systematically shattered in just a few days by a quiet, damaged policeman who believed no one cared about him.

The trouble was, Everett did care about him. He cared about Patrick Wrexham more than he'd ever cared for anyone in his life. Getting off with the man the night before had been a thousand times more intimate than the most invasive, tangled sexual encounters he'd had in the past. Waking from one of his interminable nightmares to find himself in Patrick's arms had been like being wrenched out of hell and into the embrace of an angel. But he couldn't confess to it. He couldn't let the man who had captured his imagination and his heart know how pitiful he truly was, couldn't let him know that the reason he hated sleeping alone was not for the pleasure of it, but to keep the nightmares at bay. He couldn't go on living if Patrick stopped adoring him.

"We'll find Adler today, I'm certain of it," he said with pretend bravado as they paid their fee and entered the carnival for the second day.

Patrick nodded, grunted, and fell into step behind him. Whether the movement was intended to be subservient or a way to punish him for behaving like such an arse that morning, Everett bristled. He adjusted his pace so that Patrick was forced to walk beside him instead of trailing behind like a puppy. Or rather, like a lean and powerful mastiff with a cock that sent shivers through him every time he thought about it. Which was almost constantly since....

He let his thoughts drop listlessly. Now he was lying to himself. As beautiful and awe-inspiring as Patrick's body, including his cock, was, that wasn't where Everett's thoughts kept returning. What he truly couldn't get out of his head was the way Patrick had smiled and laughed the day before. He couldn't forget the blissful ache in his chest when Patrick winked at him after mastering the test-your-strength game. God help him, he'd started calling him "Patrick" in his thoughts instead of the infinitely less personal "Wrexham".

He was besotted. After only a few days in the man's company. And not for carnal reasons. Well, not *exclusively* carnal reasons. The magnetic attraction he felt for Patrick was a thousand times more dangerous than Adler, or any of the impossibly high-born men who were responsible for the child trafficking ring.

They'd traversed half the carnival, Everett glancing over at Patrick every few minutes, neither speaking a word, before Everett couldn't stand it anymore.

"Are you bound and contracted to be a police officer for your whole life?" he asked as they turned a corner and started down a row of tents that held everything from fortune-tellers to freak shows.

Patrick peeked sideways at him, his handsome face set in a frown. "It's my employment," he said.

"For the time being." Everett shrugged. "If you had an offer for other employment, could you take it?"

"I have no other offers of employment," Patrick said, scanning the area rather than meeting Everett's eyes.

"But if you did," Everett pushed on, pretending to search the carnival as well. "Could you walk away from Scotland Yard without so much as a by your leave?"

"I would have to give notice," Patrick said. Something near one of the tents caught his eye. He craned his neck as they passed before giving up and searching forward once more.

"So if, for example—and this is merely an example—if a highly sought-after performer who is constantly being hounded by the public decided he needed a bodyguard to keep him out of harm's way, could you leave your position with the Metropolitan Police for that sort of private employment?"

Patrick jerked his head toward Everett, eyes wide and cheeks pink.

Just as Everett was convinced he would answer, Patrick's gaze slid right past him. He hardened his jaw, then cut in front of Everett, marching toward something.

"Is that him?" Patrick asked.

Everett turned, so caught up on tenterhooks from his question that it felt like the effort would snap every bone in his body. That brittleness turned to terror, as though he'd been struck across the face, when he spotted Adler peering out from around the corner of a red and yellow striped tent. Vile hatred welled up within him.

"That's him," he seethed, and launched into action.

He was fast, but Adler was faster. Adler spotted Everett and Patrick pushing their way through the carnival-goers and rushing toward him. His face registered a split-second of surprise before he turned tail and ran.

"I'm not letting him get away," Everett snapped as he and Patrick broke into a run.

Winding through the crowded rows of men, women, and children enjoying themselves at the carnival was challenging enough, but as they ducked between two tents in pursuit of Adler, Everett and Patrick had to contend with tent pegs and ropes, piles of supplies and tools for the games and food stalls, and people and animals of every kind, none of which took kindly to three men sprinting into their private realms.

Adler knew where he was going and moved with far more certainty than Everett and Patrick. He kept well ahead of them, jumping crates and darting suddenly around corners, attempting to lose them in the maze of the inner world of the carnival. Everett kept up as best he could, but it was Patrick who kept them on track and within sight of Adler. He leapt the same crates Adler did with amazing speed and agility. As effective as Everett was at parting a crowd of admirers, Patrick proved that he had a knack for forcing bystanders out of the way with nothing more than a glance when he was in pursuit of a criminal suspect. The man might have blended into the woodwork the vast majority of the time, but when it came to a police pursuit, he shone brighter than anyone Everett had ever shared the stage with.

It was solely because of Patrick that they managed to catch up with Adler near the far corner of the carnival's fencing, just as he was about to leap over the edge and escape into Brighton. Without a word of warning or triumph, Patrick grabbed Adler by the back of his collar and wrenched him away from the fence. He had the man on his back, pinned to the ground, so swiftly that Everett ached with jealousy—not for Patrick's strength and agility, but with the wish that he was in Adler's place pinned under the handsome copper.

It was Everett who announced with ridiculous bravado, "We've got you now, Adler. Your days of getting away with kidnapping and debauchery are over."

"I don't know what you're talking about," Adler panted. He attempted to fight his way out of Patrick's grasp, but gave up. Even a devil like Adler knew when he wouldn't be able to overpower his adversary.

"There should be Brighton police nearby," Patrick said in a calm voice, though he was panting with exertion. "Fetch them to help."

The absolute last thing Everett wanted to do was to leave Patrick's side, particularly when everything about Patrick—from the strain of his muscles to the fierce set of his jaw—was so captivating. Everett blessed his good fortune when he glanced around and spotted two, uniformed officers patrolling the fence line nearby.

"You!" he called to them, projecting as though on stage in Hyde Park, attempting to be heard by the residents of Kensington Palace. "Over here!"

The Brighton policemen noticed Everett waving at them and immediately rushed forward.

"What's all this about?" one of them asked as they drew near.

"This is Officer Patrick Wrexham of the Metropolitan Police," Everett announced with a sudden, broad smile, swimming with pride. "We've apprehended a suspect that Scotland Yard has been chasing for months, and we need your help securing him." He had no idea if that was strictly accurate, but it didn't seem to matter.

"He's lying," Adler gasped. "These men accosted me. They're thieves."

"If you would hold this man, I can show you my credentials," Patrick said in an even voice.

One of the officers secured Adler long enough for Patrick to stand and take a small wallet from the inside pocket of his jacket. He showed the paper inside to the second officer, who nodded and grunted, as though everything were in order.

"How can we help, Officer Wrexham?"

"What charges do you have against me?" Adler protested. "What authority do you have here in Brighton?"

Ever one for the drama of performance, Everett stepped forward, reaching for the buttons of Adler's jacket. He undid them, then tore Adler's shirt open, revealing a crude tattoo of a Lion on his breast.

"You see?" he told Patrick with a wide grin. "Here he is. The man with the lion. Just as Miss Logan said."

Adler burst into laughter that set Everett's teeth on edge. "That's why you're treating me like a dog in the gutter?" He sneered at Everett the way he had time and time again, years ago, when Everett was a sore and bruised child, begging to be rescued. "You're the dog, mate." Adler turned to Patrick. "And you're barking up the wrong tree."

Patrick scowled, moving to stand toe-to-toe with Adler. He didn't say a single word.

As it turned out, he didn't have to. Adler shrank away from him and said, "If it's the man with the lion you're after, it ain't me. You've let this sodding fool lead you on a merry chase. He's the one you should be arresting, you know. For lewd acts of the most abominable sort. Let me go and I'll make sure you have enough information to lock him away forever."

Adler was the sodding fool, as far as Everett was concerned. Though the tiniest part of Everett worried that Patrick was so angry with him that he'd actually consider turning him in for gross indecency, as hypocritical as that would be.

Instead, Patrick grabbed the front of Adler's unbuttoned shirt and growled into his face, "You think only one charge can be brought against you?" His voice was low and menacing. It made the hair on the back of Everett's neck stand up almost as much as his prick threatened to. "We've been tracking you for years, Adler," Patrick went on. "Scotland Yard has a list of charges against you as long as my arm, lion or no lion."

Adler looked as though he might soil himself. "Please. Let me go. I'll tell you anything, give you any information you want."

"You'll do that anyhow," Patrick said. He glanced to the officer who held Adler's arms behind his back. "Are you willing and able to take him into custody at a Brighton jail until transportation to London can be arranged?"

"Yes, sir." The officer nodded.

Patrick nodded back, then turned to Everett. "Return to the hotel and pack our things. Meet us at the train station as soon as you're done. I'll find a telegraph office and let Scotland Yard know we're coming in this afternoon."

"Right. Yes, sir." Everett felt as though he should salute Patrick instead of merely nodding. His heart ricocheted through his chest, and he couldn't stop himself from smiling. He turned to go do as he'd been told, but at the last minute, he twisted to call over his shoulder, "Do be careful."

It was a maudlin way for the two of them to part, especially under the circumstances, but when Patrick responded with a faint smile and a nod, Everett was over the moon. Perhaps he hadn't ruined everything between him and Patrick after all. Now that they had Adler in custody, perhaps they could put their fears aside for good and come to an understanding that would satisfy them both.

CHAPTER 10

*P*atrick hadn't pursued a life in law enforcement accidentally. He'd known long before he was old enough to leave the orphanage and strike out on his own that he would dedicate himself to helping the helpless and bringing criminals to justice. The sense of satisfaction he had from apprehending Adler and returning him to London to face charges was deep enough that it overrode his continuing confusion over Everett and whatever was happening between the two of them, which was saying a lot.

"You're a bloody fool for wasting your time with me," Adler grumbled as the train from Brighton rolled into Victoria Station late in the afternoon. "I'll have the last laugh in the end, you'll see."

"Shut your ugly face, Adler," Everett snapped, unusually petulant. "Your sins are legion."

Patrick eyed Everett sideways. Everett sat at the far

end of the seat beside him in their first-class compartment, arms crossed, scowling. They'd already purchased the first-class fare before nabbing Adler—who sat on the seat opposite, flanked by two Brighton policemen. The journey was likely the most luxurious Adler—or the two Brighton policemen—had ever taken. Even Patrick had to admit he was enjoying himself immensely. The only one who wasn't pleased with the way the situation had unfolded was Everett.

"Still bitter about the past, eh, Jewel?" Adler sneered.

Everett's eyes flared wide. "Bitter is hardly the word."

Adler laughed. "You settled into your life quite nicely, I see. Everyone knows how much you enjoy it. You should fall on your knees and thank me for brokering that deal."

Patrick promptly stood up, lunged forward, and punched Adler across his leering face.

Adler didn't see the blow coming. It jerked him to the side. A tooth flew out of his mouth, landing in the lap of one of the Brighton officers. Both policemen and Everett were stunned to the point of freezing. Without meeting any of their eyes, Patrick sat back down, relaxing his shoulders and massaging his hand, as though nothing had happened.

Inwardly, he blossomed with satisfaction as he watched blood ooze from Adler's mouth and nose. The man deserved far worse for what he'd just admitted. Patrick would have kicked him repeatedly in the balls before garroting him with his own shoelace if he could have gotten away with it.

But underneath the murderous satisfaction of the moment, a far more visceral thought consumed him. No one would ever hurt Everett again if he had anything to do about it.

They all remained silent as the train came to a stop. Evidently, Scotland Yard had communicated with the station ahead of time. The porters kept the passengers in their cars and compartments for a moment as four armed officers met Patrick on the platform. Adler was wrenched out of their compartment and handed over to those officers before anyone else was allowed to disembark.

"He attempted to escape," Patrick lied when one of the Met officers glanced askance at Adler's state.

That was enough of an explanation for the man, and Adler didn't argue the point. He cowered away from Patrick instead, putting up no resistance when the Met officers grabbed hold of him and marched him along.

Patrick started after them, intent on seeing things through to the end, but Everett stopped him.

"I have to go to the theater," he said, a strange mix of reluctance, pride, and anxiety in his eyes. "It's one thing to allow my understudy to go on for a single performance, but they're not paying me to skive off."

A hollow feeling filled Patrick's chest. "Do what you have to do." He nodded. "Once I find out which jail they're taking Adler to, I'll send someone to the theater with a note."

"I'll join you there after the performance," Everett said.

For a moment, they stood there, face-to face, a wealth of unspoken emotion crackling in the air between them. Patrick was filled with the undeniable certainty that Everett wanted to kiss him goodbye, no matter how dangerous the simple gesture would be. The mad thing was, he could barely restrain himself from doing the same. It felt as though hardly anything had happened between them in the thirty or so hours that they'd been together—aside from what they'd shared the night before—but it also felt as though the world had tipped on its axis and begun spinning in a different direction.

The longer Patrick lingered, the more suspicions would be raised, so he nodded to Everett, then turned and marched after the police officers escorting Adler. He thanked the Brighton policemen for their service and made certain they had fare for their journey home, then accompanied Adler and his entourage out of the station and into London.

Patrick was as surprised as Adler when he realized he was being taken to Pentonville.

"The order came from Lord Clerkenwell himself," one of the officers murmured to Patrick as Adler was loaded into a police carriage. "Clerkenwell thinks the man knows a great deal about a great many things, and that he's more likely to sing if he thinks his fate is sealed."

Patrick nodded. Lord Clerkenwell was probably right.

He stayed with Adler through the trip to Pentonville, as he was processed, and still, once he was assigned a cell and locked away tightly. The hour grew late, and as the sun went down, Patrick's stomach grumbled with hunger, but he didn't dare to break into his stashed bread and sausage. He'd been far hungrier in his life. It wasn't time for desperation yet.

"You seem like a sensible man," Adler said from inside his cell as Patrick stood against the far wall, contemplating his hunger and wondering when Everett would get there. Patrick turned to him, keeping his expression as bleak as stone. "I'm surprised a man like you would be taken in by a queer like Jewel." There was a cunning glint in Adler's eyes that made Patrick want to punch him again.

All the same, prickles broke out down Patrick's spine. He stared silently at Adler, knowing that a villain like him wouldn't be able to keep his mouth shut for long.

Sure enough, Adler pressed himself up against the bars of his cell, beckoning to Patrick. "I can tell you things," he whispered. "Things about Jewel and the sins he's committed. Sins stretching back to his wicked youth. Wouldn't you like to be the man that brought down one of London's most infamous actors?"

Patrick crossed his arms, narrowing his eyes at Adler, daring him to go on.

"He's a sodomite, all right," Adler laughed. "But more than that. He's been a darling of a certain set of perverted noblemen for years. You wouldn't just be bringing Jewel down, you'd be tumbling some of the most powerful men in this kingdom at the same time."

Patrick's heart raced. He could feel his face heating, which was a terrible tell.

Adler must have sensed he was provoking Patrick in some way. His grin widened. "Don't think that those men are too well-protected either," he said. "It's a funny world we live in. The highest in the land can get away with murder, rape, and pillaging, but call a man out for being a fag and it won't just be the law that will take him down, it will be his nearest and dearest too."

Adler bit his lip, as though trying to figure out whether he was getting through to Patrick. Whether he believed he was or not, he went on.

"I can give you names," he whispered. "Names of men who bought what I was selling and paid good money for it. Not just in the past, but now."

The hair on the back of Patrick's neck stood up. Adler could be the key they needed to bring Chisolm and the others down. But was the word of a petty criminal and pimp truly enough to stand against peers of the realm? He doubted it. Justice was far from blind when faced with a class system that had protected the undeserving for centuries. But Adler's information, if added to everything David Wirth and Lionel Mercer already had, might just be enough to achieve the impossible.

"Let me go," Adler whispered seductively. "Or give me some sort of reprieve. I'll tell you everything, as long as I go free."

Before Patrick could answer, a commotion from the far end of the hall broke the tension. The door flew open, and Everett marched into the room as though making a grand entrance of operatic proportions. He still wore stage make-up from the performance he'd run off to do. The sight of his enhanced beauty made Patrick weak in the knees.

Everett wasn't alone, though. David and Lionel charged in behind him, David looking determined and excited, and Lionel as cool and commanding as a winter wind. Alistair Bevan, Lord Farnham, and Joe Logan followed them.

"Well, well." Adler pushed away from the bars of his cell, stepping out of arm's reach of anyone not in the cell while pretending to have courage. "Isn't this a lot of motley fools. Queers, every one of them."

Still, Patrick kept his mouth shut, in spite of the fact that Adler glanced to him as though he would be shocked and use the situation to his advantage. He was grateful that Adler didn't have a clue that he was cut from the same cloth as the rest of them.

Patrick's moment of smugness was dampened as Logan said, "That's not him."

Everett suddenly looked crestfallen. "But it is him. Adler is as guilty as sin."

"I'm sure he is," Logan said. "But he's not the man with the lion."

No one aside from Everett looked surprised. Even Patrick wasn't entirely shocked. He'd figured there was a good chance Everett was pursuing Adler for personal reasons and not just because he was convinced Adler was the leader of the kidnapping ring.

Adler burst into cruel laughter. "Didn't I tell you? Fools, the lot of you." He snorted.

"I'd be careful about who you choose to call a fool," Lionel said, sliding menacingly toward the cell.

Adler flinched slightly, but recovered, trying to appear unimpressed. "And you," he sneered. "Swanning about, thinking you're better than everyone else, simply because you've had more important dicks up your arse than anyone else in London."

Lionel's eyes flashed with malice, but he absorbed the insult, standing straighter. "Men talk when they're balls-deep in a willing partner." He moved closer to the bars. "Some of them say things about inconsequential swine when they're in the throes of passion. Things that would make that swine squeal as he dangles from the end of a rope."

Adler blanched and backpedaled to the far side of his cell. Lionel's countenance was enough to make Patrick wary as well. A man who wasn't afraid of his sins was the most dangerous creature imaginable.

"You...you can't keep me locked up if I'm not the man you're looking for," Adler stammered, one last attempt to wriggle out of the trap he was in.

"You're exactly the man we're looking for," Lord Clerkenwell said as he strode into the room.

A pair of hulking officers followed him, though

Clerkenwell's presence alone was enough to part the rest of them. Patrick had never seen men as strong as David Wirth or Lord Farnham step out of the way so fast. Even Lionel nodded graciously to Clerkenwell and moved to stand by David's side, as far away from Everett as he could get.

"Barnaby Adler," Clerkenwell announced. "You are officially under arrest, charged with pandering, theft, kidnapping, fraud, and probably murder too. Anything we can find to stick to you will be stuck, mark my words." Clerkenwell didn't wait for his reaction. He turned first to Patrick, then to the others, nodding at them. "Thank you for your help, gentlemen, but this is a matter for Scotland Yard now."

There was nothing they could do but shuffle out of the room as Adler burst into sobs and begged for his life. Patrick couldn't decide if he felt vindicated or disappointed as he showed the others to a small, mostly empty room one hallway over. It was generally reserved for prisoners to speak to their advocates or families, but it would allow them to speak without being overheard.

"I was so certain Adler was the man with the lion," Everett hissed, rippling with disappointment, as soon as Patrick shut the door, giving their group privacy. "The man is evil. He's been exploiting children for decades."

No one disagreed with him, though Lionel and David exchanged a wary look. Patrick fought the urge to step into Everett's path to stop his pacing by sliding an arm around his shoulders. He hadn't attempted to comfort anyone since he was a lad of twelve, doing his best to stop the younger girls at the orphanage from crying when every last morsel of supper had been wrenched away from them by the larger, stronger children.

"The man with the lion is one Montague Williamson, Earl of Castleford," Logan said after allowing Everett a few seconds to stew.

Everett jerked to a stop and glared at Logan. "Who?"

Logan glanced to Lord Farnham, let out a sigh, then faced Everett with squared shoulders. "Lord Castleford owns an estate in Yorkshire, near where Lily and I grew up, close to Leeds. Along with being one of the most gothic and reprehensible men I've ever had the displeasure to know, he keeps a menagerie of exotic animals on his estate. Lily and I were particularly fascinated with the lion he kept prisoner in a pit."

"The man with the lion is a gentleman with an actual lion?" Everett asked, incredulous.

"He is." Logan nodded.

One quick glance around the room was enough to tell Patrick that everyone but him and Everett already knew the full story.

"I have no trouble whatsoever believing that Castleford would be the mastermind behind a child kidnapping ring," Logan went on. "If you'd met him, you'd feel the same way."

"The man is a macabre nightmare," Lionel agreed, his jaw tight, his eyes shining with hate. Patrick could only imagine what kind of interaction the two must have had in the past.

"We go after Castleford, then," Everett said, marching for the door.

"And just how do you expect to do that?" Lionel stopped him, sharp with animosity, the way he'd been at the club days before.

Everett whipped back to him, looking ready to pick up their fight where they'd left it. "Any action I take would be a damn sight better than whatever coy and cunning plan you think you might have."

It was pure luck that Everett stood close enough for Patrick to place a hand warningly on his arm. "Don't pick the wrong battle," he cautioned in a low voice.

Lionel's brow shot up as he studied the two of them. He huffed a curt laugh and shook his head, but didn't comment further.

"If Castleford is the ringleader," David said, meeting Lionel's, then Everett's, then Patrick's eyes, "then we'll need to find evidence to prove it."

"What sort of evidence?" Patrick asked, speaking directly to David as though the rest of them weren't in the room. David was the only one of them who could still address the kidnapping ring as a crime without drawing years of personal pain and humiliation into the mixture.

"We found papers, receipts, and correspondence, at Chisolm's house," David said. "None of it was specific enough to stand as iron-clad evidence against any of the men involved. Surely, Castleford would have similar papers, concrete evidence with names, dates, and other relevant information. Proof of financial interactions, if nothing else. His estate is remote, is it not?" He glanced to Logan, who nodded. "It is entirely likely that he thinks the barrenness of Yorkshire is an adequate hiding place for whatever damning evidence the ring may have."

"Particularly if he is, in fact, the ringleader," Lord Farnham added.

Patrick felt they were right. He also believed there was an even chance a man like Castleford would be clever enough not to leave any sort of evidence at all. But if there was even a slim possibility that the evidence they needed to bring down the kidnapping ring existed, it would be in Yorkshire.

"So what can we do?" Everett asked, still bristling with fire and energy. "Do you propose we journey to Yorkshire and simply invade Castleford's estate, wrestle the lion, and demand that all evidence be handed over?"

"Of course not." Lionel smirked, seeming to revel in the fact that Everett was agitated while he was calm. "You'll simply pay a visit."

Everyone, including David, looked askance at him. "We cannot just make a social call on Castleford without any sort of introduction or cause. He'd know in an instant something was wrong."

"Not us." Lionel shook his head. "That would be far too suspicious. No, they'll have to be the ones to go." His lip curled as he nodded to Everett.

"Why would Castleford throw open his doors and

welcome Jewel and Officer Wrexham with open arms?" Lord Farnham asked.

"Not them precisely," Lionel answered, his grin growing wider by the moment. He let the tension in the room reach towering heights before saying, "Niall Cristofori."

They all stared at him. Patrick remembered the handsome playwright from The Chameleon Club, but beyond that, he was clueless.

"Niall Cristofori," Lionel repeated, beginning to pace as though he were the one on stage, for a change, delivering the final monologue that would untangle the impossible plot. "Years ago, at university, Niall Cristofori had a, shall we say, *tendre* for one Blake Williamson, Duke of Selby."

"Williamson?" Patrick said, catching the connection.

"Castleford's eldest brother," Lionel answered the suspicion. "His only brother, actually. As far as I know, the two are on reasonable terms, though Selby never much cared for Castleford, if I'm not mistaken."

"Wait." David held up a hand, as though trying to piece things together. "Selby isn't a member of The Brotherhood." He said it as though making a deeper statement about the man's proclivities.

Lionel seemed to catch his meaning. "Trust me. It doesn't make a lick of difference that Selby appears as pure as the driven snow, that he married a perfectly vile but well-connected dollar princess from New York, or that they have three lovely children. Niall is the one he dreams about at night."

"So you're privy to men's dreams now?" Everett sneered, crossing his arms.

Lionel shifted to bore into him with a glance. "I know what you dream about, love."

The color drained from Everett's face and his eyes went hollow. Patrick's pulse kicked up. He knew what Everett dreamed about too. Jealousy flared within him, like shards of glass cutting his soul.

"We need to speak to Niall, then." David cut through the flaring tension in the room, and not a moment too soon. "If Niall still has a connection with Selby, and if Selby can assist us in securing an invitation to Castleford's estate, then we might be able to destroy the ring once and for all."

"We can corner Cristofori at The Chameleon Club," Lord Farnham suggested. "He's there most afternoons, working on some play he plans to produce next year."

"A play I'm set to star in," Everett added, sending Lionel a smug look.

"Agreed," David said in a take-charge voice. He turned to the others. "It's late. Go home for the night and rest. We'll meet at the club tomorrow for luncheon. Then we'll speak to Niall and enlist his help."

CHAPTER 11

*E*verett felt like a powder keg ready to explode as he and Patrick left Pentonville. He'd rushed the two of them out ahead of the others, striding swiftly along the dark street in front of the menacing prison to put as much distance between him and the others, specifically Lionel, as possible. He didn't ask for it, but Patrick kept up with him.

The fact that Patrick silently matched his pace, walking by his side instead of a step or two behind, wasn't lost on Everett. He was certain that three days ago, Patrick wouldn't have dared to fall into step with him. Three days ago, Everett wouldn't have cared one way or another. Now, on the other hand, if Patrick had trailed behind him, like any other hanger-on who either wanted to bask in his perfection or suck his cock as a means of paying homage, it would have been a sacrilege.

"You don't know anything about this Lord Castleford, do you?" he asked, knowing Patrick wouldn't have the first clue. He needed something to distract him from the way his breath hitched in his chest at the sound of Patrick's shoes against the pavement in unison with his, the acute awareness he had of Patrick's body only inches from his, and the horrific certainty that Lionel wasn't the only one who knew what he dreamed about every fitful night of his life.

Patrick shrugged, thrusting his hands into his jacket pockets as they turned a corner and headed vaguely in the direction of Drury Lane. "I was hoping you knew something about the man."

He should have stopped at the next corner and attempted to hail a handsom cab. A gentleman wouldn't make someone as glorious as Patrick walk halfway across London after midnight. But a cab would get them home faster, and Everett wanted to spend as much time as he could with Patrick.

"I could tell by the look on Mr. Logan's face that, whoever the man is, he's a nasty piece of work," Everett said.

Patrick merely grunted in agreement.

"Unfortunately for him, I've a wealth of experience with nasty pieces of work. They don't frighten me." Everett stood straighter, squaring his shoulders as he walked.

One, doubting glance from Patrick and he felt himself wither from the inside.

"All right," he admitted in a quiet voice, laced with tension. "Men like that terrify me."

Patrick turned his head slightly toward Everett, his brow lifting.

"You're surprised," Everett said.

"No." Patrick shook his head. "I'm shocked to hear you say it is all." He paused. "I knew you were afraid."

A chill passed down Everett's spine that started as petrifying shame that squeezed his throat closed, but ended as a warm, electric feeling that settled in his groin. He struggled against both sensations, trying to throw them off like a costume that didn't fit. He'd never been afraid before—at least not in a way he was willing to admit to himself—and he'd never felt so much like handing that fear into another man's hands for safekeeping. It unsettled him more than the shadowy alleys and hushed, menacing streets they passed.

"My entire life is a shock right now," he muttered, turning up the collar of his coat against the damp chill that seemed to pervade the foul, London air. "It isn't going to keep me from following through with whatever plan vile Lionel decides on for luring Castleford into a trap of his own making."

He had a feeling that he sounded ridiculously overdramatic. Patrick merely walked on, though. Apparently, he knew where they were going. Everett didn't actually care where they ended up, as long as he wouldn't be alone once they got there.

Another, awkward silence fell between them. Everett peeked sideways at Patrick several times as they hurried along. It was as clear as day Patrick had something he wanted to say or something he needed to ask, but he kept his lips tightly shut. Everett could still remember the taste of those lips when he'd stolen a kiss the night before. Patrick's mouth would haunt his dreams for the rest of his life, whether he ever experienced it again or not. For a man wound as tightly as his dear Officer Wrexham was, he had a generous and sensual mouth. Everett longed to teach Patrick how to use it. The desire to learn was most certainly there. Drawing out Patrick's natural talents would be the stuff of fantasy.

"How was your show tonight?" Patrick asked, almost half an hour later, as they crossed through a slightly more respectable part of London, not terribly far from Everett's flat.

Everett blinked at the question. "I was disappointing at best," he admitted. "I wouldn't be surprised if half the audience asked for their money back."

"I doubt it." The ghost of a smile touched Patrick's lips.

Everett was seized by the need to perform for him, even if the performance was simply pretending to be in a light-hearted mood. "Oh, no, I was terrible. My thoughts were scattered in a thousand directions. I dropped my lines at least three times, possibly more. And I failed to indulge the audience with a song after taking my bow, as has become my custom. I'm surprised they didn't throw rotten fruit at me."

Patrick laughed softly. "I'm sure it wasn't as bad as all that. The audience probably thought you were ill, if they even noticed you were less than stellar."

"Oh, they noticed," Everett said with exaggerated gloom.

Patrick shrugged. "Your understudy went on last night. Theatergoers are aware of that sort of thing. They likely assumed you were in the throes of some malady, attempting to push through regardless."

"You are too kind to me, Patrick," Everett said, letting his hand brush against Patrick's. "Far too kind." His heart felt as though it were straining to leap free of his chest and curl against Patrick's own heart. The sort of kindness Patrick showed him was unlike any of the praise or accolades that were tossed at him by adoring crowds, and as unlike the so-called kindness of the man who had dressed him in silks, fed him delicacies, and allowed him to pursue the theater, all while sharing him with his elite group of friends, as cheese was to mercury.

"If you're planning to travel to Yorkshire with me, your understudy will have to go on again," Patrick said.

Several parts of the statement hit Everett simultaneously. Patrick was right, of course. His understudy would have to take his place, likely for most of the coming week. That would set tongues wagging and rumors flying, but he didn't care. The fact that he didn't care, that he looked forward to a brief holiday from performing, was as much of a shock as lightning striking out of a blue sky. Performing was his life. He genuinely loved it. But the middle bit of Patrick's statement was what wrapped around him, sparking the same sort of energy stepping out onto the boards in front of a sold-out house usually gave him. With Patrick. He would be traveling to Yorkshire with Patrick. They'd share a train compartment again, and if he had his way, they'd share a hotel room as well. And a bed. It didn't matter how dastardly Castleford was, if he had a chance of sleeping in Patrick's arms again, he would march into Hell itself.

He stopped short in the middle of the street.

"Something wrong?" Patrick asked.

Everett blinked. His first thought had been of *sleeping* with Patrick, not of the two of them fucking each other until they passed out from exhaustion.

He glanced around, searching for a way to shy away from the too-tender emotions closing in on his heart.

"Good Lord," he said, a different sort of surprise hitting him. "This is my building."

"You only just realized that?" Patrick stared at him with a teasing grin, the light of the streetlamps reflecting like stars in his eyes.

Everett's mouth hung open for a moment before he found words to say. "Did you...did you just walk me home? Like a debutante out for her first stroll with a suitor?"

The corner of Patrick's mouth twitched. "Are you calling yourself a debutante?"

Something treacly-sweet broke loose in Everett's soul.

"I certainly feel like one at the moment," he said, breathlessly.

Patrick chuckled and walked on. They only had a few more yards, and then they reached the door to Everett's building. "Well," Patrick said. "Here you are."

Everett advanced on him faster than Patrick could think to back away. He slipped one arm to the small of Patrick's back and brought his mouth to within inches of his. "Come up with me," he whispered. "Stay the night."

"I—" Patrick glanced desperately around, as though a dozen torches would suddenly be uncovered, exposing them mid-sin.

"The street is empty," Everett told him. "And even if it weren't, they know me here." He trusted Patrick would know the full implication of those words. "Come upstairs," he whispered against Patrick's ear, pausing to brush his lips against the throbbing pulse in Patrick's neck.

Patrick let out a long, shaky breath. The energy that radiated from him had Everett's heart racing. Need crashed through him so intensely that if Patrick rejected him, he might die on the spot.

Instead, Patrick nodded slowly.

Everett wanted to shout in victory. He grabbed Patrick's hand, rushing up the steps and into his building. The doorman behind the desk who was paid to keep followers from rushing the place and disturbing the theatrical luminaries who owned flats in the building snored loudly, his head resting on his hands. Everett dragged Patrick past him, dashing to the stairwell and pulling Patrick up at a pace that left both of them practically wheezing for breath once they reached the top floor.

Everett wasn't sure how he found his key and let himself and Patrick into his flat. He could hardly focus on anything as he shut the door and locked it, then slammed Patrick against it. The position they found themselves in was a fascinating mirror of how they had shared their first kiss the night before, but this time, Everett was determined to have the night play out differently.

"Before you say it," he panted, fumbling with the buttons of Patrick's coat. "You can and you will."

Patrick let out a strangled groan, but Everett wouldn't let it form into words. He brought his mouth crashing over Patrick's, throwing every bit of pent-up passion and soul-deep longing for the man that he had into schooling him in the proper use of lips and teeth and tongues. Patrick's head thumped against the door, but he didn't seem to mind. He lifted his arms to Everett's sides.

Everett's first thought was that Patrick would tear his clothes off in order to have his way with him, like dozens of other men had before. When those strong, capable arms closed around him, fingertips digging into Everett's back with an urgency that was both carnal and tender, it brought an unaccountable sting to Everett's eyes. He made a sound against Patrick's mouth that was half moan, half sob, and pressed his body against Patrick's.

He took a breath, forcing himself to slow down, to savor the moment. It wasn't about racing to an invisible finish-line, it was about kissing the man in his arms—a man he would have given his life for, if only to see him smile. He pulled back on the insistence of his kiss, caressing Patrick's lips with his own instead of demanding pleasure, teasing instead of punishing. He had things to teach Patrick, after all, and, God help him, Patrick had things to teach him. He hadn't realized there was anything left to learn about pleasure until he heard the restless, pleading sighs that whispered between them. Some of those sounds came from him.

"Let me show you," he murmured, moving from Patrick's mouth to kiss the pulse that throbbed at his neck and the unassuming place where his neck curved into his shoulder. "Let me show you what it means to love a man. Let me show you all the things I want you to do to me." He tugged the hem of Patrick's shirt out of his trousers as he spoke.

Patrick answered with a tight nod, moving his hands around Everett's sides to rest on his chest. For one, terrifying moment, Everett thought Patrick would push him away. He didn't, he brushed his trembling hands to the buttons of Everett's jacket, undoing them with deliberateness. The awkward action was a declaration that could have been painted across the sky in vibrant colors, for all Everett was concerned. Patrick wanted him, and he wasn't going to hold back this time.

They shed their clothes with unsteady hands while moving gracelessly through the front rooms of Everett's too-large flat to the lavish bedroom whose windows looked out at the starry sky. Patrick's face flushed and his eyes hazed over as they removed the last of their clothes, tumbling onto the bed in a tangle of limbs and overheated flesh.

"We'll go slowly," Everett whispered against his ear, rolling Patrick to his back. He wanted to touch the man all over, from the width of his broad shoulders to the chiseled planes of his chest and stomach, to the hard thickness of his cock as it jutted between them. God, the man's cock was the stuff of erotic poetry. A far more careless version of himself would have wrenched Patrick's legs apart and gone straight to swallowing that cock until Patrick exploded. But it felt almost obscene to speed toward the end when the journey was about to be so wonderful.

Everett nestled himself between Patrick's thighs, bracing one arm on the bed to give himself some leverage, and bent down, intent on kissing Patrick until they were both in danger of passing out.

"I don't want to do anything wrong," Patrick stopped him in a voice that made him sound more like a boy than a man.

It was killing Everett. His heart was ready to rip itself into pieces with sentimentality. "Love, you couldn't possibly do anything wrong," he whispered endearingly, stroking Patrick's tousled hair and stubbly cheek. "Let me do everything tonight. Your only job is to enjoy it." He captured Patrick's lips in a soft kiss, but jerked up again and added, with one eyebrow arched, "And to learn, of course. Because everything I am about to do to you tonight, I want you to do to me at some point. And more."

He dipped down to suck another, heady kiss from Patrick's mouth, grinding his hips against Patrick's in a way that rubbed their pricks together. But again, he jerked up.

"I'll let you in on a carefully-kept secret," he said, barely able to stop from giggling at the intimacy of what he was about to reveal. "I actually prefer to take the submissive role when I'm with a man. Most of the lovers I've had assume it's the other way around. It isn't."

Patrick nodded slightly, and Everett lowered his mouth to Patrick's once more. He reveled in the way Patrick relaxed and imitated the way he kissed, growing bolder by the moment. He really would be the most amazing kisser, with enough practice.

Everett stopped, pulling up again.

"Just to put your mind at ease," he said, feigning seriousness when he felt as though he might burst apart with joy, "I'm not going to fuck you in the arse tonight. If you're under the impression that that's all men do together, you're wrong. It takes some working up to, at any rate."

He moved to resume their kiss, but stopped himself.

"I want you to be comfortable, after all, since I fully intend—"

"For the love of God, Everett. Get on with it," Patrick growled. He grabbed a handful of Everett's arse with one hand, sliding the other hand up his side to dig into his back. "You talk too much."

"I know I—"

Patrick pushed up, slanting his mouth against Everett's and thoroughly shutting him up. Everett didn't know whether to laugh or moan at the sudden aggression. He wanted to encourage it, nurture it, until Patrick was confident enough to turn the tables and master him. The thought of Patrick with enough self-assurance to have his way with him left Everett so aroused he jerked his hips against Patrick's, worried he might come long before either of them were ready.

He moved his hands so that he could thread his fingers through Patrick's hair, mussing it to the point where Patrick looked ready to be debauched. He broke away from Patrick's mouth, but only received a moment of protest as he trailed kisses across Patrick's shoulder to his chest.

"Remember this," he said, planting a light kiss over Patrick's heart before shifting to one of his nipples. "I will insist you do this to me later."

He brushed his tongue over Patrick's nipple, earning a gasp and sigh of enlightenment as Patrick realized all of the things that were possible between two lovers. Everett caressed his sides and hips with gentle, insistent strokes, taking his time and worshipping the man's body before continuing to rain kisses across his abdomen. He stole a peek at Patrick's face and found him deliciously transported by his introduction to pleasure. His eyes were half-closed, but not for long.

Everett slipped a hand between Patrick's thighs, teasing his fingers toward his arsehole for a moment before cupping his balls. Patrick's eyes flew wide open, then fluttered closed again with a moan as Everett stroked the length of his cock. Patrick's hips jerked as Everett learned his length and girth with as gentle a touch as he could. Patrick's tip was already shining with pre-cum, and Everett instinctively knew the darling wouldn't last long. Only the most stubborn man had the power to hold out long during his first time, and Patrick wasn't half as stubborn as he made himself out to be.

"This," Everett said, heat and urgency in his voice. "I most certainly want you to do this to me at some point."

He closed his mouth over the head of Patrick's cock, raking it with his tongue. He moved deeper, teasing just the right spot at the base of Patrick's head and drawing the most delicious moan of pleasure from the man that he'd ever heard.

"I can't—" Patrick gasped.

It wasn't a fearful insistence that he couldn't move forward, it was a frantic warning that he couldn't hold back.

Everett tensed in anticipation, bearing down on him and taking as much of Patrick into his mouth as he could. And he could manage far more than most. He set a fast pace, but it didn't last long. Patrick's thighs and groin tensed under Everett's hands, a guttural cry erupted from him, and warmth hit the back of Everett's throat. He swallowed reflexively, slowed his pace, and did his best to prolong the experience to the fullest for Patrick.

As Patrick's body loosened into a puddle of satisfaction, Everett pulled back, catching his breath. "That was beautiful, my love," he panted, shifting so that his body covered Patrick's.

It didn't take him long to find a position that would provide the friction he needed as he rocked against Patrick. He was so aroused from watching the darling man in his arms come undone and from feeling the power of his orgasm that what would have usually taken a strong hand, a mouth, or a tight arse, only needed the crook of Patrick's thigh where it met his hip. Everett came with a cry of satisfaction, spilling himself across Patrick's hip. He was enough of a cocky bastard to feel as though he'd marked his territory with his seed, and a wicked grin spread across his face.

"That was...." Patrick failed to form his thoughts into words as Everett shifted them to their sides so that they could curl into each other's embrace.

"I know," he said with a sly grin. "And would you believe that's barely scratching the surface of all the things we can do?"

Patrick looked at him with sated amazement, his brow inching up. The response was so typically, beautifully Patrick that Everett burst into laughter. He spent the next several minutes kissing Patrick, their arms and legs wrapped around each other, making bets with himself about whether they would fall asleep or get hard again first.

Surprisingly, sleep won, though after the day they'd had, it was no surprise. For once, Everett didn't dread the demons that would circle in on him in the night. They wouldn't dare, not with Patrick there to protect him. For perhaps the first time in decades, Everett fell asleep with a smile on his lips and peace in his heart.

CHAPTER 12

Patrick awoke in a panic the next morning. He sat bolt-upright, causing a still-sleeping Everett to spill to the side. A wave of tenderness passed through Patrick's gut at the sight of Everett, relaxed and sleep-tousled, as he stirred awake. Patrick still felt the warmth of Everett's body where they had entwined in sleep as the cool, morning air hit him. His heart hiccupped in his chest at the memory of everything they'd done. But the joy and the sweetness was short-lived.

He threw the bedcovers aside, leaping out of bed and rushing to the sitting room outside Everett's bedroom, where half of their clothes were strewn from the night before. He spotted the pouch he always carried on his belt and practically dove for it. Only when he opened it with shaking hands to see that the sausage and heel of bread were still there, unmolested, did the panic subside.

Shame rushed in to take the place of panic. Patrick slumped onto an overly-ornate, peacock blue settee. He wanted to throw the damn pouch aside, but he couldn't let go of it to save his life, like it was a vital organ he would die without. He hunched his shoulders, rubbing a hand over his face, and fought to remind himself for the umpteenth time that he wasn't about to starve, he had steady employment in a respectable position, and now he had a wealthy and famous lover who took food for granted to the point of throwing it out on a whim. Everett wouldn't let him starve.

Unless he grew tired of him.

"Was it something I said?" Everett asked from the doorway to the bedroom.

Patrick flinched, twisting to face him. His heart dropped hard into his stomach at the sight of Everett wrapped in a black kimono decorated with blue, pink, and green birds. His dark hair was a mess, his face slightly puffy from sleep, and a day's growth of scruff around his usually impeccably trimmed beard had him looking debauched and glorious. But genuine fear hovered just behind the light of his violet-blue eyes.

"No." Patrick rose, forcing himself to set his pouch aside. "It was something...." He didn't know how to explain, so he made a useless and awkward gesture.

Everett's gaze fell on his pouch for a moment before sliding across his body. The corners of his mouth tipped up in a wicked grin. Only then did Patrick realize he was stark naked. Self-consciousness lashed him, but there was nothing he could do, nowhere he could hide.

"You're forgiven, then." Everett sidled closer, hips swaying, grinning at him with a cockiness that would have been better suited for gloating over a prize he'd won.

Patrick couldn't figure out what to do or how to move fast enough. Everett swayed right up to him, looping an arm around his waist, and pulling him close for a kiss. There was no reason why Patrick should have been surprised by the action, but he was. He was shocked. It made no sense that a man like Everett could want someone as pathetic as him, but there he was, kissing him with tongue and dropping his hand to caress Patrick's backside. And, God help him, Patrick responded enthusiastically. In spite of the voice in the back of his head that warned him to protect himself.

"Shall we go back to bed?" Everett asked, a rakish gleam in his eyes. "I still have so much I want to teach you."

Patrick wanted to say yes more than anything in his life, but his gaze shifted to the clock on the mantle behind Everett. "It's already half eleven," he said, hoarse with desire.

Everett reacted as though someone had doused him with cold water. "Half eleven?" He stepped away from Patrick, staring at the clock with wide eyes. "We slept all morning?"

"We needed the sleep," Patrick said, though he had

the feeling the real shock was not in how long they'd slept, but how peaceful that slumber had been.

"Fuck." Everett marched toward his bedroom. "God damn Lionel Mercer and his mad plan to meet Cristofori at the club for luncheon."

They washed and dressed as fast as they could. The intimacy of sharing a washstand with Everett and borrowing his razor wasn't lost on Patrick. Nor was the significance of Everett picking out one of his own clean shirts and a pair of his drawers for him. It was mad to think that wearing Everett's drawers felt more intimate than the way their sweating bodies had slid together the night before, but it did. His shoulders were broader than Everett's, so the shirt was tight across his chest. The emotions that accompanied everything were just as ill-fitting.

"I do love a man in a copper's uniform," Everett sighed happily as they finished their ablutions. He stood in front of Patrick, straightening his uniform collar and brushing his shoulders with a delighted grin. "You are the picture of dignity, my darling," he said, then stole a quick kiss from Patrick's lips before marching out of the bedroom.

Patrick followed, feeling as though he'd stepped into a whirlwind. Everett had dressed in a colorful, fashionable suit of dark blue that set off the color of his eyes. He'd outlined those eyes with kohl as Patrick shaved, and now he looked as though the world was a stage and he was about to make a grand entrance. Patrick could only scoop up his pouch from the settee, fasten it to his belt, and follow.

Whether Everett planned it deliberately or not, using the excuse that Patrick was a bodyguard hired to protect him from his legion of admirers made it so that not a single soul questioned the two of them walking out together. The ruse proved especially helpful when they left Everett's building only to find a particularly passionate young man, dressed in imitation of Everett's costume from his current show, brandishing a poster from said show and begging Everett to sign it. Patrick played his role as expertly as any actor, keeping the young man at bay while Everett scrawled his signature across the poster with the pencil he kept tucked in his inside jacket pocket.

"I was serious the other day when I said I would hire you as my personal copper," Everett said as they walked on, Everett waving at a handsom cab waiting on the corner.

"You never said such a thing." Patrick tried to keep the thrill in his chest from exploding onto his face.

"I implied it." Everett fixed him with a teasing look. "Strongly."

He had, but Patrick wasn't quite ready to contemplate the cataclysmic shift in his life that leaving Scotland Yard to work for Everett would mean. He bristled at the idea of being a kept man. As beautiful as the last few days had been, Patrick still found it all unbelievable. As in, he didn't believe any of it. He couldn't.

Having Everett open the Pandora's Box of his sexuality meant one thing to him, but he was certain it meant something vastly different to Everett—something less meaningful.

"Stop scowling," Everett told him as they climbed into the hired carriage. Everett gave the driver the address of The Chameleon Club, and as soon as they were moving, he went on. "You've nothing to scowl about. We're working together on a mission of utmost importance, and we will succeed in this endeavor. And then we will succeed in a great many exotic endeavors that will put a smile on that handsome face of yours you won't ever be able to wipe away."

Patrick glanced sideways at him, all of his clothes uncomfortably tight. Success wasn't a word he would ever have applied to himself.

"Have I ever told you about the time I performed for the queen?" Everett asked, stretching and settling into his seat.

"You have not," Patrick answered.

"It was a special performance at Buckingham Palace for Princess Vicky's birthday. She'd come over from dreadful Germany for a visit, and would you believe it, the darling thing asked for me specifically."

Everett blathered on, telling a story about Victoria and Vicky that Patrick was reasonably certain he'd completely made up. He let Everett talk without interrupting him, though. The man soothed himself with the sound of his own voice, and who was he to deny him that pleasure? Besides, he rather liked listening to Everett spout shit with a smile.

By the time they reached The Chameleon Club, Patrick was actually smiling. That smile was short-lived, though.

"I don't care how viciously you harangue me, Lionel, I'm not doing it," Niall Cristofori was in the middle of saying as Patrick and Everett strode into the club's dining room.

Lionel's pale face was splotched pink, and he practically vibrated with frustration. Patrick had never seen the powerful man in such a state.

"For God's sake, man. You know what is at stake here," Lionel seethed, glaring at Cristofori. "You would see the lives of children put in danger because you don't have the balls to face a former lover?"

"Lionel," David warned him, raising a hand. David stood between Lionel and Cristofori beside a table strewn with Cristofori's papers and scribblings.

Lionel wasn't the only one beside himself with irritation. Cristofori was flushed, all of the composure Patrick usually admired about the man gone. "You know full well it's not as simple as that," he argued.

"How complicated could it be?" Lionel threw his arms out. "You wanted him, he left you. That's hardly a cause for cowardice when young lives are in danger."

"What is this?" Everett barged forward, a deadly light in his eyes as he stared hard at Lionel. "Is that the pot calling the kettle black that I hear?"

Dread swooped through Patrick's stomach so fast he thought he might be sick. He nodded to David in greeting, but neither of them had time for more.

"Bloody hell, Everett. Not now," Lionel snapped, attempting to turn back to Cristofori.

"You're accusing this man of being a coward because he doesn't want to step back into the morass of a failed love affair, if the little I heard upon entering the room is correct."

"It's more complicated than that," Cristofori said through a clenched jaw.

Neither Everett nor Lionel seemed to hear him. "Don't you start on me, Everett," Lionel snapped. "We both know that I've never been afraid of facing you. Why would I be when I best you at every turn?"

Everett barked a laugh that sent a chill down Patrick's spine. Minutes ago, Patrick had felt like the center of Everett's world, but the moment Lionel Mercer was in the room, he was back to being an invisible speck on the wall. It stung like a thousand wasps.

"The only way you have ever bested me is when I let you." Everett strode to stand toe-to-toe with Lionel.

"A likely story," Lionel snorted.

"Please," David said in a long-suffering voice, pinching the bridge of his nose. "For Christ's sake, could we please not turn this into yet another cock-measuring contest between the two of you?" Patrick edged his way around the table to stand beside David. "Every fucking time," David murmured to him. "It's like a disease with these two."

There was more than just irritation in David's eyes. Patrick could see the same sort of hurt in their brown depths that he felt within himself.

"I'm not the one who exhumes the horse to beat every time this jackanapes is in the same room as me," Lionel said, pulling himself to his full height and picking an imaginary piece of lint from the sleeve of his expertly-tailored, dove-grey suit.

"Please," Everett sneered. "You're the one who can't stop gagging for me years after we parted ways."

"I do not," Lionel sniffed.

He was lying. Patrick winced as soon as he saw it. A sick knot formed in his stomach. He peeked sideways at David. David knew Lionel was lying too. Though Patrick wouldn't have come close to calling it love, Everett held Lionel captive in some way. And how was he possibly supposed to compete with a man of education, finesse, and power like Lionel Mercer?

"Could we please stick to the matter at hand," David said, rubbing a hand over his face. He turned to Cristofori. "Niall, please reconsider. We need your connection to Selby in order to gain access to his brother. You yourself said that Castleford fancies himself a patron of the arts. If you could only ask Selby to provide you and Everett with an introduction so that you can appeal to Castleford to finance your play next year, it would give us exactly the foot in the door that we need."

Patrick's brow lifted slightly. They'd arrived late, but the plan that David and Lionel had evidently come up with in their absence to infiltrate Castleford's estate was a good one.

"I will use whatever other contacts I have to get you into Castleford's good graces," Cristofori said, "but I cannot contact Blake personally." His face flushed a deeper shade of red at his statement and he avoided everyone's eyes. "That door is closed. I can't open it again."

"Where have I heard that before?" Everett muttered, crossing his arms and narrowing his eyes at Lionel.

"You were the one who was finished with me," Lionel shouted, startling everyone within a twenty-foot radius of the conversation.

"My, my. A bit touchy about the past, are we?" Everett's eyes went wide, as if he were ready for a fight. "And for your information, that's not the way I remember things. You were through with me."

"Not true," Lionel snapped. "I needed you." He jabbed a slender finger into Everett's chest, leaning toward him, pain in his eyes. "I needed you and you waltzed off with some toff from Scotland."

Everett's cocky smirk dropped into an ashen look. "It wasn't like that. And you never needed me. You never needed anyone but yourself."

There was far too much uncertainty in Everett's eyes for Patrick's comfort. He swallowed, battling hard against the feeling that Everett was sand in his hourglass, and it was about to run out.

"I needed you," Lionel repeated, hoarse and barely audible. "You left."

Everett shifted uncomfortably. "Is there something you aren't telling me?" he asked, warm tones seeping into his voice. "Something you didn't tell me then?"

"Is there something you're not telling me now?" David echoed, but with a deeper level of intensity.

Patrick held his breath, glancing between the three men, feeling as out of place in their tangle as a lark at sea.

Lionel held Everett's stare for so long that Patrick felt he should look away, but he couldn't. When Lionel shifted to look desolately at David, a dark pit formed in Patrick's gut.

"I can't stay here," Lionel croaked at last. He glanced to Cristofori. "Be a man and get over your disappointments. Children's lives are at stake."

Without another word, he marched off, picking up speed as he crossed the dining room until he was nearly running. He raised a hand to his mouth as he turned the corner into the hall, and Patrick could have sworn that his face was pinched with tears. The great and mighty Lionel Mercer, usually the epitome of commanding serenity, had been reduced to tears by the past. By a former lover, to be exact. By Patrick's current lover.

The ground he thought he stood on shifted beneath him like quicksand. If Everett truly had thrown Lionel Mercer off in his hour of need because another man came along, what would he do when he realized how pedestrian Patrick was?

"Whatever's got his goat—" Everett started.

David cut him off with a sharply-raised hand. "Don't," he warned. "I'm through with your arrogance and your selfishness. If you ruin all of the work Lionel and I have done over the past few months because you cannot pull your head out of your arse long enough to put others before yourself, so help me God, I will obliterate you."

Patrick knew the look of a man suffering under the lash of love when he saw it. He wasn't sure if he should pity David Wirth for being so hopelessly in love with Lionel as it was clear he was, or if he should curse himself for getting so deeply involved with a man like Everett—a man who basked in applause and adoration and stomped on the hearts that were thrown at his feet.

"I wasn't—" Everett began, his expression genuinely baffled, and also pained. He didn't go on, even though no one cut him off.

David bored into him with a look. Everyone held their breath, even men at the tables around them who had no part in the argument. Finally, David pushed forward without a word, walking past Everett and bumping his shoulder hard with his own as he passed.

Patrick watched David leave, feeling like he'd been left with a mess to clean up but no mop and bucket. Everett watched David go, clearly at a loss, then turned to Patrick with an appeal in his eyes.

Patrick turned away from him, facing Cristofori. "Mr. Cristofori, may I have a word with you in private?"

Cristofori had been silent since the argument had shifted away from him and onto Everett and Lionel's tumultuous past. He met Patrick's eyes now with deep wariness. "Of course."

Patrick drew in a breath and forced himself to look at Everett. He'd never seen Everett look so at a loss for words. "This isn't my fault," Everett said, his voice unusually thin. "Patrick, you have to believe me." He took a step forward.

Patrick held up a hand to ward him off, stepping back. "Let me speak to Mr. Cristofori alone." He hesitated, shifting his weight from one foot to the other and back. "Perhaps you should go to the theater."

"I don't have to be there until this evening," Everett said.

"Then perhaps you should go home." Patrick's eyes bored into his, turning his suggestion into an order. "I'll send word about our next step as soon as things are sorted."

Everett's jaw worked soundlessly for a moment. Patrick knew full well what it meant to him to be dismissed. He knew that Everett truly didn't understand what had just happened, or where the two of them stood. Patrick wasn't sure where they stood either, only that he couldn't feel safe and secure with a man who had a string of broken hearts trailing behind him. Even though he understood that not everything in Everett's past was his fault.

At last, Everett's shoulders dropped as he let out a breath. "All right," he said, as close to a cowed schoolboy as Patrick had ever seen him. "I'll go. You know where to find me." He turned and took a few steps before pivoting to say, "Please find me," in a whisper.

Patrick's throat closed up. Dangerous though Everett was to his heart, he had a feeling it was already too late to save himself. He nodded, his mouth twitching into the closest thing to a smile that he could manage. Everett hovered where he was for a moment before nodding in return and marching on.

"You'll have your hands full with that one if you keep at it," Cristofori said. The comment wasn't unkind, but it stung all the same.

Patrick shifted to face him. "What is there between you and Lord Selby that would prevent you from stopping innocent children from being kidnapped and sold into slavery—both for manual labor and as sexual toys for evil men?"

The question was blunt enough that Cristofori stumbled back, hitting his thigh against the edge of the table. He lowered his head for a moment before drawing in a long breath and standing straight.

"I loved him," Cristofori admitted. He glanced up to meet Patrick's eyes. "Blake. I loved him as I have never loved anyone. And I believe he loved me." He swallowed, the depth of his pain on display as if it were a monologue in one of his plays. "He not only left me, he denied everything we had, everything he is. He married for money and to please his family, slamming the door in not only my face, but in his own as well. I cannot forgive him for that." His voice grew hoarse. "He turned his back on everything."

"Like you are turning your back on children who need you?" The question bubbled up from the wounded part of Patrick that had watched adult after adult turn their back on him and the rest of his peers at the orphanage, refusing even to give them scraps from their table when they went begging. It came out with so much raw emotion that Cristofori flinched.

"I hadn't thought of it like that," Cristofori said, barely audible.

"Then think of it," Patrick said. "Children are helpless, especially against men like Castleford and his friends. What would you have given for a savior to sweep in and rescue you from the pain you experienced?" The image of himself as he was now, marching into that blasted orphanage and raising hell until every child in the place had enough to eat and love to envelope them, had Patrick's eyes stinging with unshed tears. "You could be that savior," he managed before words failed him entirely.

Cristofori lowered his head, raising a hand to shield his eyes as his face pinched. "All right," he whispered. He stayed frozen in that position for a moment before sucking in a breath, raising his head, and squaring his shoulders. "All right," he repeated, looking miserable. "I'll do it. I will unravel my sanity by ripping my heart open to all that again if it means those children might be saved."

Patrick managed a sympathetic, though grim, smile, clamping a hand on Cristofori's shoulder. "You won't regret it," he said. Though he was beginning to regret everything that had trapped him on his current path as he did.

CHAPTER 13

It took everything Everett had not to fall into his old habit of biting his nails as the train he'd been riding for hours approached the central station in Leeds. He'd slept terribly, yet again, without Patrick beside him the night before. Three times in the night, he'd been awakened by violent nightmares. Only, instead of the usual horrors of his past that played themselves out like macabre stage shows with a leering audience, he dreamed that the men of his past were chasing him as he frantically searched for Patrick, but couldn't find him.

"I apologize in advance for how awkward this meeting is about to be," Niall said from the seat across from Everett. He glanced to Everett, then to Patrick, who sat beside him. "I haven't seen or spoken to Blake in nearly ten years, aside from the telegram I sent yesterday explaining the bare minimum of our plan."

"You say he plans to meet us at the train station?" Patrick asked, stoic and unreadable.

Niall nodded and sighed, rubbing the back of his neck. "And again, I apologize. It's going to be extraordinarily uncomfortable."

Everett gave up trying to resist his impulse and raised a hand to chew at the corner of a fingernail. Extraordinarily uncomfortable was exactly how he'd felt since the bizarre confrontation at The Chameleon Club the day before. Everything had happened so fast. He had given it so little thought as it was unfolding. Lionel was simply being Lionel—though Everett was willing to admit that he'd been Lionel on a level that he hadn't seen in years. The bastard couldn't actually still hold a candle for him, could he? The idea was preposterous. They'd gotten what they needed from each other for as long as they'd needed it, then moved on.

Hadn't they?

He forced himself to drop his hands, studying Patrick across from him instead. In retrospect, it wasn't particularly wise to have a tiff with a past lover while his current lover was standing right next to him. There was nothing for Patrick to be jealous of, as far as he was concerned. But Patrick *was* upset. Deeply. He radiated disapproval, even now, as the train whistle sounded and they began to slow. But what had Everett done to earn such disapproval?

Guilt roiled in his gut, even though a specific answer to the question failed to materialize in his mind. His past was not his fault. Making light of horror was how he had survived. Loathing to sleep alone didn't mean he was willfully immoral. But for every excuse he came up with, guilt wrapped itself tighter around his heart. Patrick deserved better than a used piece of costume finery like him.

"Annamarie Cannon brought a small fortune with her as dowry from her father's plate glass business."

Niall had gone on speaking while Everett was lost in his thoughts. Everett had resumed chewing his nails as well without being aware of it. He folded his hands stiffly in his lap and forced himself to pay attention to whatever story Niall was telling.

"The marriage was brokered without Blake ever having met her," Niall went on, dark circles under his eyes and a hard set to his jaw. "Still, he could have refused the alliance. I fully expected him to, after the things the two of us said to each other."

"So you were lovers?" Patrick asked.

Niall let out a sad breath. "I thought we were more than that. We took to each other from the moment we met at Oxford. I'd written and was staging a musical play. Blake auditioned for the lead. He was perfect for the part—handsome, talented, and charismatic. We had so many similar likes and interests that it was as if I'd finally found my other half.

"Of course, he didn't know that he had an inclination to love men," Niall went on with a shrug. "It had never dawned on him. But we became fast friends, and then...."

His sentence trailed off, and he glanced out the window as the city of Leeds slid past at a slower and slower pace. "Everyone knew there was something between us," he continued in a far-away voice. "I played opposite him in the musical, and the connection was obvious for all the world to see, fellow players and audience alike. For a short and glorious time, we were lovers, though never publicly, never openly. When asked about it, we'd laugh it off, pretend it was ridiculous, mock people for even suggesting it." Again, he paused, lowering his head. "I cannot tell you how much pain that caused me."

"Selby was unwilling to own up to your relationship." Patrick made the statement with a frown.

Niall winced. "Part of me thinks that he would have had to come to terms with it eventually. But his father came to Oxford to attend the final performance of the musical. He informed Blake of his impending nuptials and his duty as a future duke. And blast him, Blake didn't fight it. Not one bit. We argued. I pleaded with him, cursing him for turning his back on love. He insisted there was no such thing between us, only youthful folly, but his eyes told a far different tale than his lips. It didn't matter, in the end. He graduated and retreated to Yorkshire to marry his dollar princess, and I moved to London to begin my career as a playwright."

"And you haven't spoken since," Patrick finished the story for him.

Niall shook his head. "Not a single word. Not in ten years." He shrugged, the weight of his broken heart clear on his shoulders. "I've seen him in London several times—at the theater, in the street, at balls and such—but only from a distance." The train whistle sounded again, as did the screech of brakes as the train pulled into the station. "We're about to speak the first words we've said to each other in a decade."

"Shakespeare himself couldn't have written a more poignant tragedy," Everett said with a sympathetic smile.

His gaze slipped sideways to Patrick, who was studying him with his own sort of wistfulness. Everett would have given his right eye to know what exactly he had said or done to put Patrick off of him so thoroughly. All of the hard-won openness between them had vanished. It was as though Everett was forced to peek at Patrick through a crack in the thick wall between them.

"So, once more," Niall said with a sigh, standing when the train came to a full stop, "I apologize for what is doomed to be a brittle and stilted reunion."

"As long as Lord Selby is willing to give us an introduction to his brother, it doesn't matter how awkward things are for us," Patrick said, standing as well.

Everett rose last, turning to fetch his suitcase from the rack above his seat. As soon as he had it in hand, Patrick took it from him. Their hands brushed on the handle, and a jolt of longing shot through Everett.

"I am perfectly capable of carrying my own bag," Everett said.

Patrick shook his head. "I'm here as your bodyguard and assistant. I should carry the bags."

Everett swayed closer to him. "You know you're so much more than that, love."

The jumble of emotion that came to Patrick's eyes was almost unbearable to look at, chiefly because doubt was among the most readable emotions there. Everett didn't have time to comment on it, though. Niall opened the door and stepped down onto the platform. Everett followed, Patrick right behind him with their luggage, bracing himself for a confrontation between Niall and Lord Selby.

"Niall? Is that you?" a jovial voice rang out from farther along the platform.

Everett and Patrick—who had reached his side—turned to find a dazzlingly handsome man in an impeccable suit beaming at Niall as though angels on high were singing. He started forward at a swift pace, hazel eyes shining, sunlight catching in his unfashionably long curls.

"It's so good to see you, my friend." Joy rang in Lord Selby's musical voice as he reached Niall and drew him into a tight embrace.

Everett's brow shot up, and he glanced from the friendly reunion to Patrick as if to say, "That was unexpected."

Patrick glanced back at Everett with the same sentiment in his eyes, whatever tension existed between the two of them temporarily forgotten.

Only Niall remained on edge, hugging Selby back before breaking away and putting deliberate distance between the two of them. "You look well, Blake," he said.

"I feel well, now that you're here," Selby answered, smiling and staring at Niall as though seeing a vision. "It's been far too long. Come. I have my carriage waiting."

Everett exchanged another look with Patrick before the two of them moved along, trailing Niall and Selby as though they were suddenly supernumeraries in someone else's drama.

"I'm sorry if this is an inconvenience," Niall said as they crossed through the station and out to the street, where several carriages were lined up, ready to whisk newly-arrived passengers off to their final destinations. "I wasn't sure where else to turn. My play is so close to completion, but without the proper funds to mount it, it might never see the light of day. And since your brother claims to be such a patron of the arts, I owed it to Mr. Jewel here and everyone else invested in the production to leave no stone unturned in bringing the play to the stage." Niall stuck rigidly to the story they'd devised to gain entry into Lord Castleford's estate.

"Yes, yes, of course." Selby waved the explanation away as he led the three of them to his carriage. "I would do anything for you, you know that." He glanced back to Niall with so much fondness in his eyes that Everett smirked. The man was a fool if he thought he was hiding anything. Or so he thought until Selby went on with, "I wish you would come up to Brayton Park, though. Annamarie and the children would be so delighted to see you. Annamarie hasn't been able to talk of anything else but you since I mentioned I was coming here to meet you and take you to Montague for an introduction."

Again, Everett turned to Patrick to see what he thought. Selby would never have had the audacity to speak of his wife—the woman who had come between him and Niall—with so much enthusiasm, and right in front of Niall's face, unless he were either prodigiously stupid or being deliberately cruel. Selby didn't seem to be either, though. Everett prided himself on knowing people and being able to read them. It was a professional skill that helped his acting craft. And Blake Williamson, Duke of Selby, seemed like nothing more than a merry soul with a cheerful disposition whom he would very much like to stay up all night drinking and carousing with.

"Where are my manners," Selby said, his energy seeming to increase with every step, as they reached his carriage. "I haven't properly introduced myself. Blake Williamson." He extended a hand to Everett, who took it. Before Everett could return the greeting, Selby went on with, "It is a pleasure indeed to meet you at last, Mr. Jewel. I saw you in Hamlet a few years ago, and in more than a few musical reviews before and since. Your talent is astounding."

Everett beamed from ear to ear before he could think better of it. At least Patrick already knew how much of a conceited prat he was. "I'm glad I could entertain you, Lord Selby," he said, letting go of the man's hand and executing a dramatic bow.

"None of that." Selby made a dismissive gesture. "I'm

Blake to my friends, and it would be a great honor for a man of your prominence to call me a friend."

"But of course." Everett grinned. When Blake's gaze shifted to Patrick, he said, "Allow me to introduce you to my own personal copper, Officer Patrick Wrexham."

Patrick held both his suitcase and Everett's in his hands, so could only nod in acknowledgement. "My lord," he said, then slunk around to the back of the carriage to hand the suitcases off to the driver.

The whole thing put Everett's teeth on edge. Patrick should not be bowing and scraping, like a servant. He was as worthy as the rest of them, probably more so.

"I once entertained delusions of running off and making a life on the stage for myself," Blake went on, ushering them all into the carriage, then knocking the ceiling to signal to his driver they were ready to depart. "But, of course, a duke cannot make a life on the stage." For a fraction of a second, his affable demeanor cracked, and Everett caught a glimpse of real regret. The man seemed to be deliberately avoiding staring at Niall, who had taken a seat beside him, but squashed himself into the far corner so that no parts of their bodies touched. "I haven't had a chance to act in years, but I keep up with the piano and play and sing to entertain my friends whenever possible."

Everett arched an eyebrow. Hadn't had the chance to act in years, indeed. The man was acting up a storm right before their eyes. Everett could see it now.

Before he could make a comment, Blake rushed on

with, "Niall's great-great-great-great-something-like-that-grandfather invented the piano, you know."

"Did he?" For what felt like the thousandth time in the last ten minutes, Everett's brow went up, and he turned to Patrick to gauge his opinion.

"Yes. Bartolomeo Cristofori," Blake said. "He was Italian, of course, but we can forgive him for that. Right, Niall?" He laughed as though sharing a joke.

Niall laughed as well, but the sound was brittle and uneasy.

"You should have seen the first time I played for Niall," Blake continued. "I took him utterly by surprise. No one expects a future duke—my father was still alive at the time—to play like that."

Everett settled back in his seat, covering his mouth with one hand and trying not to look as though he were laughing at the hapless Duke of Selby. The man was clearly every bit as nervous as Niall, though he had the endearing habit of hiding his anxiety with frivolous talk and the sound of his own voice. Everett knew the tactic well. It was one he employed himself, one that got him into trouble more often than not. It was a revelation to have someone else taking up every inch of the space in the carriage besides him for a change. Patrick seemed downright stunned by the number of words Blake managed to squeeze out in the twenty minutes it took them to travel from the train station to the edges of a walled and gated estate on the edge of what he supposed was a moor of some sort. In those twenty minutes, Blake spoke more words than Patrick had likely spoken in his lifetime.

"This is Montague's estate." Blake shifted the topic of his endless, cheerful monologue from the theater and his and Niall's university days—managing not to divulge so much as a hint of what their relationship might have been during those years as he spoke—to the landscape around them. "It has the hopelessly dull name of Castleford Estate. That's far more of an encyclopedic description than a proper name for such a vast and unique property."

"Unique?" Patrick asked, his expression betraying nothing.

"Well, there's the menagerie, of course," Blake said. "Montague always was interested in animals, ever since we were boys. He was forever keeping things in cages in the nursery. It's unfortunate that so many of those things ended up dying."

Everett's eyes went wide and a chill shot down his back. "Unfortunate indeed."

"I might have entertained the idea of running off to make a life on the stage," Blake went on, "but I'm certain, if he hadn't had the title and estates of an earl thrust on him, Montague would have joined the circus. He would have made the perfect lion-tamer."

Several bells sounded in Everett's mind. The man with the lion indeed. "One thing I learned about your brother whilst researching various men who would be patrons of the theater was that he keeps lions on his property. Is this true?"

"Only the one," Blake said with a nod. "The lion and a few monkeys, along with several exotic birds, are all that remain of his menagerie now. He has far too many other concerns these days to maintain what he once had."

"Other concerns?" Patrick asked. "What might they be?"

Blake shrugged. "I'm not entirely certain. My own affairs—my estate, my business ventures in London, and my wife and children—have kept me preoccupied." The same hollow flash of guilt and sadness that had flickered around the edges of his expression returned. It was disconcerting on a variety of levels to Everett. He couldn't shake the feeling that Blake was the sort of man who lived so deeply in denial about so many things, covering that denial with the veneer of a genial man, that he was no longer aware of any sort of truth at all.

"Oh, look," Blake said, sitting straighter and glancing out the window. "Montague has come out to greet us. And he didn't even know I was bringing you here today."

Everett's gut clenched so fast that he reached for Patrick's steadying hand without being aware of it. Patrick pulled away just as swiftly, leaving the gaping pit in Everett's stomach twice as wide. The carriage stopped, and the four of them exited, approaching the terrace in front of Montague Williamson, Earl of Castleford's rather gothic-looking home.

"Blake." Castleford narrowed his eyes at his brother. "What are you doing here, and who are these people?" His peevish expression jolted to surprise as he laid eyes on Everett. The recognition there relieved Everett. Castleford must truly have been a theater aficionado. Lionel's plan wasn't some sort of half-baked notion, meant to send them into the proverbial and literal lion's den on the weakest of pretenses after all.

With that in mind, Everett turned on every ounce of charm and stage presence he could muster. "Lord Castleford, it is such a pleasure to meet you at last." He advanced up the stairs to meet Castleford on his terrace as though they hadn't just been formally introduced already, but as if they were old friends of equal rank. He extended his hand and flashed his most seductive smile. "And what a fascinating estate you have. Your brother pointed out several of its most interesting features to us just now, as we made our approach."

Castleford was just intrigued enough by the role Everett was playing to take his hand and shake it without seeming the least bit offended. The second their hands touched, however, Everett wanted to turn and run. Montague Williamson was as different from his brother as night was to day. Where Blake was all warmth, good cheer, and, as Everett suspected, willful ignorance, Castleford was frosty, withdrawn, and conniving. There were no other words for the feeling the man gave Everett, except perhaps "disturbed". Castleford's hand was physically cold, and the man was so pale as to appear bloodless. He had the same hazel eyes and dark, curling hair as Blake, but they made him seem like a specter instead of a friend.

"I was just telling them about Leo." Blake stepped forward with a bright smile. He crossed to his brother, embracing him and thumping him on the back. Castleford remained stiff as a statue as he was hugged, but when Blake stepped back, he continued to grin as though the two of them were the best of friends.

Everett didn't know whether to roll his eyes at Blake or feel deeply sorry for him.

"Why are you here?" Castleford asked with the same formal bluntness as before. "I'm expecting company."

"I simply had to introduce you to an old university chum of mine," Blake explained. "This is Niall Cristofori, the esteemed playwright."

The barest hint of surprise registered in Castleford's icy expression. "Niall Cristofori. I've certainly heard of you. I very much enjoyed *Fate's Consequences* when it was staged in eighty-seven. Though I was less enamored of *Lady Jezebel* last season."

"I'm flattered that you know my work, my lord," Niall said, stepping forward. He had remained silent since the initial greeting at the train station, but fell into the part he'd been asked to play as seamlessly as though he were vying for Everett's place at the top of the bill. "It's why I called in a favor from an old university chum to ask for an introduction," he said, echoing Blake.

"Oh?" Castleford appeared genuinely intrigued.

"Yes, my lord," Niall went on with a somewhat forced smile. "In short, I am on the verge of mounting an all-new musical play next season, *Love's Last Lesson*, which will star Mr. Jewel here. But our most important financer has backed out, and I'm afraid we've been forced to travel door-to-door begging for funds in order for the production to continue."

In spite of his sinister demeanor, Castleford seemed flattered. "And you thought of me as a potential patron?"

"Of course," Everett said, playing up to the man in every way possible. Out of the corner of his eye, he spotted another carriage rolling up the drive toward the house. "Your reputation precedes you, my lord. Everyone told us that you were the first person we should consult with for advice on how to proceed with the production."

"I would be happy to discuss offering whatever help I can," Castleford said, though his attention shifted more and more to the arriving carriage. "Your timing is less than desirable," he went on. "As you can see, I was expecting other company. But I am certain my friends would be more than happy to meet such a fascinating and well-known personality."

He stepped away from Everett, heading down the stairs to meet the newly-arrived carriage. Everett kept his smile firmly in place, nodding encouragingly to Niall, then risking everything to wink at a stony-faced Patrick.

His excitement for the ruse and optimism about its possible outcome shattered completely just seconds later as one of Castleford's footmen opened the door to the newly-arrived carriage and Chisolm stepped out.

CHAPTER 14

Castleford Estate gave Patrick chills. He'd felt an air of menace about the place from the moment Selby's carriage passed through the elaborate gate and onto the property. It may only have been his imagination, but the colors throughout the landscape seemed darker, and the great house itself looked like something out of a nightmare. As Everett, Cristofori, and Selby chatted, Patrick studied everything around him with narrowed eyes and a quickened pulse.

The first thing he spotted that chilled his blood were the spiked gratings underneath all of the windows on the ground floor. The spikes were sharpened and the gratings positioned in such a way that anyone who thought to escape from the house through the windows would be in serious danger of impaling themselves. Beyond that, the garden that was just visible around the left-hand side of the house had its boundaries marked by hemlock hedges.

Patrick wondered how many of the other plants in that garden were deadly. Around the right-hand side of the house he could just barely make out the edges of tall cages. They were likely the former home of whatever animals had made up Castleford's menagerie, but instinct told Patrick they'd been put to a more chilling use.

"Your timing is less than desirable."

Castleford's words jolted Patrick back to attention. He dragged his assessing gaze back from the edges of the house and focused on the man for a moment. In spite of his fine clothes and elegant demeanor, he was the last man Patrick would have wanted to meet alone in the dark.

"As you can see, I was expecting other company. But I am certain my friends would be more than happy to meet such a fascinating and well-known personality."

Patrick turned to the approaching carriage at Castleford's words. He caught a look of mild curiosity on Everett's face—a face that was otherwise smiling and jovial, as if he were trying to woo Castleford into spilling all his secrets. Patrick had to give Everett credit for being a brilliant actor.

No sooner had the thought popped into his head than it was challenged. Chisolm and Eastleigh alighted from the carriage. The moment Everett spotted Chisolm, all color drained from his face. It didn't matter that Patrick was so frustrated with Everett that it felt as though he might crawl out of his skin. It didn't matter if he was jealous of Everett's careless attitude toward his past lovers, or if he doubted the man's intentions toward him. The memory of how Everett had reacted to the sight of Chisolm at Batcliff Cross Docks was enough to prompt Patrick to step up to Everett's side.

"Steady on," he murmured, touching a hand to the small of Everett's back.

Everett sucked in a breath and nodded tightly. He then cleared his throat and rolled his shoulders as Castleford marched down the steps to greet his guests.

"Chisolm, Eastleigh," Castleford said with a smile like icicles jutting from a roof in the dead of winter. "Welcome to Castleford Estate."

"Castleford." Chisolm nodded, shaking Castleford's hand.

Eastleigh shook his hand as well. There didn't seem to be a lick of warmth between the men. Patrick found that paradoxically encouraging. They were business partners, not friends, which meant, if push came to shove, they could be turned against each other.

"Who do we have here?" Chisolm asked as Castleford escorted him and Eastleigh up to the terrace. His eyes bored into Everett's with the sort of cunning reserved for a dog he'd already beaten and knew would cower before him.

"Unexpected visitors," Castleford said, moving to stand between the new arrivals and Everett, Patrick, and the others. "Surely, you have seen Mr. Everett Jewel perform."

"Oh, I most certainly have," Chisolm said in a low purr.

Every muscle in Patrick's body tensed, ready for a fight. His mind was quick to write the story of what must have happened between the two men in the past.

"My wife dragged me to that monstrosity of a play you're in right now," Eastleigh said, studying Everett with interest, clearly more impressed with him than he let on.

The insult seemed to shake Everett out of his stupor. He grinned wickedly at Eastleigh and bowed dramatically. "Your words are too kind, my lord." His expression was teasing when he straightened, but his eyes maintained the hollowness of a frightened child. "I will be certain to reserve a box for you for opening night of my next show."

"A show which Mr. Jewel and Mr. Cristofori here have asked me to finance," Castleford said, puffing with pride.

"Is that so?" Chisolm narrowed his eyes in suspicion.

"It seems my reputation as a patron of the arts precedes me," Castleford said. "Of course, we all know that I have always been a fan of spectacle." He sent Chisolm and Eastleigh a knowing look that had the hair on the back of Patrick's neck standing up.

The air around them all sizzled, like the last moments of calm before a battle. Patrick willed himself to be as invisible as possible as he studied the noblemen in front of him. They all had an aura of evil about them, but Patrick was certain they each had chinks in their armor.

Castleford had preened like a girl receiving her first compliment when asked to finance Cristofori's show. His weakness was either renown or the theater itself. Lionel had been beyond clever to send them up north with Cristofori's show as their ruse.

Chisolm's weakness was harder for Patrick to accept. It was Everett, but not in the same way that Everett was swiftly becoming his own weakness. With Chisolm, it was something far more sinister. The words "power" and "control" flashed through his mind.

Eastleigh was harder to read, but as the noblemen fell into conversation, Castleford introducing his brother and Cristofori as their group retreated into the house, Patrick wondered if arrogance and a feeling of superiority as a peer were Eastleigh's Achilles' heel. The man only seemed interested in conversing with Selby—a duke—and ignored the rest of them—even Everett—the same way he ignored the servants.

"It's such a lovely day," Castleford said as their group wandered into a conservatory decorated more like a funeral parlor than the scene of light musical events. "Why don't we take tea in the menagerie. That way, I can show you Leo."

"And how is good, old Leo these days?" Selby asked, his smile far wider than the brittle tension around them warranted. Then again, Patrick had decided within minutes that Lord Selby was the sort who would rather smile in ignorance and be considered a dolt than weep in the face of reality.

"As well as could be expected," Castleford said, leading their group across the conservatory to a pair of French doors that led out to another terrace. "I am determined to find him a new friend one of these days. The trouble is, he keeps eating the friends I give him." Castleford laughed as though he'd shared a cunning riddle.

Everett laughed with him, though the sound hit Patrick's ears more like the shriek of a kettle hitting its boiling point and letting out steam. He kept his eyes on the stiff lines of Everett's back as they proceeded out into a shady section of the garden. How Everett had managed to keep his composure so far was a testament to his inner strength. In spite of everything, Patrick's heart warmed.

Within seconds of stepping out onto the terrace, Chisolm and Eastleigh separated themselves from the others. They inclined their heads together and exchanged a few, quick words while staring at Everett and the others.

"I always used to enjoy visiting Montague's menagerie when it was at its height," Selby explained to Cristofori and Everett. "Didn't you have an elephant at one point?" he asked his brother.

"At one point," Castleford said with a nod. "And a giraffe, camels, several hyenas."

The corner of Patrick's mouth twitched. He would expect a man like Castleford to keep hyenas caged on his property.

"What ever happened to the giraffe?" Selby asked with a puzzled smile. "She was a beauty," he added for

Cristofori. "I wish you could have seen her. It's a shame you never had the opportunity to visit Yorkshire with me."

Cristofori's mouth dropped open, but he didn't reply. Patrick detected a great deal of incredulity in the man's expression, along with heartache that Cristofori failed to hide and that Selby either couldn't see or was deliberately ignoring.

At the same time, Everett's mouth was clamped shut, and a green pallor had replaced his pale shock. He eyed Chisolm as though he were the lion who was about to pounce.

All in all, it made for a painfully awkward gathering.

"Where is Leo at any rate?" Selby asked, walking to the edge of the terrace and craning his neck to look around at the rows of empty cages. "You used to keep him right up against the house. I remember the way he would roar at night."

"Alas, I've had to move him back to the pit." Castleford gestured for them to follow him off of the terrace and through a row of empty cages to a knee-high fence surrounding a pit at the end of the garden. "He's turned vicious, I'm afraid. There was no way to get close enough to the cage to feed him without one of the footmen losing an arm. So I had him moved here."

They reached the edge of the pit. Castleford grinned down into it, like a vengeful god surveying his supplicants.

Patrick's heart squeezed with pity in his chest at the

sight that met him. There was indeed a lion in the pit. The poor thing was emaciated. It paced restlessly from one end of the surprisingly large pit to the other. Its misery was palpable. The moment it spotted the odd assortment of humans standing over it, it charged toward them, roaring and attempting to leap to freedom. Selby cursed and jumped backward, grabbing Cristofori and dragging him back as he did. But the pit was too deep for the starving lion to jump out of, though dozens of lines of scratches in the stone walls lining the pit hinted that he continued to try.

"I should probably feed him," Castleford said on a sigh, as if he didn't truly care. He turned toward a pale footman standing on the terrace they'd just left. "Norris, see if you can't purchase a sheep from one of the local farmers for Leo. I believe we're out of monkeys."

The footman nodded, then disappeared into the house. Moments later, a stony-faced maid brought a tray set for tea out to the terrace, placing it on a table in the sun.

"At least *we* won't go hungry," Castleford laughed, turning away from the pit.

Patrick spared one last glance for the pitiful lion. The beast looked up at him with vacant eyes, too consumed by hunger to think about anything else. Patrick knew how it felt all too well. He touched a hand to the pouch on his belt, shame welling within him as he turned to follow the others to the terrace.

"Jewel, tell us all about this new play of yours,"

Castleford said once the gentlemen were settled in chairs around the terrace as Patrick stood in a shadow against the wall, hands clasped behind his back, observing.

"Yes, *Jewel*," Chisolm echoed with a grin. "Tell us what you've been up to."

"The show is Cristofori's," Everett answered in a hoarse voice, doing his best to smile and preen as usual but falling short. "I will merely be delivering his words. You should get him to tell you about it."

"Yes, I, for one, am eager to hear all about this new show," Selby said, shifting in his seat to face Cristofori. He went so far as to rest one elbow on the arm of his chair and his chin on his hand as he gazed at Cristofori with rapt interest.

"It's a comedy of manners," Cristofori explained, glancing uneasily from Selby to Everett, then on to Castleford. "The action takes place during a summer holiday at the country house of one Lord Applebaum, who is desperate to make a match for his spritely daughter, Abigail."

As Cristofori explained the plot of his creation to the gentlemen, Patrick took a moment to study the house itself. Aside from the gothic architecture, there was nothing that set the house apart from a dozen other country estates. The menagerie and deadly garden were telling, but the house itself—or what Patrick could see of it through the windows—was furnished normally. He found that encouraging, though. If the layout of the house was no different than the standard fare for a country house, that meant it contained any number of parlors and offices. Any one of those rooms could contain the material evidence David and Lionel needed to bring down the kidnapping ring once and for all.

The other, paradoxical encouragement quickening Patrick's pulse was the presence of Chisolm and Eastleigh. Combined with the chilly way the three noblemen interacted with each other, the fact that all three of them were present was a dead giveaway that something important was on the verge of happening with the ring.

That, however, brought with it the worry that, if they didn't act fast, the ringleaders would get off scot-free. They had to know David and Lionel were closing in on them, which meant they would be fools if they weren't planning to destroy whatever evidence would implicate them in any wrongdoing.

"Gentlemen, that sounds like a lovely endeavor," Castleford said, slapping the arm of his chair and standing.

Patrick flinched. He'd been so involved in his observations that he hadn't followed the conversation. The others rose along with Castleford, indicating that their conversation was over. Everett stood on shaky legs, glancing warily in Patrick's direction.

"I would be more than happy to invest," Castleford went on. "Send me your address in London, and I'll pay you a call as soon as possible."

"Thank you, my lord." Everett pretended to be thrilled, but as he edged toward the door leading into the conservatory, it was clear to Patrick that all he wanted was to flee.

"Why wait to discuss the matter in London?" Chisolm asked, striding closer to Everett.

Everett froze for a moment, terror filling his eyes as Chisolm circled him. Patrick watched the deliberate way his expression changed to feigned ease. His heart went out to Everett, and he cursed the distance between them that kept him from rushing to Everett's rescue.

"Why don't you stay here for a night or two," Chisolm went on, grinning at Everett and ignoring Cristofori and Selby. "Send your man back to London on business, but you stay." Chisolm nodded in Patrick's direction, but Patrick had the feeling he didn't really see him.

"I couldn't possibly," Everett laughed. The sound set Patrick's teeth on edge. "I'm needed in London. The show must go on."

Patrick's expression tightened. He attempted to tell Everett with his eyes that he was making a mistake. The whole point of traveling to Yorkshire was to find the evidence against the ring, and they'd barely begun that search.

"Nonsense," Chisolm said, as though issuing an order. "You'll stay here. We're having a shooting party tomorrow. You must join us."

Everett glanced desperately at Patrick. There wasn't a thing Patrick could do but meet his eyes with a steady gaze and hope he remembered why they'd come in the first place.

"I...I suppose," Everett started, furrowing his brow as though attempting to read what Patrick was trying to tell him. He turned back to Chisolm. "But I already have a hotel reservation in Leeds. I couldn't disappoint the staff there." He burst into one of his most charming smiles.

"You should come stay at Selby Manor," Selby suggested with a broad smile. "I would love to have you there, and I'm sure Annamarie would jump at the chance to entertain."

"No," Cristofori answered, a little too sharp. "Jewel is right. We've already committed to staying at the hotel in Leeds."

"But you must come back tomorrow for our shooting party," Castleford said. "We have so much more to discuss."

Everett checked in with Patrick once more. "Yes, that would be lovely," he said, sounding as though it were anything but.

More pleasantries were exchanged as Castleford led them all through the house and back out to the front. Selby's carriage still waited by the stairs, as though the driver knew the visit wouldn't be a long one. Patrick had never felt so much relief as when he climbed back into the carriage and watched Castleford Estate disappear behind them as they returned to Leeds.

CHAPTER 15

*E*verett couldn't shake the feeling that he was swimming through a thick, foul fog, even as the carriage whisked him away from Castleford Estate and Chisolm. His ears felt full of cotton as Selby and Niall chattered through the short journey to Leeds.

"I really wish you would stay at Brayton Park," Selby said, pleading in his eyes. "We've so much to catch up on."

"It would be out of the question," Niall mumbled.

"At least come visit," Selby insisted. "I would love for you to meet my children."

A part of Everett wanted to make some sort of joke or pointed observation about how obtuse Selby was being, but the fog reduced that impulse to a flat buzz at the back of his mind. It was hard to fault a man for fighting desperately to ignore the past when he'd just been smacked in the face with his.

Chisolm had been so smug. The man had grinned and snickered at Everett as if the years had fallen away and he still held Everett's life in the palm of his hand. The sickening part was that he did. All of the acting and posturing on Everett's part hadn't wiped away the fear that Chisolm would expose him, make demands of him, and leave him hurt and humiliated. And though it was unlikely the man would have tried anything untoward in front of the others, the terror was still there. Chisolm still controlled him.

He shook out of his thoughts with a sharp intake of breath—not realizing he'd forgotten to breathe—when Patrick rested a hand on his thigh. Heat rushed through Everett, and his eyes stung. Mostly because he was certain Patrick was still angry with him, but there he was, attempting to give comfort all the same. Patrick was a thousand times the man he was.

Whether the others noticed how unusually quiet he was as they reached the hotel, Everett couldn't tell. None of them seemed in much of a mood for conversation.

"Shall I reserve us a table in the hotel's dining room?" Selby asked with cheer that was almost grating.

"I'll take supper in my room," Everett said, leaving the others to cross to the front desk.

He ordered a light supper from the concierge for him and for Patrick, even though he had no appetite at all. Once that was done, without taking his leave of the others, he marched to the stairs and started up to the suite he'd reserved.

Patrick caught up to him just outside of the suite's door. "Selby insists on meeting us here tomorrow and returning to Castleford Estate with us," he said.

Everett nodded, exhausted, as he fit his key into the door.

"I'm not sure if the man will be a help or a hindrance to our investigation, but at least he can provide a distraction," Patrick went on.

Everett agreed, but the aftereffects of fighting for his life not to crumple into a cowering mess at Chisolm's feet back at Castleford Estate had him too weak and weary to do more than push open the door and shuffle inside.

"I consider it a promising sign that the gentlemen paid me no heed at all," Patrick went on, taking the key from Everett once they were safe in the room. He closed and locked the suite door, keeping an eye on Everett as he crossed to an elaborate sofa that faced a wide window framed by cheery curtains. "I would say the chance of me slipping away into the house while the rest of you are shooting tomorrow is a good one."

Everett nodded, then sank into the sofa. He let out a breath as he leaned his head back, closing his eyes, and willing himself to evaporate. He listened as Patrick put the key down on a table somewhere with a click, then walked around the sofa to stand near him.

"Usually you're the one talking up a storm while I merely nod."

Everett opened his eyes slowly. His heart swelled in an odd, broken way as he gazed up at Patrick's concerned face. He wasn't wearing his police uniform, but the simple drabness of his suit was just as no-nonsense.

"Are you still angry with me?" he asked in a pathetic voice. God, he really was reverting to his younger self.

Patrick's expression barely changed, but his eyes filled with compassion. "It's hard to be angry with a man who looks like he's just seen a ghost."

Everett blinked before falling into a bitter laugh. "You didn't answer my question."

"You only asked it to avoid talking about what happened at Castleford's estate," Patrick fired back.

Everett's heart leapt with affection at the same time as his stomach churned. "I'm merely attempting to ascertain your feelings so that I might come up with a way to beg for your forgiveness." He closed his eyes and leaned against the back of the sofa once more, stretching his arms along its top.

"I don't know my feelings." Patrick sat gingerly on the far end of the sofa. "I've never been in a position like this before. But obviously, you have." His voice was stony and clipped.

Everett hummed in exhaustion. "I see." He pressed his lips together, caught between hating himself and indignation over being judged for a thousand things that happened before he knew Patrick existed. "You're jealous."

"Of course, I'm jealous," Patrick laughed.

Everett popped his eyes open. He'd expected a denial and defensiveness.

"Who knows how many past lovers you have to judge me against?" Patrick went on. "Lovers who, it seems, you've had no problem throwing off once you grew tired of them."

"Lionel." Everett shook his head bitterly. "Don't believe a word he said. He knew what sort of an agreement we had, and he was just as much a party to ending it as I was."

"Which is precisely the point." Patrick's voice took on a brittle edge. "You wear your lovers like a costume that is changed and discarded at the end of each performance."

"I do not," Everett snapped.

Except that he did. But not for the reasons Patrick seemed to think.

He turned his head away, staring out the window at the sunset-streaked sky. "You don't understand."

"I bloody well *don't* understand," Patrick said. "You love everyone. I love no one."

Everett whipped to face him again, his heart squeezing in his chest. Both sides of Patrick's statement stung, and both left him miserable for their respective lots in life.

He didn't have a chance to answer the statement. A knock sounded at the door. Patrick leapt up to answer it, receiving a covered tray containing their supper from a member of the hotel staff. He set the tray on the table at the end of the sofa, then returned to lock the door.

"Did you tip the man?" Everett asked, scooting to the edge of the sofa to look under the tray's lid.

"Did I what?" Patrick walked back to the sofa.

"Tip the man." Everett grinned, already knowing the answer. He shook his head. "You've a lot to learn about staying in hotels, love. I'll make sure to leave a large gratuity before we check out."

Patrick flushed as he drew one of the room's chairs to the side of the table. The feast that had been sent up for them was probably magnificent, but Everett's appetite was nonexistent. He picked at the roast pheasant and potatoes. Patrick ate as though it were his duty, but Everett had the sense that he didn't taste anything. He supposed there was no such thing as not having an appetite for someone who had come so close to starving as a child.

That thought brought him full circle. All of his bottled-up fear and misery from seeing Chisolm that afternoon overflowed, spilling its contents through him.

"It's all about power," he began in a barely audible voice, eyes downcast.

Patrick stopped in the middle of chewing to stare at him.

"It's not about love—or even sex, and certainly not pleasure—at all," he went on, feeling as though he were in danger of gagging at any moment. "I'm sure that someone, somewhere would rush to call Chisolm out for being a queer if they knew what happened all those years ago, but it wouldn't be accurate. He didn't love me. He didn't even like me. He doesn't like boys, girls, or anyone. He got off on the knowledge that he held complete sway over every aspect of my life and he could do with me as he pleased."

Patrick set his fork down and faced Everett squarely. "Tell me."

Everett dragged his eyes up to meet Patrick's. The stony anger he saw there was strangely relaxing. "I've told you that my father sold me to Adler for the price of a few bottles of gin when I was eight years old."

Patrick nodded and swallowed.

"Adler sold me to Chisolm for ten times that amount within a week." Everett's gaze lost its focus. "At first, I couldn't believe my own luck. I was taken to the country, where I'd never been before. I was scrubbed, given a haircut, and dressed in fine silks. Everything around me was beautiful and clean. Chisolm discovered right away that I could sing and put me to work entertaining his guests. I was convinced the whole thing was a miracle.

"Until I ended up in his bed." He fought down a wave of nausea at the memories. His whole body began to shake. "I will spare you the details of all the ways a grown man can use a small boy. If you aren't aware of what they are, then I would rather die than put those things in your mind. But rest assured, Chisolm left no depraved stone unturned. He made no secret of his desire to break me. Young fool that I was, I believed that if I went along with everything he demanded, he would consider me broken and stop."

Everett paused, hearing the screams of his younger self, the way he'd begged for mercy.

"He never did stop. Far from it. And he insisted on sharing his toy with guests to his estate." Everett raised his eyes to Patrick with a shaky grin. "But he continued to dress me in silks and to order me to sing for his guests. And then to perform in various bacchanals and plays as I grew older. He threatened to turn me into a eunuch on several occasions as well. Thank God he didn't." He laughed ironically. "I think I proved too valuable to him as a virile youth, very much sought after by his political allies and those he wanted favors from, to damage the goods."

"I assume you got away from him eventually," Patrick said after a long pause.

"Did I?" Everett made a sour face. "Did it look to you like I've gotten away from him when the two of us stood face to face this afternoon?"

Patrick glanced sympathetically at him.

Everett shook his head. "I made several attempts to escape, starting when I was twelve. The punishments for each failed attempt were harsh. I still bear the scars." He sucked in a sudden breath to steady himself. "I finally succeeded in getting away when I was fourteen, one of the few times Chisolm took me to London. Lucky for me, I'd befriended a rather well-known actor who enjoyed participating in Chisolm's debauched weekends. It was rather like jumping out of the frying pan and into the fire, but at least I felt as though what I was doing was under my control instead of forced."

"But you were only fourteen," Patrick said.

"And as any bull-headed youth of fourteen will tell you, even the illusion of being in control of your own body and your own destiny feels like immeasurable freedom after being a slave for six years."

Patrick flushed, looking sick. "I'm sorry."

"For what? You weren't responsible. You were likely mired in your own problems at the time."

Patrick nodded.

Everett shrugged, feeling as though a slight weight had been lifted from his shoulders. "Every rotten thing that happened to me after escaping from Chisolm felt like a gift from God. I threw myself into a life on the stage with so much enthusiasm that I'd made a name for myself within years. And honestly, the rest of the story from that point is anticlimactic. I made my own decisions. I commanded the stage. I took lovers when I wanted them to prove that no one would control me, body or soul, ever again." He paused. "But that was all a lie. Chisolm always has and always will control me."

"He will not," Patrick insisted, suddenly vehement.

The show of anger on his behalf was so endearing that Everett laughed. "Yes, he will, love. He set out to break me all those years ago and he succeeded. You saw that much for yourself today."

"I refuse to accept it." Patrick stood, shifting to scoot across the sofa to Everett's side. "You are the master of your own destiny. That's what attracted me to you. Whatever hold Chisolm continues to have over you is an illusion. You have to believe that."

"I have to believe it, do I?" Everett lit with amusement, pivoting to face Patrick. Their knees bumped. Even that cursory contact was a comfort to him. "Forgive me, darling, but you don't know what you're talking about."

"Don't I?"

Before Everett could reply, Patrick took his face in hand and swayed in for a kiss. It wasn't the clumsy sort of kiss he would have expected from a man of almost no experience. It was passionate and heartfelt. Patrick's mouth was hungry for his, and Everett instantly gave him everything he needed. He moaned deep in his throat and reached for him, teasing Patrick's lips with his teeth before brushing their tongues together. In the space of a heartbeat, he went from cowering in fear at his own memories to longing to feel Patrick as a part of him in every way.

As suddenly as their kiss began, Patrick stopped. "You see?" he panted, eyes alight with lust. "You tell me if Chisolm still has power over you when I can spin your head with just one kiss."

Everett wanted to laugh. Patrick was the sweetest, most desirable, most precious thing he'd ever had in his life. He was pure goodness in a world filled to the brim with evil. "How could you ever doubt that I want you to have and to keep or think I would grow tired of you, you silly man," he said, launching himself into Patrick's arms.

Their mouths met again in a furious kiss that had both of them panting for breath in no time. Everett pushed Patrick flat to his back against the cushions scattered across the sofa. He drew wild groans of pleasure from Patrick as he ravaged his mouth with lips and tongue. His hands spread across Patrick's unforgivably dull suit, undressing him as fast as he could while so overwrought with need. As soon as he unbuttoned Patrick's jacket and waistcoat and pushed them open, then undid the buttons at the top of his shirt, he dragged his lips and teeth down over Patrick's neck, nipping, tasting, and sucking as he went. Without a lick of shame, he deliberately left a mark on Patrick's shoulder, just below his collar, that would remind both of them that they belonged to each other.

Patrick struggled to push Everett's jacket off of his shoulders and to unbutton his waistcoat, but Everett didn't leave him much room to maneuver. Their clothes were askew and their bodies already overheating when Everett propped himself above Patrick and said, "Let's continue this in the bedroom."

Patrick nodded and rolled off the sofa, staggering to his feet, so quickly that Everett laughed. He stood as well, grabbing Patrick's hand and leading him on to the pristine, hotel bedroom. As soon as the door was shut behind them, they rushed to throw off the rest of their clothes and shoes, stealing kisses and touches as they went.

Everett finished with his clothes first and moved to pull back the bedcovers on the room's large bed. He was taken utterly by surprise when Patrick came up behind him, embracing him tightly and kissing his shoulder. Better still, his thick, hard cock fit snugly into the cleft of his arse, sending a jolt of lust through him that had him as stiff and erect as a monument. With a burst of utter frustration, he realized he hadn't brought anything with him that would ease that sort of congress.

"You have the most magnificent body I've ever seen," Patrick murmured in his ear, apparently unfussed when Everett didn't immediately bend over and beg to be fucked. "I could spend a lifetime learning it."

The sweetness of the statement was a thousand times more alluring than any quick and deep thrust. He inclined his head toward Patrick's, nuzzling against him, then took hold of one of Patrick's hands. "Please do, darling," he whispered, sliding Patrick's hand down his abdomen to grasp his prick.

Patrick sucked in a breath as Everett guided his movements. The man was a fast learner, and within seconds, he was stroking Everett in a way that had his knees ready to buckle with pleasure. He intended to compliment Patrick on his dexterity, but all that came out was a shattering moan of pleasure. At the same time, Patrick jerked against him, pleasuring himself against Everett's arse.

Neither of them could keep up the coordination needed to carry on that way. Everett rolled out of

Patrick's reach, flopping onto his back on the bed and dragging Patrick with him. He sighed with pleasure as their bodies made contact in a thousand places. They ground their hips together in a way that sent shivers through Everett, even as he grasped Patrick's face and held it as still as possible so he could kiss him. Their tongues did what their cocks couldn't without preparation, but it was enough for him.

"I'm yours," Patrick growled, breaking away from Everett's mouth and shifting to kneel between his legs. "And you are mine."

Similar words had been used to batter and threaten Everett years ago, but coming from Patrick's lips, they left him feeling utterly transported with joy. Almost more so than the shattering jolt of pleasure as Patrick pushed his knees aside and bent to draw his cock into his mouth. Everett's eyes flared wide for a moment as Patrick teased his head with his tongue and tested how much he could take. It didn't matter that his attempt was clumsy and hesitant or that he didn't seem brave enough to go more than an inch or so, it was the most erotic thing anyone had ever done to him. Everett threaded his hands in Patrick's hair, tugging slightly and letting out a sound of appreciation.

"I'll get better, I swear," Patrick said, panting, as he straightened a bit.

"Love, you're wonderful," Everett said, or at least tried to say. Patrick closed his hand around his cock, working him with such a deft stroke that a powerful orgasm snuck up on him before he could finish his sentence.

He felt that orgasm through his entire body as seed erupted from him. It shook him to his soul, spreading fire through his veins. If that wasn't bliss enough, as the bone-deep contentment of pleasure radiated through him, turning his body to a useless but satisfied mass of jelly, Patrick straightened, planting his knees on either side of Everett's hips, and took himself in hand.

Everett's heart raced at the erotic vision above him. The transported expression on Patrick's face as he jerked into his hand, stroking himself at a punishing pace, was enough to ignite all sorts of sparks within him. He couldn't tear his eyes away from the sweat that glistened on Patrick's chest, the power in his thighs, and above all, the absolute pleasure that pinched his face. Patrick wasn't shy about vocalizing what he was feeling either, and by the time he let out a cry, spilling himself across Everett's abdomen with an impassioned curse, Everett groaned right along with him.

As Patrick collapsed to his side, Everett felt as though they'd shared the wildest forms of intimacy instead of something young boys merely experimenting would have laughed at. Everett didn't care. He wiped his abdomen with the corner of the bedsheets, then curled into Patrick, entwining their bodies.

"I love you," Patrick panted as he nuzzled against Everett's neck. His words were hazy and soft, as if spoken in a dream.

"I love you too," Everett said with a smile, though he was fairly certain Patrick was already asleep and couldn't hear him. It didn't matter. Patrick had proven the point he'd set out to make. For the first time since his fractured childhood, Everett wondered if Chisolm truly controlled him after all. In Patrick's arms, he felt free.

CHAPTER 16

The bed beside him was empty when Patrick awoke the next morning. For a moment, he wondered where he was. Sunlight streamed in through a window to his left. The sheets encompassing him were crisp and cool and had the scent of lavender and musk on them. The bed itself was soft and comfortable, which was a sure sign he wasn't at home. Only when he rolled onto his back and rubbed his eyes did the reality of his situation flood back in on him.

He blinked up at the ceiling, letting a faint smile play across his lips for a moment. He couldn't believe that those lips had been wrapped around Everett's cock the night before. Never in a hundred years would he have considered himself brave enough to follow his urges like that. He was certain he'd made a mash of things, but it had felt good. The whole, carnal encounter had been natural and wonderful, as wonderful as sleeping soundly with Everett at his side. Everett hadn't woken in a panic once during the night.

Patrick's cozy thoughts dampened. He knew all the reasons Everett had nightmares now. His whole body clenched with misery at the thought of the abuse young Everett had suffered. He wanted to push the vague ideas of everything Chisolm, and who knew how many others, had done out of his mind, never to consider them again. How Everett had gone through all of that and come out with even a shred of sanity was a mystery. It proved to him that Everett had reserves of strength that he had only begun to see.

He stretched in an attempt to banish the pain and tension of thinking about Everett's life, then pushed himself to sit. Every instinct within him wanted to find Everett and just be with him. But as he swung his legs to the side of the bed to get up, Everett marched through the door wearing an elaborate silk robe, a tray in his hands.

"Don't get up," he said, alarm in his expression that was almost innocent in its eagerness to please. "Stay right where you are, love."

Patrick let out a confused breath and sat back against the pillows and the headboard. "What's that?" He nodded to the tray Everett carried.

With all the pride of a child presenting his elders with a particularly choice frog captured from a pond, Everett set his tray over Patrick's legs and removed the silver dome covering its contents. "*Voila!*"

Patrick sucked in a breath at the sight that met him,

utterly overcome with emotion. So much so that tears stung his eyes. The tray in his lap contained a pile of eggs, several sausage links, slabs of ham, beans and mushrooms, toast with butter and jam, and tea. It was a feast the likes of which he had never seen, something he had barely dared to dream was possible. The rich, savory scent of it wafted over him, whispering of home, security, and love, things he'd never had.

"I wasn't sure what you liked, so I ordered everything the hotel serves," Everett explained with a casual shrug, sitting on the bed beside him. "I know how important a good meal is to you, so I splurged." He swiped a finger across the jam spread over the toast, then sucked his finger seductively.

The teasing in Everett's eyes turned quickly to distress, though.

"Heavens, darling, why are you crying? It's only jam."

Patrick shook his head, trying his best to be grateful and to appreciate the loving gesture, but he couldn't stop himself from sobbing. He hid his face in his hands, shame and adoration and a sense of wild, unfathomable love filling every fiber of his being.

"No, sweetheart, don't cry, please." Everett pulled Patrick's hands away from his face, leaning in to rain light kisses across his lips and cheeks. "Whatever I've done wrong, I didn't mean it, I swear." He kissed Patrick several more times before the tray started to slip sideways, putting the cup of tea in danger of spilling.

"Here, let me take this away," he said, reaching for the tray.

"No!" Patrick stopped him a little too loudly, closing his hand over Everett's on the tray's handle. He forced himself to look into Everett's eyes, knowing the full force of his affection and his shame were on vibrant display. "My whole life, all through my childhood, I had to fight for every scrap of food I had. You've just laid a feast out for me like...." Words failed him. There was nothing like the beautiful gesture Everett had just made for him.

Understanding dawned in Everett's eyes. He smiled, gently at first, but within seconds, that smile turned into a typically wicked grin. "If I had known how easy it is to touch your heart, I would have brought you breakfast in bed much sooner."

He leaned in to plant a passionate kiss on Patrick's lips, then inched back and plucked a piece of toast from the tray.

"Open up, love," he said with a flicker of one eyebrow, bringing the toast to Patrick's lips. "With me, you'll never go hungry again. I will satisfy all of your appetites."

Patrick laughed. The reaction was as powerful and as unfettered as his tears. He let Everett feed him a bite of toast, his heart so light it could cause the sun to rise, before shaking his head and nudging Everett away.

"I'm not going to let you feed me breakfast like I'm a baby," he said, reaching for one of the forks on the tray.

"Then you will leave me in a state of utter disappointment," Everett said with a look of mock offense. "But I will be consoled as long as you share your feast with me."

"I would share everything with you," Patrick said from the bottom of his heart.

"What an intriguing statement." Everett eyed him with a look of hunger that went beyond the delicacies on the tray between them.

They ate the incomparable breakfast together, chatting about inconsequential things as they did. Everett insisted on feeding Patrick a few bites of what he considered particularly tasty, and Patrick let him. It was as delightful to indulge Everett's whims as it was to have his own needs satisfied. Although, there was something to be said for satisfaction. As soon as breakfast was finished, Everett set the tray aside, threw off his robe, and straddled Patrick as he nestled back against the pillows in a delightful state of fullness.

Everett had only just begun to kiss him madly while reaching between them to stroke his hardening prick when there was a knock at the door.

Everett hissed a curse, slumping, his forehead resting against Patrick's. "Just as I was about to treat you to dessert."

The knock sounded again.

"Perhaps it's only the hotel staff asking for their tray back," Patrick suggested.

Everett hummed as he climbed off the bed. "There's only one staff I'm interested in at the moment." He glanced pointedly to Patrick's cock, then bent to retrieve his robe.

Patrick listened to Everett cross through the suite's main room to answer the door, then sighed with disappointment at the sound of Cristofori's voice.

"It's already ten o'clock. Blake has been waiting downstairs for the two of you for fifteen minutes."

Patrick swore and climbed out of bed. Dessert would have to wait for later. Once again, he'd let the delicious distraction of Everett sidetrack him from the mission that formed the entire basis for their being together. There was no time for him to indulge in a sexual awakening—or even a new discovery of love—when helpless children's lives were at stake.

By the time Everett returned to the bedroom, Patrick was already halfway through washing in the basin that sat in the far corner of the room.

"I suppose it was a dream we had to wake from eventually," Everett said with a maudlin sigh. His eyes continued to shine with affection and mischief, though.

"Another day," Patrick said. "Once Chisolm and the others are rotting in prison, as they deserve to be."

It was as though Patrick had blown out a candle. Every bit of happiness vanished from Everett's expression. He moved through washing and dressing like a man who had just been reminded he was on his way to the gallows. Patrick did his best to stay close to Everett's side as they dressed and shaved and prepared for what was bound to be a difficult day.

"We'll make this as brief as possible," he said as they descended the stairs, on their way to meet Cristofori and Selby in the hotel lobby. "I'll take the first opportunity to slip off into the house to search for the evidence we need against those men." He deliberately didn't use Chisolm's name. "Remember, you are London's most brilliant actor. Your character is a man who is not under that villain's sway."

They reached the bottom of the stairs, and Patrick paused, grabbing Everett's shoulders and turning him to face him.

"He does not control you, Everett. You told me yourself last night. You took back control of your life from him." He paused, jealousy still licking like flames in his gut, even though he understood so many more things now. "The lovers you've had, they were your way of claiming yourself. You have nothing left to prove. The lover you have now is all that matters, and he could break Chisolm's neck with a single twist if he wanted to." He held Everett's gaze with deadly seriousness.

Everett nodded, though Patrick could see it would take a great deal more time and work for Everett to believe everything he had just said.

Neither of them said more as they crossed the lobby to meet Cristofori and Selby. Selby was full of his usual, overly-cheerful greetings. He expressed his regrets that Cristofori and the others hadn't stayed with him during the night as they made their way out to his carriage and started off to Castleford Estate. The more Selby nattered on, though, the more Patrick had a sense that something had gone wrong for the man.

"Annamarie was furious, I can tell you that much," he said, fidgeting with the hem of his sleeve and not quite looking at Cristofori as the carriage jostled on. "She accused me of all manner of things by hiding you from her." He peeked up at Cristofori. "I didn't know what to say in the face of her fury."

Patrick arched an eyebrow at Everett, who returned the look subtly. He had a feeling they'd stumbled into someone else's story, a story that might be on the verge of a boiling point. There wasn't time to inquire about it, and if Patrick were honest, he wanted nothing to do with what was clearly a wealth of unresolved emotions between Niall and his duke. He had far more pressing things to concern himself with as Selby's carriage pulled up to the terrace at the front of Castleford's house.

"Remember," Patrick whispered to Everett as they alighted and were greeted by Castleford's butler. "He does not have power over you. You are a brilliant actor who can distract the lot of them for as long as you need to. We're doing this for the children, so not another soul has to go through what you went through. We will beat them."

"God above, I love you," Everett groaned quietly, squeezing Patrick's hand for the briefest of moments before striding forward to enter the house by Cristofori's side.

Patrick froze, eyes wide and stunned, watching Everett's

back as the others entered the house. Everett loved him? He'd thought that was a dream. It couldn't possibly be true. But if it was, Patrick had even more of a responsibility than ever to bring down the man who had hurt his love so much.

"Ah, brother of mine, I see you've brought your friends back." Castleford met them in the conservatory they'd passed through the day before on their way to the garden and the menagerie. Chisolm and Eastleigh were there as well, dressed in tweed and examining several hunting rifles with the help of a few of Castleford's footmen. Patrick hung back as much as he could to observe the proceedings without bringing attention to himself.

"We never would have passed up an opportunity to spend time in such august company," Everett said with all the gusto he used to greet his admirers at the stage door.

"I'm happy to see you so enthusiastic, Jewel." Chisolm broke away from the footman he was working with to stride up to Everett's side. He thumped Everett's shoulder. "You'll be my shooting partner this afternoon."

Patrick balled his hands into fists, wishing for the opportunity to snap Chisolm's neck the way he'd told Everett he could. His deeper concern was for Everett, though. Some of the color had drained from Everett's face, but he continued to smile. Patrick swelled with pride in him, even as he boiled with fury at Chisolm.

"Will you be needing me while you shoot, sir?" he asked, stepping up to Everett's side. The gesture was intended to underscore his role as Everett's bodyguard, but he wanted to look Chisolm in the eyes and dare him to lay a finger on what was his.

Chisolm sneered at Patrick. "Quite a determined bulldog, isn't he?" He glanced down his nose at Patrick. Whether he understood the true nature of Patrick and Everett's relationship or not, he clearly considered Patrick so far beneath his notice as to be laughable.

Which was exactly what they needed to further the investigation, even if it infuriated Patrick even more.

"I think I should stay with you, sir," Patrick went on. It was a gamble, but the more he gave the impression of wanting to stay glued to Everett's side—which was, in fact, what he would rather have done in every way—the less suspicious the gentlemen would be when he disappeared.

"We don't need supervision, do we, Jewel?" Chisolm asked, turning his back on Patrick.

Everett met Patrick's eyes. More than a hint of panic flashed in their violet-blue depths, but with it was understanding. Everett knew what Patrick was up to.

"Why don't you take a rest and enjoy yourself, Wrexham," he said, feigning ease. "There won't be anything for you to do on a shooting trip anyhow."

"Yes, sir." Patrick didn't have to fake resentment as he took a step back. He glared at Chisolm, but the man didn't see him. He was too busy glancing Everett over, as though he were a slice of cake Chisolm intended to devour. It was all Patrick could do to remind himself of why he was really there.

"Gentlemen, shall we go out to the shooting range?" Castleford asked as he crossed the room, heading out the open French doors.

The gentlemen followed him. Everett sent Patrick one last look over his shoulder. Patrick nodded reassuringly, but his insides roiled. He stood where he was for a moment, waiting to see whether anyone would acknowledge him or whether he'd just been abandoned to the house.

"If you will come with me, sir," the butler, Norris, said in a dry tone from the door leading to the hallway. "I'll show you to the servants' hall below-stairs where you can wait for your master."

Patrick hid his disappointment with a stony nod. He followed Norris through the house, observing everything he passed and searching for ways he could leave whatever waited for him in the servants' hall as quickly as possible.

It was a stroke of luck that few of Castleford Estate's servants were in the servants' hall and those who were seemed far too busy to pay him any mind. Patrick fell back on his ability to blend into the background, sitting quietly in the hall and pretending to find a book someone had left on the long dining table interesting. Once he was certain not a soul was paying the slightest bit of attention to him, he set the book down and quietly walked out of the room and up the narrow back stairway to the main part of the house.

The house itself was quiet. Whatever duties the servants were about, they weren't anywhere to be seen. That set Patrick's nerves on edge. The house had a sinister feel to it. He'd felt it the moment they'd arrived the day before. It had sorrow in its walls and villainy in the floorboards. As he passed carefully from room to room, barely making a sound as he walked, he was certain that it wasn't a matter of *if* he would find some sort of incriminating evidence against Castleford, but *when*.

His search took longer than he anticipated. The huge house had more rooms than he would have guessed from the outside. Most of the rooms were impeccably tidy, as if they were rarely used. The furnishings were all dark and gothic. Several had taxidermied animals of all descriptions posed in ferocious positions. Each unfortunate creature gave Patrick chills. There was no doubt in his mind that they had all lived in the cages of the menagerie at one point or another. It made him wonder how long it would be before Leo joined the others.

At that thought, Patrick reached instinctively for his pouch of food. He'd filled it with the remnants of the breakfast Everett had brought him that morning. Heat flooded his face and guilt curled in his gut at the force of need he felt for the scraps in his pouch. After everything that had passed between him and Everett, after the care Everett had shown, in spite of the fact that his mind was convinced he would never go hungry again, his instincts couldn't let go of that pouch.

He was teetering on the verge of letting those thoughts take over when he stepped into a dark office adjacent to a parlor containing several hairy, stuffed boars. The room was as tidy as every other in the house, but it had a used feeling to it. The curtains were closed, leaving it shadowy and menacing. Patrick knew he'd found the right place.

He strode into the room, pulling open the curtains on one window to let just enough light into the room for his investigation. He would have to work fast and leave no stone unturned or cabinet unlocked if he was going to find the concrete evidence he needed to bring Chisolm and the others to justice.

Or so he thought.

Lying in the center of the desk, open to the most recently-used page, was a ledger containing names, dates, locations, and prices. Patrick's eyes went wide at the sight of it. Every row and every column of the ledger was neat and precise, as if whoever wrote it was maniacally organized. Patrick guessed what it was in an instant, but it wasn't until he spotted Lily Logan's several pages back along with columns reading "London", "September 4th, 1889", "Leicester", and "£5" that he was certain. His stomach squeezed at the sheer volume of names and the prices they'd all been sold for. Worst of all, the most recent names had only been entered the day before.

"What are you doing in here?"

Patrick jerked straight and slammed the ledger shut as Selby's voice cut through his thoughts. Of all the men who could have caught him red-handed, Selby was not the one he would have expected.

"My lord." He bowed tightly. "Rest assured that I am here with the full authority of Scotland Yard, conducting a police investigation."

"Police investigation?" Selby stepped farther into the room, his brow knit in confusion. "What sort of a police investigation?"

Patrick narrowed his eyes as he studied the man. He wasn't half as chipper on his own as he had been in Cristofori's company. He had dark circles under his eyes and the air of a man who was so defeated by life that he didn't know how to fight back anymore. Patrick knew the look well. Until he'd met Everett, he was sure he looked the same way.

With an unexpected wave of compassion, he stepped around the desk, approaching Selby. "I regret to inform you, my lord, but your brother, Lord Castleford, along with Lord Chisolm and Lord Eastleigh, is at the center of an investigation into a child kidnapping ring."

Shock pulled Selby's features tight. "Child kidnapping?"

Patrick nodded. "I've just found what I believe to be irrefutable evidence proving his involvement. I'm certain that this room contains all manner of proof." He paused, pitying the way Selby gaped and glanced around, as though faced with a horror that he didn't want to see.

"Hundreds of children have been kidnapped over the course of several years and sold into slavery of the worst sort."

"No." Selby shook his head. "It couldn't possibly be. Montague would never—" He paused, swallowing hard, a sickly pallor coming to his face. He met Patrick's eyes with the look of a man who knew the truth, but couldn't comprehend it. "I would have noticed," he said, his voice hoarse. "I would have seen something, done something. I...I would never have allowed evil like that to continue in my family, would I?" His question was fraught and painful.

"I am sorry, my lord." Patrick truly did feel sorry for him, but the longer they stood there, the more anxious he grew. There wasn't time for a duke to test his conscience when children's lives were at stake. He needed to gather as much evidence as he could to take to David and Lionel. They needed an iron-clad case if they were going to bring down three peers. They needed—

He blinked, inspiration striking. "My lord." He took a step closer to Selby. "We may need your help with this case. The sharpest difficulty we face right now is bringing accusations like this against members of the nobility. We can provide all the evidence in the world, but what we will need, ultimately, is a high-ranking member of the nobility to testify against the men who are at the center of this ring if the case goes to the House of Lords, which it inevitably will."

Selby continued to gape vacantly for a moment

before snapping his mouth shut and focusing on Patrick. "You want me to testify against my brother to the House of Lords on a matter of child kidnapping?"

Before Patrick could answer or explain, Castleford's voice sounded from the parlor. "Blake, dammit, where have you gone? I only sent you in to find Ross, and now —" Castleford stopped just inside the doorway to the office. His eyes narrowed bitterly as he glanced from Selby to Patrick. "What is the meaning of this?"

A thousand excuses shot through Patrick's mind, but before he could voice any of them, Selby said, "This man is trying to tell me that you are involved in a child kidnapping ring. Montague, is that true?"

Patrick could have screamed in frustration. One glance from Castleford, and he knew the game was over. Castleford's expression said that he comprehended everything in an instant, from Patrick's purpose in the office to their sudden arrival the day before.

"Of course, that's not true," Castleford said with a vicious, toothy smile. "Whyever would you believe something like that? Come along, now. We're waiting for you outside." He grabbed Selby's arm and dragged him out of the room. "You too, Wrexham. I think it was unwise of Mr. Jewel to go off shooting without you after all."

Patrick said nothing as he followed. There was nothing he could say and nothing he could do. He glared at Selby as they made their way through the house and out through the garden to the shooting range. The only possible bright spot in the disaster happening all around him was that Selby eyed his brother as though considering whether the accusations could be true. The veil of congeniality that Selby had so deliberately wrapped himself in was clearly torn, proving that the man wasn't as stupid as Patrick had thought he was. He might just break and see the truth, and if he did, he might just act on it. But that did nothing to help the cause now.

They reached the shooting range within minutes. Everett was watching Chisolm take a shot at a target while Niall stared blankly at Lord Eastleigh. Everett's bitter smile dropped the second he spotted Patrick.

It vanished altogether when Castleford said, "Gentlemen, you'll never guess what scurrilous accusation my brother has just made against me."

CHAPTER 17

It was a poor actor who couldn't stay in character for the length of a performance. Everett knew that a thousand things depended on his ability to convince Chisolm and the others that he was nothing more than the vain, vapid personality everyone thought him to be as they strolled out to the shooting range set up beyond the empty cages of Castleford's menagerie.

"What a pleasant afternoon." He smiled up at the sun, eyes closed for a moment, praying that Patrick would find whatever evidence they needed and that they could flee Castleford Estate and the north as quickly as possible. "It does one good to get out of London now and then," he went on, exchanging a friendly look with Niall. "Particularly in the summer."

Niall failed to take the bait and start up an innocuous conversation. He was too busy frowning at Selby, who walked by his brother's side. Selby looked as though he were explaining something difficult to Castleford, but attempting to do it with a smile. Castleford could have been deaf for all the change in his expression.

"I know how much you enjoy the country," Chisolm said, falling back from Eastleigh's side to match steps with Everett. "You always did thrive in the summer sun."

Everett fought tooth and nail to keep from withering under the man's devilish grin. He smiled in spite of the inescapable memories of outdoor entertainments Chisolm had hosted at his estate before Everett was old enough to resist. "Sunlight is good for all God's creatures," he insisted as though he had no idea what Chisolm was talking about.

Chisolm laughed. "I'm surprised you're fool enough to believe in God."

So much was implied in Chisolm's dismissive tone, but underneath the chiding was the man's belief that, as far as Everett should be concerned, he was God.

"I most certainly do believe in God." Everett let his joviality vanish for a moment. "A God of Justice."

His meaning wasn't lost on Chisolm. The man snorted and shook his head. "You always were a beautiful dunce."

They reached the shooting range. The footmen who carried their rifles were already in place, setting up targets and performing last-minute checks on the weapons. Everett had half a mind to snatch up one of the rifles leaning against a rack and to use it to send Chisolm to his great reward. He only barely managed to hold back by closing his eyes, taking a deep breath, and remembering what truly mattered—Patrick's mission inside the house.

"I haven't been shooting since last summer," Selby said, his usual cheer more strained than ever as he selected a rifle. "I never really was one of the sporting set, though Annamarie insists that I should take it up and get out of the house more often." His sentence trailed off and his smile plummeted. "I suppose that doesn't matter now."

Everett stared hard at the man for a moment, wondering what he meant, before glancing to Niall. Niall seemed just as taken aback by the comment as he was.

"I've always enjoyed a good fox hunt," Eastleigh said, grabbing a rifle and striding to stand opposite the target farthest to the left. "They're a reminder of man's place in the hierarchy of nature." He raised the rifle to his shoulder and took aim, but paused. One of the footmen was still adjusting targets at the far end of the range, though Everett was surprised that stopped Eastleigh from shooting.

"Come stand with me," Chisolm said, picking up a rifle of his own. He narrowed his eyes at Everett, his mouth tugging into a grim smile. "You've always brought me luck in the past."

"What need do you have for luck this afternoon?" Everett moved slowly to stand off to the side, close enough to Chisolm to make him think his order had been obeyed but far enough away to be out of arm's reach. "Do you have some sort of wager running?"

Chisolm laughed as he raised his rifle to practice his aim, then lowered it again. He turned to Everett. "I'm certain we could make some sort of wager that both of us would find interesting."

"Perhaps a wager that could end with all of the gentlemen present financing my production next season," Niall said.

Everett was grateful for both the interruption and the reminder that not everything revolved around Chisolm and his sick notions of power and superiority.

"I think that's a capital idea," he said, nodding at Niall. "What do you say, Lord Eastleigh? Shall we wager for the fate of Mr. Cristofori's show?"

"Leave me out of that nonsense," Eastleigh said. "I have far better ways to invest my money than in theatricalities." He raised his rifle once more and shot at his target, hitting it square in the bull's eye. The footman on his way back from arranging the targets jerked into a run to get out of the way.

"Pity we can't aim at more interesting targets," Chisolm said, raising his gun and firing as well.

Everett's lip curled in disgust. He was surprised Chisolm had even those scruples, after all he knew the man was capable of. He checked the silver watch tucked into the pocket of his waistcoat, praying that time would pass swiftly and Patrick would find what he needed.

"It's a pity we don't have a bit of tea on hand to make

the afternoon complete," he said, tucking the watch back into his pocket and clasping his hands behind his back.

"Tea would be a good idea," Niall mumbled, eyeing Everett as though trying to figure out the purpose for that particular topic of conversation.

"If it's tea you'd like, I'd be more than happy to fetch some for you," Selby chimed in, his smile returning as he studied Niall. "I'm certain I could find one of Montague's maids to prepare some."

"Don't bother," Castleford said. "Cook knows to send tea out at two."

"But if Mr. Cristofori wants tea now, he shall have it," Selby insisted, turning to start back to the house.

"No, really," Niall tried to stop him. "I can wait until two."

"Nonsense." Selby continued toward the house, turning to walk backwards. "If you want tea, I'll get you tea. It would be my pleasure." He turned and jogged on, as though unwilling to be stopped.

"My brother is as mad as a hatter," Castleford muttered, watching Selby's retreating back. "Ross, go after him and see that he gets what he needs," he ordered one of the footmen.

Everett arched one eyebrow at the man. Calling Selby mad was rather like the pot calling the kettle black, as far as he was concerned. At least Selby's madness seemed harmless, whereas Castleford's....

"Did you ever secure supper for your lion?" Everett asked, pretending lightheartedness. He'd forgotten about the lion until that moment. He was surprised the poor creature hadn't already died of hunger.

"My butler sent a letter to one of the farmers this morning," Castleford answered, a sly light in his eyes. "We should have quite a show later today."

Everett swallowed hard. For weeks, somewhere in the back recesses of his mind, he'd wondered what sort of men could organize an endeavor to kidnap children and sell them into unimaginable lives. Between Chisolm's desire for power and Castleford's lust for blood, he had his answer. Men like the ones in front of him seemed far better suited to the pages of some far-fetched and spine-chilling novel, but even the most macabre characters had their origin in reality. And if life had taught him only one thing, it was that the truth was stranger and more horrific than fiction. Evil really did exist in the world.

Castleford let out a sudden hiss of irritation that startled Everett out of his thoughts. Without a word to the rest of them, he turned and marched toward the house after his brother.

"Where are you going?" Chisolm called after him.

"To clean up the remnants of the game we left out yesterday evening," he called back.

Chisolm muttered something indistinct, raising his rifle and firing at his target with what seemed like extra venom.

Everett's heart sped up and his thoughts flew back to the house, to Patrick. God, he hoped the man had already found what he needed and was somewhere that would prevent him from being caught. He hoped that Castleford's comment meant he and the others had been careless enough with their business to give Patrick and the rest of them a leg up. And he hoped that he could hold things together long enough to give the side of good the victory it so desperately needed.

"Stand here, boy."

Everett's eyes snapped wide at Chisolm's order, delivered in the same voice of cold command he'd used decades before. Chisolm stood with his rifle in hand and his legs slightly apart. His expression held no doubt that Everett would do exactly as he said.

Everett hesitated. He needed to buy time without raising suspicion. Patrick's voice whispered in his head, reminding him that Chisolm had no real power over him. He wasn't certain he believed that, although as he stepped forward, moving to the spot that Chisolm indicated, he insisted to himself that he was doing it not because Chisolm had issued an order, but because he chose to make the man think he still had power.

"Do you still remember how to reload a rifle?" Chisolm asked.

"It involves a great deal of ramming things down a barrel, does it not?" he answered, refusing to let Chisolm get the upper hand.

Chisolm laughed. "An activity you always enjoyed." He thrust his rifle out. "Reload."

Everett met Chisolm's order with a grin that might actually have appeared flirtatious. If he could throw the man off his game, he might have a chance of coming out of the afternoon with his sanity intact.

The shooting continued without much comment from either Eastleigh or Niall. Eastleigh was enjoying his practice a little too intently, and Niall seemed lost in a world of his own thoughts. That left Everett feeling as though he and Chisolm were alone for the moment.

"I never had a chance to tell you how disappointed I was when you left my service," Chisolm said as Everett handed his reloaded rifle back to him. Their hands touched on the cold metal. It was all Everett could do not to recoil.

"And I never told you what a perfectly miserable time I had as your slave," Everett said with an icy smile.

The light of challenge sparked in Chisolm's eyes. "Feisty," he said. "That's why I liked you the best, you know. It's always more fun to tame someone with spirit."

"Tame, you say?" Everett's hands shook with rage as he took a step back. "And how many spirited souls have you tamed?"

Chisolm chuckled, returning to his mark and raising his rifle. "Every man must have a hobby."

Everett bared his teeth at the man, eyes narrowed, as he aimed and fired. He would be doing England and the world a favor if he snatched up one of the extra rifles from the rack behind him and bashed Chisolm's head in with it.

"Your hobby is about to come to an end," he said instead.

Chisolm flinched away from studying his target, frowning at Everett instead. For one glorious moment, Everett had him on the back foot. He grinned, ready to tear the man down.

"Gentlemen, you'll never guess what scurrilous accusation my brother has just made against me."

Everett whipped sideways to find Castleford marching Selby across the lawn toward them, Patrick following. His gut clenched in fear at the anxious expression Patrick wore.

"I'm not the one making the accusations...precisely," Selby said, wringing his hands. He glanced to Niall, pleading for help.

"What is going on?" Eastleigh thrust his rifle at the footman who had moved in to help him and strode toward Castleford.

"My friends, you'll never believe it." Castleford had a mad light in his eyes as he glanced from Eastleigh to Chisolm. "We've been accused of operating a child kidnapping ring." He laughed, but there wasn't a lick of humor in his eyes.

Neither Eastleigh nor Chisolm so much as cracked a smile.

"I told you this trip would bring problems," Chisolm growled.

"There's an easy way to solve them," Eastleigh said, snapping his fingers at the footman holding his rifle. "We can call it a shooting accident. They stepped out into the line of fire without warning us."

Everett's eyes popped wide. He jerked toward Patrick, as though he'd have to protect him, before stopping himself. "You cannot be serious," he told Eastleigh, laughing as though the whole thing were a joke or a misunderstanding.

"Did you just threaten the lives of my friends?" Selby gaped at Eastleigh, then turned his incredulity on his brother. "What in the devil's name is going on here, Montague?"

Everett opened his mouth to explain, but hesitated, debating how much it would be useful for Selby to know. Niall didn't seem to have any more of a clue what to do or say in the situation than he did.

Patrick was the only one with the courage to take the situation in hand.

"Scotland Yard has been tracking your activity for weeks, gentlemen," he said, stepping forward and looking every inch the hero. Everett's heart ran riot as he continued. "Enough evidence has been obtained proving your involvement in the child kidnapping and trafficking ring that formal charges will be brought. There's nothing you can do to escape the consequences of your crimes now."

For a chilling moment, silence reigned. It was followed moments later by Castleford bursting into laughter. Chisolm and Eastleigh exchanged pale-faced looks before falling uneasily into laughter with him.

"My dear boy, you couldn't be more mistaken about our activities," Castleford said, continuing to laugh.

"Mistaken?" Patrick looked downright incredulous.

"I know what I saw, my lord. I know what I have seen these last few months."

"It was all a game, man," Castleford insisted, snorting. "Isn't that right, gentlemen?"

"A game," Eastleigh said through a clenched jaw.

"An elaborate one," Chisolm added.

"I have experience with your games," Everett seethed. "I'm not sure Scotland Yard will care what you call it. You are all criminals."

"We are nothing of the sort." Castleford shook his head, as though the whole thing really were a misunderstanding. He waved a hand as though swatting a fly. "Whatever it is you think you may have seen in the house, you are wrong. Come." He crossed to his brother, clapping a hand on Selby's arm. "Come back to the house and I'll show you the game board and explain the rules. You'll see that it's all a harmless fabrication."

"I—" Selby glanced to Niall, helpless with confusion. "Come with me," he pleaded.

Niall let out a breath, glancing quickly to Everett. Whether that look was intended to tell Everett he was on his own or not, that was exactly how he felt when Niall marched humbly along behind Castleford and Selby as they returned to the house.

The four of them that remained watched until Castleford and the others had nearly reached the house. Everett wanted more than anything to charge to Patrick's side so that the two of them could take on the remaining villains together, but the calculating look in Chisolm's eyes stopped him, particularly as it was directed at Patrick. To Chisolm, Everett might have worth of some sort, but Patrick was expendable.

Everett would rather have returned to the hell that Chisolm had put him through than see a hair on Patrick's head hurt. And he had a feeling that was exactly where he was about to go.

"Kill them," Eastleigh said with a shrug, marching to the rifle stand. "It'll save us time in the long-run."

Everett's heart shot to his throat. He drew on every last bit of talent he possessed to shrug and say, "Why bother? Wrexham is as dumb as a post. He'll say or not say whatever I tell him to."

It was a horrible gamble, and one that he regretted as soon as he made it. Patrick's expression pinched with hurt before he schooled it into stony stillness.

"I don't care if he's a simpleton who doesn't speak English," Eastleigh said, selecting another rifle. "Kill him, and we won't have to worry about the truth getting out. Kill this popinjay as well."

Twin bursts of victory at Eastleigh's admission of guilt and terror at the thought of Patrick being killed rocked Everett. His head spun, but he managed to say, "All this for a silly game? I can think of much more interesting games to play." He swayed closer to Chisolm's side, sliding a hand up his arm. Touching the blackguard made his skin crawl, but he would endure anything if it meant Patrick had a chance of getting away.

Chisolm studied him with a wicked grin. "This is an

interesting turn of events." He grabbed Everett by the throat, forcing his head up and turning it from side to side, as though studying merchandise. Everett's whole body went numb at the sense memory of where the gesture had always led in those nightmare years of his past. "It's been far too long since I enjoyed this particular sport."

Eastleigh let out a grunt of disgust. "I want no part of your perverted pastimes, Chisolm. We had contingencies in place, and this wasn't a part of it. I wash my hands of this." He threw his newly selected rifle down and marched off toward the house. Something in the speed of the way he walked made Everett wonder if it was only disgust that caused him to flee or if he felt threatened enough to attempt an escape of a far bigger sort.

Either way, he didn't have the time to find out.

"I've been waiting for this for more than a decade," Chisolm purred, tightening his grip on Everett's throat. "I'm going to enjoy this particular reunion."

Part of Everett wanted to weep in terror, like the boy he had once been. Behind that swell of emotion, a part of him roared with indignation. It was bitterly unfair that he could still be made to feel every painful sensation that his younger self had been helpless against. He should have been past that. He should have left it behind when he escaped Chisolm the first time.

But he had escaped, Patrick's voice within him whispered. Feeling something, no matter how acutely, was not reality.

He sought out Patrick with his eyes the best he could with Chisolm holding him so firmly in place. "Go," he said as dismissively as possible. "I don't need you for this."

"I'm not going anywhere." Patrick took a step forward.

Goddammit, how he loved the man. But now was not the time for Patrick to put himself in danger. Not when the lives of so many children who were far more deserving than him were at stake.

"I can assure you, Wrexham, I'm in no danger here," he lied, praying Patrick would catch on and just go. "This is all quite normal."

"Like hell it is," Patrick growled. "I won't let you do this."

"Be gone with you." Everett did his best to sound bored. "The choice to engage in this interplay is all mine."

Patrick hesitated.

Chisolm yanked Everett forward, forcing him to stumble to his knees. "Go away, boy," he said. "Leave your betters to their entertainments."

"For God's sake, Wrexham, just go," Everett snapped, his heart racing so fast the edges of his vision started to go dark. "I don't want you here."

Patrick took a step back, his expression unreadable. Everett could only see him out of the corner of his eyes as Chisolm shoved his back, forcing him to plant his hands on the grass in front of him. He could bear whatever humiliation Chisolm had in mind for him as long as Patrick got away and sought out the help they would all need.

"Whenever you're ready, darling." He winked up at Chisolm, hoping Patrick would see and take the hint.

Whether he did or not, Everett's prayers were answered. Patrick turned on his heel and ran.

CHAPTER 18

It wasn't right. It didn't matter what sort of a ruse Everett was attempting or that Everett was clearly trying to keep Patrick from harm. Patrick's head told him to act strategically, to play along, and to focus on the mission, but his heart couldn't help but be hurt. He fled from the shooting range, feeling as though a boulder were lodged in his gut. He should stay by Everett's side so that he could prevent Chisolm from hurting him. His duty to the mission was at war with his duty to the man he loved, but he couldn't stop.

Patrick approached the great house, knowing every step he took left Everett more and more at Chisolm's mercy, but that the fate of the investigation hung in the balance. Everett was a consummate actor and could keep Chisolm engaged long enough for Patrick, Cristofori, and Selby to neutralize Castleford and Eastleigh and send for the Leeds police to raid the estate, but at what cost? It simply wasn't right.

Fighting to keep in motion, to stay focused on breaking the ring, Patrick dashed into the house, shooting through the conservatory and searching for Cristofori and Selby. He passed a footman in the hallway, but didn't bother asking if the young man had seen them. For all he knew, Castleford's staff was as rotten as he was and would turn on him if he so much as acknowledged them.

He thanked his lucky stars when he heard Selby's voice from the entry hall.

"But I don't understand." Selby gaped at his brother, helpless and confused, as Patrick approached. "How can this be a game? From what Niall has told me, children truly are going missing, and the things you showed me look more like financial records than pieces in a game."

"Come now, Blake," Castleford laughed, though the sharpness in his eyes was as vicious as ever. "You never did understand these sorts of things. Go back to your pretty, American wife and your darling children and play your piano like a good boy. This is none of your concern. The game is over at any rate, just like that silly game of charades you had all of your summer guests play last year."

Selby's mouth snapped shut, and he recoiled in offense, but the conversation stopped there. All three men spotted Patrick marching down the hall toward them.

"We need to leave," Patrick said, specifically to

Cristofori, meeting the man's eyes in an attempt to communicate how dire the situation had become.

Cristofori nodded once, then fell into step with Patrick as he passed, charging toward the door that led out to the terrace and the front drive.

"Hang on." Selby jumped after them, though he glanced at his brother over his shoulder as he did. "We're not through, Montague," he said before jogging to catch up to Patrick and Cristofori.

Selby's carriage and driver waited off to one end of the drive. The driver sat in the open carriage door, reading a book, but he leapt to attention at the sight of the three of them charging.

"Where is Jewel?" Selby asked as they reached the carriage. "Are we leaving without him?"

"Jewel is otherwise occupied," Patrick grumbled. He felt sick saying it, but that slender thread of hope in his chest, the hope that they could call in help and return to the estate in time to spare Everett from the worst Chisolm could do, kept him just on the right side of sanity.

"It's Chisolm, isn't it," Cristofori said with a frown. "Everett is with him."

Patrick nodded, incapable of saying more. His throat squeezed with worry and anger that was spiraling quickly into deep fear.

"He wouldn't abandon the mission." Cristofori rested a hand on Patrick's arm, steadying him with a glance. "He wouldn't abandon you."

"I wouldn't be so sure," Patrick said, voice hoarse, no time to explain Cristofori's misunderstanding of the situation or Patrick's theory of what Everett was up to.

Cristofori shook his head. "That's not your true self talking. Don't let other people's voices in your head cause you to doubt what you know for certain." He sent Selby a brief but powerful look of regret.

Patrick's mouth dropped open. Cristofori wasn't thinking about Everett at all, he was reliving his own regrets.

A flicker of movement from the corner of the house. Patrick turned and squinted in time to see a small carriage crossing from the carriage house to what must have been a kitchen courtyard. In a flash, his personal pain was forgotten.

"Eastleigh," he said, remembering his earlier suspicions over how easily Lord Eastleigh had given up the argument over whether to kill him and Everett. "It has to be. He and Chisolm spoke as though they had plans in place in case they were caught. He's going to try to flee the estate, flee Yorkshire, in all likelihood."

"If he gets away, we'll never catch him and bring him to justice," Cristofori agreed.

"What do we do?" Selby asked in a weak voice, his expression showing that the last of his resistance to the idea that something sinister was going on fading.

Patrick tried to think fast, but his heart flew back to the shooting range, and his imagination ran wild with horrible possibilities. He could swallow his pride and his irrational hurt over the way Everett ordered him to go, fight the voices in his head—voices that stretched all the way back to his childhood and the innumerable bullies that told him he was worthless and unlovable—and rush to Everett's rescue, or he could leave the estate to seek out help. Enough evidence existed in Castleford's office that even local policemen who knew Castleford would be willing to take him and the other gentlemen into custody. But only if they acted fast.

"We need to get back to Leeds," he said, grabbing Cristofori and Selby both by their sleeves and shoving them toward the open carriage door. "We need to enlist the help of the local police force to raid Castleford's house, and we need to telegraph London to make David and Lionel aware of what's going on."

The others leapt into the carriage without protest. The driver was ready, and within seconds, before Patrick could shut the carriage door, they were barreling down the drive, heading for the city.

"Wait!" Selby barked all of a sudden as they passed through the estate's gates on their way to the road. "Wait, we cannot leave the estate." The man was mad enough to lower the window and stick his head out of the carriage to shout at the driver, "Stop!"

"Blake, what are you doing?" Cristofori shouted, grabbing Selby's jacket to pull him back into the carriage. "You'll get yourself killed."

Selby's eyes were wide when he settled in his seat as the carriage jerked to a stop. "All those things my brother showed us," he said. "Things he claimed were part of his game." He waited, as though either Patrick or Cristofori would interrupt him, but neither did. "Like the game of charades at my house party last year."

Patrick blinked at him, more convinced of the man's madness than ever.

But Selby's expression pinched with alarm as whatever thoughts he was half caught up in formed an answer to some sort of question in his mind. "He's going to destroy it all," he said, voice hoarse. "Just like he destroyed the costumes and sets for the game last summer."

"Destroy them?" Cristofori's alarm matched Selby's.

"He thought it was unmanly for me to play the part of Cleopatra, even though the children and I had worked on the costume for—" He stopped suddenly, shaking his head and lunging for the carriage door. "That part of the story is irrelevant. Montague doesn't just like to keep animals in cages and watch when they're fed. He likes to burn things as well." He stumbled out of the carriage, Patrick behind him. "How could I have been such a blind fool?" Selby cursed himself.

"That doesn't matter now." Patrick took charge. "If you believe your brother will destroy the evidence we need immediately, then we need to get back to the house." He twisted back to the carriage just as Cristofori was getting out. "Go to Leeds," he ordered. "Alert the police and telegraph David and Lionel. We're going to need all the help we can get."

Cristofori nodded and pulled back into the carriage. As soon as the door was shut, Selby nodded to the driver, and the carriage sped away. Patrick headed back to Castleford Estate, Selby catching up to his side. Sure enough, the smoke billowing out from the chimneys on one side of the house was thick and black enough that Patrick wondered whether more was on fire than fuel in the house's fireplaces.

"If we manage to stop your brother from destroying his records, you will have saved hundreds of innocent lives," Patrick told Selby as they ran through the estate's gate and up the drive.

"If Niall is right—and if we make it back in time—you might just be able to save the man you love," Selby said in return.

Patrick's face heated, and he avoided the look Selby was sending his way.

"I have eyes, man," Selby said. "You're far more than simply Jewel's bodyguard. And Niall is right. You cannot let someone else's voice in your head turn you away from the truth your heart already knows."

Patrick risked a sideways glance at the man. He was surprised to find Selby's expression so serious and pinched with regret, as if the mask of amiability that he usually wore had completely cracked.

"I let those voices get the better of me," Selby went on. "I let duty and family and society come between me and love, and I've regretted every moment of my idiotic, hollow life since then." He turned his head to stare hard at Patrick as they continued to run. "Don't let the same thing happen to you."

"Believe me, I won't," he hissed, picking up his pace and sprinting toward the house. His life wouldn't just be hollow without Everett, it wouldn't be worth living.

The moment Patrick disappeared from sight, the trembling started. Everett's emotions scattered like flotsam on the sea during a storm once his anchor was gone. He was already on his hands and knees at Chisolm's feet—a position he was all too familiar with—so he lowered his head and forced himself to think of nothing but drawing breath until the trembling subsided.

If it subsided.

"If that wasn't a performance worthy of a standing ovation, I don't know what was," Chisolm said, crossing his arms and chuckling.

That chuckling made Everett's skin crawl. It was just another memory, another tool of intimidation Chisolm had used when he was a defenseless boy. It was another sound from his nightmares. Everett straightened, jaw clenched, eyes narrowed, battling with the fear that had never truly left his soul to stare up into Chisolm's gloating face.

"I cannot possibly imagine what you mean," he said, cursing how thin his voice sounded.

Chisolm snorted. "Look at you," he said with a disgusted sneer. "You, who claim to be a shining luminary of the London stage, adored by thousands, in command of crowds. All it took was one half-hearted threat against the life of that handsome bodyguard of yours, and once again, you're on your knees before me, where you belong."

Everett's heart pounded against his ribs. He couldn't tell if Chisolm had guessed the nature of his feelings for Patrick or if he merely thought Patrick was another audience member to please and deceive. It would be safer for Patrick if Chisolm believed the latter.

"I hate to disappoint my adoring public," he said with false bravado. "The man will consider me a hero for sacrificing myself to save him. Imagine the stories *The Times* will print about me now."

Chisolm's lip curled brutishly, but Everett still couldn't tell what he truly thought. "You think you're so very clever," he said in a menacing voice. "You think just because you slipped out of my grasp all those years ago that I no longer have power over you."

"You don't," Everett said with a shrug. The truth of the fear and ancient hurt turning his insides to jelly was far different than the casual appearance of his gesture.

"Don't I?"

Chisolm moved so fast Everett barely had time to react. Chisolm grabbed a fistful of hair on the back of Everett's head, forcing him to look up and expose the long line of his neck.

"I haunt your dreams, don't I?" Chisolm growled. "Whenever you feel a whisper of joy, the memory of me swoops in and destroys it, doesn't it? Whenever you experience pleasure, you remember the pain I caused. I am in your blood, in your breath, in everything about you."

Everett couldn't stop himself from shaking so hard he feared he might come apart. "Yes," he admitted freely. Not even he was a skilled enough actor to deny the scars he would always bear. "But yours is not the only face that haunts me now."

He clung to that, clung to the memory of Patrick nestled in bed beside him, snoring like a man without a care in the world. His heart conjured the image of Patrick bursting into tears just that morning when he served him breakfast in bed, the way they'd devoured the feast, knowing that it meant more than nourishment for the body. He threw everything he had into imagining the future he and Patrick might share together—Patrick watching him from the wings as he performed, the two of them taking holidays by the sea, all the lessons of pleasure he had yet to teach Patrick, and all the ways of love that Patrick had still to teach him.

He jerked his head out of Chisolm's grip and pushed himself to his feet, even though his legs felt as though they might give out under him.

"Only a pitiful man with a small cock thinks he can ruin a child's life and call himself all-powerful," Everett hissed, leaning in so that his face was inches from Chisolm's. "Evil preys on weakness and considers itself a god. But I'd like to see you try to wield your so-called power over a grown man who is more than your equal."

His insides quaked and the echo of his younger self's screams came dangerously close to bringing him to tears, but he held his ground. He would face Chisolm in a way that would make Patrick proud, in spite of the fact that the man was likely furious at him for sending him away.

Chisolm chuckled, but the sound was hollow. He took a step back, attempting to seem as though he still held all the power, in spite of the doubt that had seeped into his expression. "I'm not fooled," he growled. "The second I snap my fingers, you'll be back on your knees with my cock so far down your throat that your eyes will roll back in your head, like they always did."

Instead of cowing him, Chisolm's words infuriated Everett. "It was never about pleasure for you." He stepped back into Chisolm's space, grinning as though he'd deciphered the key to the universe. "It was never about sex. You don't have any special interest in boys or men. You just like to hurt people."

"And you like to be hurt," Chisolm countered. "Admit it. You liked being used. Your own body betrayed you. It's why you've continued to be such a slut, even after slipping away from me." He took another step back.

"Is that what you believe?" Everett stayed with him, feeling the shift in power between them with each second that ticked by.

"It's what I know," Chisolm said, though his certainty was fading. The lines on his face stood out, diminishing somehow, and his complexion turned splotchy. He suddenly appeared old and impotent.

"Go ahead, then." Everett held his hands out to his sides. "Order me to my knees. See what happens."

Chisolm pursed his lips, the corner of his mouth twitching. He held Everett's gaze, but seemed to be having trouble breathing. A shining flash of victory pulsed through Everett's heart. He could hardly believe it. His entire life, he'd lived in the shadows, lived in fear, terrified of truly being himself, but now—

"I hate to interrupt this tête-a-tête," Castleford called out, racing across the lawn toward them, "but our guests have caught on to the game."

"I'm not finished here," Chisolm hissed at Castleford, stepping away from Everett. "What nonsense are you spouting now in any case?"

Castleford looked less than pleased by Chisolm's reaction. There was clearly no love lost between the two men. "You're welcome to idle away the last few hours of your freedom enjoying what is left of my property in any way you see fit—" His glance slipped sideways to Everett with a disgusted sneer before he focused on Chisolm again. "But we're about an hour away from having the Leeds police, Scotland Yard, the army, and who knows who else descending on this estate. Either help me destroy the evidence you had the audacity to bring into my house or stay here and explain the whole thing on your own."

"Where's that bastard, Eastleigh?" Chisolm strode toward Castleford, as if the whole thing were Castleford's fault and he would ring the man's neck.

"Gone," Castleford said. "He saw the writing on the wall the moment my brother started raising questions. He's probably halfway to South America by now."

Everett caught his breath, uncertain whether to rejoice at what felt very much like the beginning of the end for the kidnapping ring or to rage against the fact that Eastleigh had gotten away.

"We have to destroy the evidence," Castleford repeated. He turned to Everett. "Starting with him."

Everett weighed his options in an instant. He could run, but with a rack of hunting rifles less than ten feet away, he wouldn't get far. He could lunge for one of the rifles, but if he killed one of the men glaring at him, the other would have a clear shot before he could reload.

Chisolm thought faster than him, snatching a gun from the rack. "He's of no more use to me anyhow," he said, raising the rifle.

"Stop," Castleford said with eerie calm. Chisolm glared at him without lowering his rifle. "I agree, he needs to die, but why not have a little fun with it?"

"Fun? Are you mad?" Chisolm looked as though he might turn his rifle on Castleford.

Castleford stepped forward, grabbing Everett's arm in an iron grip and yanking him to the side. "Why waste a bullet on a man so used to making dramatic entrances and exits when I have a starving lion just waiting for a tasty meal right over there?" He pointed across the lawn to the lion pit at the edge of the menagerie.

"You really are mad," Chisolm said, though he lowered his rifle and followed them.

"You can't possibly be serious," Everett gasped, trying to tug out of Castleford's grip and failing. "You truly intend to feed me to your pet lion?"

"Why not?" Castleford shrugged. "I'll be killing two birds with one stone, as it were. Leo still hasn't been fed, after all. And I am quite certain your death will be highly entertaining for me. Consider it your final, glorious performance."

Everett laughed. The idea was that ludicrous.

He laughed until Castleford dragged him right to the edge of the lion pit. Leo must have sensed his hunger was about to be satisfied. He paced restlessly around the bottom of the pit, looking hungrier than ever. When he roared, Everett's knees threatened to give out.

"In you go," Castleford said, attempting to push him.

Everett dug his feet in, resisting. He might be able to break free and run if he resisted hard enough.

"Wait." Chisolm stepped forward.

For one, bizarre moment, Everett thought the man cared after all and would save him from a grizzly death.

Instead, Chisolm reached into his jacket pocket and pulled out a small hunting knife. He moved to stand toe-to-toe with Everett, slashing him deeply across his cheek. Everett shouted in pain before he could stop himself.

"There," Chisolm said with a satisfied grin as blood spilled across Everett's cheek and chin. "Good old Leo won't be able to resist the scent of fresh blood. I'm looking forward to seeing Jewel's pretty little face chewed off."

"Good idea," Castleford said, as though the two were at a tea party and Chisolm had decided on current jam instead of marmalade. "Now that that's done, in you go."

Castleford pushed hard. Everett was still shocked by the pain of being cut and the audacity of Chisolm's grin. He didn't resist fast enough, and with a sickening lurch, he toppled over the side of the pit, crashing to the ground and thumping his head against the concrete. The lion roared, and the world around him went black.

CHAPTER 19

Patrick was out of breath by the time he and Selby reached the house, but there wasn't time for him to rest or recover.

"We need to gather as much evidence as possible before Castleford or the others attempt to destroy it," he told Selby, racing up the terrace steps to the front door.

The door was locked tight. Patrick took it as an ominous sign. They were no longer working against enemies who didn't know why they were there. That only meant that time was even more of the essence.

"We can enter through the kitchen," Selby said, grabbing Patrick's sleeve for a moment before running down the terrace steps and heading for the side of the house. More smoke could be seen billowing from the chimneys, and perhaps some of the windows.

They'd nearly reached the gravel path that led to a kitchen courtyard when the carriage they'd spotted being prepared earlier rolled out into their path. The driver hadn't whipped the horses into anything resembling high speed yet, but when Patrick and Lord Selby dashed in front of it, he pulled up on the reins and shouted at the horses to stop.

"What the devil is going on?" Lord Eastleigh called from inside the carriage. "We need to move!"

Patrick leapt out of the way of the horses, but kept close to the carriage. Instinct and duty took over as he wrenched the carriage door open and reached in to grab Eastleigh by the front of his jacket. Eastleigh was surprised enough that he barely resisted as Patrick yanked him out of the carriage. He spilled to the gravel.

"I'll have your head for this," Eastleigh growled. "Don't you know who I am? I could have you dismissed from your position, financially ruined, even killed. I—"

Patrick clenched his jaw as he pulled Eastleigh to his feet, then punched him so hard across the face that the man twisted in his grip, then fell, unconscious.

"Good Lord." Selby gaped at the fallen nobleman. "I've never seen anyone take a man down with a single blow like that in my life."

Any other day, Patrick might have considered gloating under the praise. Today, there wasn't time. "Don't take this man anywhere," the told the driver of the carriage. "He will shortly be under arrest for kidnapping and child trafficking, and unless you want to be seen as an accomplice, you'll make certain he stays right where he is."

The driver gaped down at the scene from his perch on the carriage. He nodded once, then sat heavily.

Patrick pushed on, dashing into the kitchen courtyard and past a pair of startled maids into the house, Selby following. He thanked what little luck he had left that he'd been shown down to the servants' hall earlier in the day and that he remembered the way to the stairs that took him and Selby up into the main part of the house. The fact that they only encountered a handful of Castleford's servants felt like the very worst of signs.

The scent of smoke met them as they hurried through the parlor that led to Castleford's office. Dread pooled in Patrick's stomach as they tore into the room only to find Castleford's butler throwing as many papers and documents onto a fire in the grate as he could.

"Stop what you're doing," Patrick warned him, sprinting forward as if to grab the documents the butler still held.

The butler shouted in terror and reeled back, spilling papers everywhere. "I had nothing to do with it. I didn't know what was going on until…I don't know what's going on." The man scrambled for the door, fleeing the scene.

"He tried to throw too many things on the fire at once," Selby said, pulling smoldering paper out of the grate. "Thus the smoke."

It was true. In his haste to destroy his master's evidence, the butler had smothered the fire. The smoke filling the room was enough to make Patrick cough, but ultimately it was a good sign. Also encouraging was the presence of the journal in which every kidnapped child's name was recorded. It still lay open on the desktop. That told Patrick that the butler was either stupid or the papers he'd chosen to burn first were twice as damaging as the ledger itself.

He started toward the desk, but a shout from the garden snagged his attention. It was a quick cry of pain and far enough from the house that it could easily have been ignored, but Patrick would have recognized Everett's shout anywhere. He abandoned the idea of gathering Castleford's papers and shot to the window.

The office had a clear view of the abandoned menagerie. In its heyday, the window would have provided a perfect view of every one of the caged animals Castleford owned. There was something bone-chilling about the empty cages and overgrown paths between them now. The true horror of the site came from the way Castleford and Chisolm stood at the edge of the lion's pit, gazing down at something of interest.

"Everett," Patrick gasped, guessing all too readily what had happened.

His fears were confirmed by Castleford shouting into the pit. "Don't just stand there, you stupid beast. That's your supper."

Patrick didn't hesitate. In spite of the fact that it was at least a ten-foot drop, he crawled out the open window, heart pounding in his ears. A fraction of a second too late, he remembered the spiked gratings that lay under each of the windows. It took quick thinking and more agility than he thought he had to place his feet in such a way that the sharp spikes didn't impale him. He was forced to throw himself clumsily to one side, crashing into the grass with a thump that knocked the wind out of him.

Jagged rocks were hidden under the grass. Patrick groaned in pain as he crawled to one side and dragged himself to his feet. He didn't want to think about how many bruises he'd sustained or how many cuts his exposed skin had received. His suit was ripped in several places, and the pouch containing his desperately-needed supply of bread and sausage was torn to the point where the heel of bread peeked out. Irrational anxiety for that food momentarily eclipsed the rest of his emotions. He stood, hands shaking as he shoved the precious food back to where it would be secure.

"What are you doing, man? Run!" Selby shouted from the window above him. "If Jewel is in that pit, he won't last long against a hungry lion."

The thought of Everett yanked Patrick back into the present, setting his heart on fire. Everett was what mattered, not his stomach or his pride. He started forward, then turned to call to Selby, "Gather up all the evidence you can. Stop it from being destroyed. We need it."

He thought he saw Selby nod as he turned to rush forward, but there wasn't time to check. All he could think about as he raced through the overgrown paths of the menagerie, body aching, one ankle in particular sore to the point of making him limp, was Everett. If Everett died, if he was harmed in any way, Patrick didn't think he could live with himself.

"Everett!" he shouted as he neared the edge of the pit.

Castleford and Chisolm flinched in surprise, wheeling back from the edge of the pit.

"What are you doing here?" Castleford asked, eyes wide.

"I'm not staying here to find out," Chisolm said. His face hardened, in spite of his eyes being glassy and his face splotched with color, like a man out for vengeance. He turned to Castleford. "If I were you, I'd run. All has been discovered."

Part of Patrick knew he should run after Chisolm as the man turned to flee. If anyone deserved to be brought to justice, it was Chisolm. The man had a thousand crimes to answer for and a thousand sins that he should be made to face. The same was likely true of Castleford, who glanced one last time into the lion's pit, winced, then cursed under his breath and dashed toward the house. Both men were so close to being held accountable for their sins.

One fierce roar from the lion in the pit below filled Patrick with a whole new kind of terror, forcing him to abandon the villains to give his everything to what truly mattered.

"Everett!" he shouted, spinning toward the pit and sprinting to its edge.

He let out a wordless cry of panic at the sight that

met him. Everett lay in a huddled heap on the filthy floor of the pit. The lion paced only a few yards away, sniffing impatiently and dancing closer for a moment before pulling back. The beast was obviously starving, but distrusted the scent of a human in the pit with him. There was no telling how long the poor thing's fear would gain the upper hand over its hunger, though.

A sharp pain gnawed at Patrick's heart. Fear and hunger. He knew both far too well. They had been his life, the same as they were likely all Leo had ever known. It wasn't the poor creature's fault that its life had been made miserable by a blackguard who kept it in a pit as a toy, just as it hadn't mattered that the men who ran the orphanage that had felt more like a prison for him and too many others were motivated by money instead of compassion. What mattered was whether the hunger that would never go away made him live a half-life or whether it gave him the strength to put himself in someone else's shoes.

"Easy there," he called down to the lion in as soothing a voice as he could. "I know you're starving, but he's not lunch." Patrick sank to his knees, then slowly sat with his legs dangling into the pit. "Everett." He needed to shake Everett out of whatever stupor he was in without aggravating Leo. "Everett, can you hear me?"

Everett moved slowly, letting out a low groan. He rolled to his back, raising a hand to his head. Patrick tried not to gasp or make any sudden moves as he saw how caked with blood and filth Everett's face was. A sharp line cut across his cheek, as though he'd been slashed, but the way he held his head told Patrick he'd hit it when he fell into the pit.

He didn't wait to see whether Everett would be able to stand or climb out of the pit on his own. As carefully as he could with his own body battered and bruised from his earlier fall, he slid down the side of the pit, landing not far from Everett's side.

Leo roared at the invasion of his prison. He continued to dance back and forth, as though trying to decide whether to flee or fight. There was no place for the poor creature to flee to, though, which meant it was only a matter of time before he pounced.

"Easy, Leo, easy." Patrick held out one hand to the lion while inching closer to Everett. "Everett, can you get up?"

"I...I think so." Everett's voice was weak, and he squinted hard at the sunlight pouring into the pit. "My head."

"Just stand up, and I'll help you out of the pit," Patrick said, eyes still locked on Leo.

Everett made a pained noise and tried to muscle himself to his feet. Patrick watched out of the corner of his eye as he got as far as flinging himself against the wall and using that as a support, all while continuing to hold his head. Blood seeped down his cheek from the cut on his face.

Leo's nostrils flared, and suddenly the lion had his full attention. Patrick could practically see the creature lick his lips. Leo's gaze shifted between Everett and Patrick, as though he was desperate for a meal but knew Patrick stood in his way. Patrick took advantage of that, shifting to block Leo's sight of Everett entirely.

"Can you reach the top of the wall?" Patrick asked over his shoulder.

Everett made a miserable sound, then answered, "No."

Patrick cursed under his breath. The pit had been built deep enough that Leo couldn't escape, but that meant neither he nor Everett could escape either. Unless Patrick could give Everett enough of a boost to heave him over the edge. To do so would mean sacrificing himself, in all likelihood, but it was a risk he had no doubts at all about taking.

"We're going to have to move fast," he told Everett over his shoulder, keeping eye-contact with Leo. "I'm going to boost you over the edge, then you need to go for help. Selby is in the house, and Cristofori went into Leeds to fetch the police."

"What are you talking about?" Everett groaned. He was directly behind Patrick and so completely out of view.

"I'm going to turn around at the count of three. Step into my hands, and I'll push you out of the pit."

"I'm not letting you—"

"One. Two. Three."

Patrick whirled around, grasping his hands together and crouching beside Everett. Everett hesitated for only a moment, only as long as it took for Leo to let out a hungry roar. He grabbed Patrick's neck with one hand and stepped into his locked hands.

As hard as he could, Patrick hoisted Everett up. Whether it was the intensity of his fear for Everett or pure, brute strength, Everett sailed up, flying over the edge of the pit. For his part, Everett had enough strength to grab the lip of the pit and pull himself fully out. He hooked one leg around the top, grunted with effort, then twisted to lay flat in the grass, still looking down at Patrick.

"Give me your hand," Everett called down, extending an arm.

Patrick didn't answer. Leo had had enough of humans for one day. He roared again, jerking toward Patrick, ready to take whatever meal he could get. Patrick backed against the wall, spreading his hands out against the sunbaked concrete.

"Give me your hand," Everett insisted a second time. "I'll pull you up."

"It's too much of a risk," Patrick said. The second he turned his back on Leo, the lion would pounce. If Everett had hold of any part of him, he would be dragged back into the pit with no way to escape. Leo might not have been hungry enough to eat both of them, but he would certainly kill them both.

"Now is not the time for you to be a hero, Patrick." There was enough anger in Everett's voice to send Patrick's heart racing with love. Only a man in love would be angry at someone like him for sacrificing themselves.

"Now is exactly the time for me to be a hero, dammit," he called up to Everett. "I couldn't live with myself if anything happened to you."

"And you think I would be able to go on without you?" Everett asked, incredulous. "If you think that, you're a fool."

"Everett, back away from the pit. Go help Selby," Patrick warned him. "You don't want to watch this."

"I love you, Goddammit," Everett shouted. "I want to spend the rest of my life with you, thumbing my nose at society and not caring a whit who knows what we are. I am not going to watch you be devoured by some demon when there's even a chance that I can do something about it."

Patrick wasn't certain whether it was Everett's words themselves or the deep, all-consuming emotion that came with them. His heart seemed to swell to fill his entire chest. It filled more than that. It eclipsed every bit of need, every cold, hungry part of himself that had ever been. Everything would be all right if he and Everett were together until the end of their days. He would be damned if he let that end come immediately.

He fumbled for the pouch on his belt, not bothering with its tight fastenings. He ripped the already damaged cloth with all his strength, spilling the bread and sausage. It wasn't much—it was a pitiful offering, really—but it felt as though he were offering every ounce of pain in his heart, every shattered dream from his childhood, and every moment he'd wasted in fear to Leo.

"I'm sorry," he sobbed, seeing too much of himself in the lion. "It wasn't your fault. It was never your fault. You didn't deserve this life."

Leo lifted his head slightly, nostrils flaring. Patrick met the lion's eyes, wishing there were a better way to tell the beast everything would end happily for him, then threw the sausage to the far end of the pit.

It was like throwing a tiny pebble into the ocean, but it was enough. Leo followed the sausage with his eyes, then leapt after it. It was hardly even a bite for him, but it gave Patrick just enough time to twist toward Everett, grab his hand, and lunge up the side of the pit with all the strength he possessed.

Between his efforts and Everett's, Patrick made it far enough to hook his leg over the top of the pit. Leo had devoured the sausage by then and saw his last chance slipping away. He roared and lunged forward, swiping his razor-sharp claws at Patrick just as he hoisted his second leg over the pit's edge. The blow came so close that Patrick felt his trousers ruffle.

As soon as he was out of Leo's reach, he and Everett crawled frantically backwards, clinging to each other and panting as though they hadn't drawn breath for days. Every bruise Patrick had earned in the last few, harrowing minutes ached as if he'd just received it. His muscles turned to jelly, and for a moment, he couldn't hold himself up. He flopped to his back, squeezing his eyes shut and clutching Everett's arm as though his life depended on it.

Everett wasn't in any better shape. He groaned as he pressed himself against Patrick's side, but it was more a groan of relief than of pain. Below them, Leo roared in fury. Continued scraping sounds indicated he was trying to get out of the pit.

"We should…." Everett panted, struggling to sit. "We should fetch one of the rifles and put the poor creature out of its misery."

"No." Patrick shook his head hard, wrenching himself to a sitting position. "No, if there's any way at all to save him and to take him to a better home, he deserves to be saved."

Everett winced, but he didn't protest. He nodded, then surged into Patrick, kissing him for all he was worth.

It was a desperate, filthy kiss. Both of them were covered in dirt and blood, but Patrick didn't mind. He needed to feel Everett against him, to know that they'd made it through the worst of it, and that they would be all right. The only thing that stopped him from pushing Everett to his back in the grass and kissing him like a madman was a commotion from the side of the house.

Patrick pushed himself to stand, though every part of him hurt. He raised a hand to his forehead as he looked to the house, finding Selby waving at them from the office window and shouting. Men in police uniforms surged around the edges of the house. Smoke issued from several windows on that side of the house, but there were no flames.

"He did it." Patrick let out a heavy breath. "Cristofori managed to send the Leeds police."

Patrick reached for Everett, helping him to stand as well. Everett leaned heavily against him as they started back to the house.

"Are you well?" he asked, concern rushing in to fill all the places where his fear had lodged just minutes before.

"I will be," Everett said, managing a smile. "That bastard, Chisolm, cut me before tossing me into the pit. I hit my head when I fell. I didn't come to until you—" He glanced suddenly around, wincing for a moment, as though the movement were too much. After a short groan, he said, "Where is he? Where is Chisolm? I'll kill him with my bare hands."

"He and Castleford fled nearly as soon as I reached the pit." Disappointment swooped through Patrick's gut. "We can only hope that Selby or Eastleigh's driver stopped them from leaving the estate."

Patrick's hopes were crushed within ten minutes.

"None of them are anywhere to be found," Selby informed them once they made it back to the house. "Half the staff has fled with them. At least a dozen small fires had been set throughout the house, but whether through poor planning, haste, or indifference on the part of the staff, they failed to create the sort of conflagration I know my brother would have loved."

The young, timid maid who had stayed behind and

now dabbed at Everett's face with a wet cloth, attempting to clean his wounds, peeked dolefully up at Patrick. "Lord Castleford knew someone would catch them someday," she said, her voice barely audible. "He's had an escape plan in place for years."

"Do you know what that plan is?" Patrick asked her.

His renewed hopes were dashed when the maid shook her head no. "Only that he planned to burn the whole house down. It's a bad house to work in, this one," she said. "Too many secrets."

She started crying, and nothing anyone could say or do convinced her to stop, even though she kept working diligently on Everett's face. None of the other servants were willing to speak up either.

"They're gone, then," Selby said with a sigh, rubbing a hand over his face. "And it's all my fault."

"You didn't know," Cristofori—who had returned with the officers from Leeds, as he'd promised—said, attempting to rest a soothing hand on Selby's shoulder.

Selby shook him off, tensing as though the touch had gone through him like electricity. "It is my fault," he said, pinched with guilt. "I turned a blind eye for too long. I should have known my brother was the worst sort of—" He pressed his lips shut, shaking his head. "I did nothing. I let everything slide past me without asking questions, without wanting to see it." He glanced pitifully to Cristofori. "I ignored everything because it was easier for me. I am the worst sort of man imaginable."

"You're not—" Cristofori started.

Selby shook his head, holding up a hand as if to ward him off, then turned and ran from the room.

Patrick watched him leave, then shifted his uneasy gaze to Cristofori. Cristofori's pained look held a lifetime of regret behind it.

As soon as Cristofori noticed Patrick watching him, he let out a defeated breath and shook his head. "I'd go after him, but I don't think it would do any good. I should head back to Leeds and find a telegraph office to let David and Lionel know what's happened and that Chisolm, Castleford, and Eastleigh got away."

"They won't get very far," Everett said, in spite of the fact that the color had drained from his face and a knot the size of an egg had appeared on his forehead. Combined with the vicious cut across his face—a cut that would leave a deep scar—it made him look a fright. But as far as Patrick was concerned, he had never looked so appealing.

"There aren't many places they can go," Patrick agreed, sinking to sit on the sofa by Everett and the maid's side. "Besides which, with all the evidence we uncovered here today, everyone across England, and half the continent as well, will be looking for them."

Everett looked as though he would argue the point for a moment, but he gave up, letting out a breath and taking Patrick's hand. "In any case," he said. "Now that this is over, all I want to do is go home."

CHAPTER 20

The roar of the crowd that filled the theater to celebrate Everett's triumphant return to the stage after a fortnight was so deafening that Patrick winced and held a hand to his ear, even though he stood in the wings, out of the direct impact of the applause. Tickets for that evening's special performance had sold out within minutes of the box office opening. If the rumors were true, resellers were fetching as much as fifty pounds and more for prime seats. All because of a few, whispered rumors that had made their way around London in the past two weeks.

"I wish he'd've let me cover up that scar," Olivia, the actress who had played opposite Everett in the previous production said as she leaned into Patrick's side, watching Everett take his bow and blow kisses to his followers. "It's just so obvious and gruesome under the stage lights."

Patrick chuckled. "He wants everyone to see it, stitches and all."

"But he had such a pretty face," Olivia sighed.

"He still has a pretty face." Patrick shrugged. More than pretty, in his opinion. Everett was the most gorgeous thing he'd ever seen, scar or no scar. "He's going to wear that scar as a badge of honor until the day he dies," he said aloud.

Olivia hummed, grinned, and rested a hand on his arm. "You're a lucky devil, Patrick Wrexham." She winked at him before swanning out onto the stage to join Everett in a comedic sketch the two of them had worked out for the return performance.

Old tendrils of anxiety wound their way around Patrick's stomach, squeezing him until he had a hard time catching his breath. From the moment they had stepped back into the theater after their jaunt to York, Everett had made no secret about what Patrick meant to him. He regaled everyone he could with tales of Patrick's heroism in saving him from the lion. Patrick could have blushed and stammered his way through that praise without thinking too much about it, but Everett also informed every one of his theater colleagues that Patrick was the love of his life, that he'd moved Patrick into his flat and into his bed, and that he was no longer interested in what he coyly called "private performances". Patrick had expected hellfire and brimstone to rain down on him at Everett's careless declaration, but the theater people couldn't have cared less. Several had congratulated him and sought to bring him into their inner circle by chatting his ear off whenever Everett was otherwise engaged.

It was an odd thing, to have friends. Friends who knew who he was and didn't care. As Everett and Olivia caused the audience to roar with laughter at the scene they played, Patrick glanced around the backstage area. He knew every stagehand and aspiring actor by name, knew a bit about their lives as well. Rob, the young man with massive forearms who manned the ropes connected to pieces of scenery in the fly space nodded to him with a friendly smile before tugging on a thick rope to change the backdrop. Emma, the costume mistress edged past him with a quick, "Sorry, love," as she positioned herself for a quick-change Olivia had coming up. The rest of the backstage crew accepted his presence as though he were one of their own.

He *was* one of them now, ever since returning from York and handing in his resignation to Lord Clerkenwell. He was Officer Wrexham no more. Now he was simply Everett Jewel's bodyguard to outsiders and Everett Jewel's lover to those in the know. Best of all, his new position came with living arrangements, enough food for him to never have to worry about going hungry again, and a variety of other benefits that he certainly wasn't going to discuss with his new friends at the theater, though he suspected most of them knew far more than he did about it.

A smile broke out on his usually stern face at the thought, but it was cut short as the buzz of whispers and soft talking drew his attention to the back of the backstage area. He frowned, sending one last glance out to the action on the stage, then marched away to tell whoever was making the racket to be quiet.

"Did you hear there was another sighting?" Jenny, a young costume woman, asked before Patrick could do more than touch a finger to his lips to get her and the two stagehands gathered around her to settle down.

"Of who?" Patrick asked, his voice a low growl.

"Eastleigh, I think," Jenny said. "Though it could have been Chisolm. I didn't have time to stay for the whole story."

"Where did they spot him?" Harry, one of the stagehands, asked.

"Trying to board a ship in Liverpool," Jenny said, her eyes wide. Even in the darkness backstage, her features stood out, bright with excitement. "He was trying to escape, to be sure. But they stopped him from going aboard."

"Did they nab him?" Roger, the other stagehand, asked.

Jenny shook her head. "He got away, yet again." She blew out a breath. "I tell you what. Those evil nobs certainly are slippery. I think that's the fourth time in the last fortnight that one or more of them was nearly caught trying to leave the country."

"I hope all three of them are nabbed, and soon," Harry said, a growl in his voice. "My bird, Betty's, cousin's friend was one of the girls taken by that lot. Right out of the position she had as a maid in some toff's house in Mayfair."

"Was she one of the ones they found?" Jenny asked, suddenly full of concern.

"She was, by the grace of God," Harry said, crossing himself for good measure. "But not before some damage was done."

Jenny made a sad noise, resting a hand on Harry's arm for a moment. "At least all the children they've rescued are being reunited with their families or moved to a safe place to recover."

"I heard they found another great lump of them at a factory in Derby," Roger said. "Two dozen of the poor things, all chained to the machinery."

Patrick's gut turned at the revelation, but his flash of misery for those children resolved into relief. It was true. Using the documentation he and Everett—and Selby, though Patrick still had his reservations about the man— had uncovered at Castleford Estate, factories and brothels across England had been discovered and raided by the police. Hundreds of children had been rescued in the past fortnight. Jenny was right about most of them being returned to their families. Stephen Siddel and Max Hillsboro had been instrumental in finding safe homes for the others.

But Stephen and Max's efforts on behalf of the children had been utterly eclipsed when word got out that Everett had earned his disfiguring scar by working with Scotland Yard to expose and attempt to arrest the three noblemen at the center of the ring. All of London had gone mad with excitement at the idea of dashing, heroic Everett using his charm and talent to wheedle his way into the confidence of Chisolm, Eastleigh, and Castleford to bring them down. The vast majorities of the rumors circulating about how the ring had been broken were false at best and patently absurd at worst, but no one who had truly been involved minded Everett getting all of the attention in the least. And Everett, of course, lapped that attention up like wine.

Another swell of applause drowned out the backstage conversation and indicated the end of the show. Jenny and the boys dashed off to their duties as the actors paraded out to the stage for their curtain calls. Patrick returned to his spot in the wings, watching Everett preen and pose for his audience. He shook his head, heart brimming with affection, as Everett made a ham of himself. That was why Patrick loved him, though. Everett was himself, through and through, and he made no apologies for it.

Patrick had to wait through the rousing applause, through Everett's traditional curtain call musical number, then through three encores before the audience would let him leave the stage. They continued to roar and demand more even as Everett dashed into the relative darkness where Patrick stood.

"You enjoyed that, didn't you?" Patrick asked, handing Everett a towel for him to mop his face. He could see from the way Everett winced slightly that his cut was stinging, but that didn't dampen his spirits in the least.

"Immensely," Everett replied with almost orgasmic enthusiasm, taking Patrick's hand with his free hand and leading him through the backstage area to the hall and his dressing room. "The stage is my home. It was agony to be away from it for so long."

Patrick laughed. "A fortnight is hardly a long time."

"And how would you feel if the two of us were parted for two weeks?" Everett asked, sending a sassy look over his shoulder as they dodged other performers and stagehands to duck into his room.

"Point taken," Patrick chuckled.

"Speaking of—" As soon as Everett tugged Patrick into his dressing room and shut the door, he pushed Patrick against the wall and brought his mouth crashing over his.

Patrick gasped in surprise, but that only allowed Everett to kiss him deeper and thrust his tongue against his. Everett's hands seemed to go everywhere at once, brushing Patrick's side and reaching for his instantly excited cock. Patrick did his best to keep up and return Everett's passion. He should have guessed that his arrogant lover would be in a state after receiving so much applause and adoration on stage.

The only thing, Patrick suspected, that kept Everett from tearing off both of their clothes and bending him over the room's settee for a quick and powerful fuck was the sound of someone clearing their throat from said settee.

Everett jerked straight and whipped around as though he'd been doused by cold water. Patrick tensed hard, glancing past Everett to see Lionel Mercer lounging, catlike, in the settee.

"Don't stop on my account," Lionel said, something sharp in his eyes, in spite of the smoothness of his high voice. "I haven't been a voyeur in ages. I've almost forgotten how the whole thing goes."

"What do you want, Lionel?" Everett snapped, chest heaving as he caught his breath.

Lionel arched one elegant eyebrow. "Is that any way to greet the man who has come to bring you good tidings of great joy?"

Everett laughed. "You're no angel."

Lionel shrugged—managing to make the gesture look like the height of elegance—and stood. "I most certainly am. A fallen angel." He fixed Everett with a coquettish look that would have made Patrick burn with jealousy, if not for the exhaustion rimming Lionel's eyes and making him seem even more pale and gaunt than usual.

"You have news?" Patrick said, stepping away from the wall and slightly in front of Everett. It was a cheap, defensive gesture, but one the part of him that still couldn't believe Everett loved him needed to make.

Lionel rolled his shoulders slightly, losing some of his cockiness. "I'm not a threat to you," he told Patrick quietly. As quixotic as Lionel Mercer was, Patrick knew him absolutely to be a man of his word. He let his defensiveness drop as Lionel went on with, "David thinks he knows where Chisolm has run off to." He stared hard at Everett.

Everett swallowed noticeably. "It's not good news until you tell me he's dead," he said in a hoarse voice.

Lionel tipped his head to the side and made a thoughtful sound. "He will be if I ever see him face-to-face again."

Patrick's brow shot up. To look at him, he wouldn't have thought Lionel Mercer was the sort to kill anyone. Then again, the man did have that edge of danger to him.

Everett narrowed his eyes. "What did Chisolm ever do to you?"

Lionel's expression changed in an instant from the elegant dandy about town to a mask of stone and steel. He stared at Everett for a long time, the air in the room crackling, before taking an almost whimsical breath and smiling. "I just thought you would want to know that the man's reign of terror is at its end. You may rest easy from now on, knowing that past injustices have been righted and every dog will have his day."

With a nod for Patrick, Lionel headed for the door.

"Why did you really come here?" Everett asked before he made it across the room. "You could have told me all that next time you saw me at the club. You could have sent a note."

Lionel glanced over his shoulder at Everett as he neared the door and reached for the handle. There was something faded and wistful in his expression that reminded Patrick a little too much of Leo—starving and abandoned. "I just wanted to make sure you were well," he said, his voice lower, less artful. "I wanted to make certain you were happy." He glanced past Everett to Patrick, nodding. "You are."

For several, long seconds, Lionel held Patrick's gaze. It felt to Patrick as though some sort of torch were being passed. Finally, Lionel glanced back to Everett, his smile returning. He winked, then threw open the door and left the room.

Everett stood where he was for a moment before shaking his head. "I will never understand Lionel Mercer as long as I live."

Patrick swallowed the lump in his throat. "I understand him," he said, barely above a whisper.

Everett turned to him, mouth pulled sideways, as though he were about to make a joke. He remained quiet when he saw the look on Patrick's face, though.

"Let me just remove this make-up, and we can go home," he said, crossing to the vanity on one side of the room. "Unless you'd rather join the raucous crowd at The Cock and Bear tonight."

"You know I'd rather go home." Patrick took a deep breath, letting the awkwardness of the moment pass. He moved to sit on the edge of the vanity, grinning at Everett as he washed his face. "With you, I'd always rather go home."

Everett met his affectionate smile with one of his own

that promised every sort of sin once they were safely in their own flat. He hurried through his ablutions, working gingerly around his scar, which had a long way to go before it was completely healed. When that was done, Everett changed into his street clothes, and they made their way to the back of the theater to make a grand exit.

It felt as though half of the audience had crowded the alley behind the theater to greet Everett at the stage door as they left. Everett played his role perfectly, preening and welcoming the attention with open arms. Patrick, for his part, had the chance to show off his strength and to prove to anyone who may have doubted why Everett Jewel suddenly had his own, personal bodyguard why he was needed. Patrick held off overzealous admirers as they rushed in for an autograph. He kindly removed people who came too close or crowded Everett too much. He cleared a path for them to slowly make their way out of the alley. And once they reached the street, he hailed a cab and held the door open, blocking anyone who thought Everett was still in the habit of taking his followers home with him for the evening from leaping into the carriage.

"You've earned your keep today, Wrexham," Everett laughed once they were safely inside the carriage. "But you'd best be sure I will require you to earn it even more once we return home."

Patrick laughed—half at Everett's joke and half at the shiver of nervousness that shot through him at the suggestion. On the one hand, three weeks seemed like the blink of an eye for their budding romance. On the other, it felt as though he had belonged to Everett and Everett had belonged to him for their whole lives.

It felt as though he'd lived in Everett's flat for a lifetime, as though the flat had always been his as well, once they reached home and shut themselves away in their own private paradise.

"All in all," Everett said, shedding his clothing piece by piece as he walked across the main room toward the bedroom, "I'd say that tonight was a success."

"The audience certainly enjoyed the performance." Patrick followed him, picking up each discarded item with a smirk and draping it over his arm in a growing pile. "So did you."

By the time they reached the bedroom, Everett was down to just his shirt and trousers, which were already unbuttoned. "The only performance I'm interested in tonight is yours, Officer Wrexham."

Patrick shook his head with a smirk. "I'm not an officer anymore, remember?"

Everett plucked his discarded clothes out of Patrick's arms and tossed them onto a chair in the corner of the bedroom before turning back to Patrick and sliding his arms over Patrick's shoulders. "You'll always be my own, personal copper," he said, mischief and flirtation in his eyes. "And seeing as I have been a shameless reprobate tonight, I think you should punish me with the full force of the law."

Patrick laughed and shook his head. "You are a fool,

Everett," he said, then circled his arms around Everett's trim waist. "But you're my fool, and I rather like you foolish."

"Good," Everett hummed. "Because my character isn't likely to change anytime soon. Unless—"

Patrick tugged him flush against his torso, slanting his mouth over Everett's to stop whatever new nonsense he was going to suggest. He might not have been half a fraction as experienced as Everett, but in the past fortnight, in spite of bruises, cuts, and bodies battered from the events at Castleford Estate, they'd spent enough time learning and exploring each other that Patrick knew what Everett liked. And at the moment, he was more than inclined to give Everett all of that and more.

Patrick teased his mouth, nibbling on his lower lip and sucking his tongue before invading Everett's mouth with just enough force to have Everett moaning for more. Everett hadn't been lying when he'd intimated to Patrick weeks before that he enjoyed playing the more submissive role. It was erotic to watch the way he came undone as Patrick used his strength to ply Everett against him and ultimately to shove him toward the bed. In a way, it didn't make sense to Patrick that someone who had been so badly abused as a youth would enjoy being overpowered by a man larger and stronger than him. On the other hand, being overpowered was only an illusion. They both knew that Everett had as much or more control than Patrick ever would, because everything they did was his choice and his alone.

"I don't think I'm going to last long tonight," Everett panted as he undid the buttons of Patrick's jacket and waistcoat, shoving them aside. He tugged Patrick's shirt free of his waistband and spread his hands along his hot sides as well. "I'm wound too tight from the performance as it is."

"Fortunately," Patrick said, shrugging out of his clothes as he nudged Everett toward the bed, "whether either of us lasts long or not, all we need is a short rest and we can go at it again. As many times as you'd like, in any way you like."

Everett let out a shaky breath. "God above, I love you," he sighed, looping his hand around Patrick's neck and pulling him in for a kiss.

They shed the rest of their clothes somehow—Patrick was far more engaged by the taste of Everett's lips and the way he moaned with pleasure as he kissed and nipped his way down the line of Everett's neck—and tumbled into bed. It still felt odd on several levels for Patrick to be on top, with Everett spread and aroused beneath him. There were so many things he wanted to do, so many ways he wanted to tease and treat Everett's body, that he didn't know where to begin. Fortunately, he would have the rest of his life to do everything and then some.

"I can't wait," Everett panted as Patrick kissed his shoulder and teased his hand between them, stroking Everett's prick in a way he knew was far too gentle. "I want you in me. Now. I want you to make me yours."

"You are mine," Patrick said in a gruff voice, teasing his tongue across one of Everett's nipples before shifting to crash their mouths together. He ground his hips against Everett's for good measure, earning a passionate groan from both of them. Every inch of their bodies that touched was alive with pleasure. "You are mine, and you always will be."

He had half a mind to draw things out as long as possible and to make Everett crazy with lust in the process. Everett was positively wicked when he wanted it so badly he lost his mind, as Patrick had learned a few nights before. But he pushed to the side, reaching for the jar of ointment sitting ostentatiously on the bedside table. Keeping that jar there was Everett's way of loudly announcing to the world that he wouldn't hide who he was or what he liked, and what he liked was being fucked.

Luckily for Everett, Patrick was fully willing to embrace the fact that he liked fucking. He used a generous amount of the ointment on his throbbing and expectant cock before teasing Everett's arse with what was left on his fingers. Everett made a sound of utterly transported delight at the teasing, dropping his knees to the sides and lifting his hips in invitation. Patrick wasn't in the mood to wait, lifting Everett's hips and spreading him even more before guiding himself home and thrusting with a satisfied groan.

It was far more beautiful than any ignorant outside observer could possibly know. Patrick moved slowly until he found his rhythm, then picked up his pace and intensity, giving Everett everything he wanted. It was more than just two bodies satisfying each other, it was two souls becoming one, two beings entwined and entangled with each other. True to his word, Everett climaxed with lightning speed, spilling his seed between the two of them with a moan that Patrick felt all through him. Patrick took longer to finish, slowing down on purpose as soon as Everett's body softened with post-orgasmic bliss. The way they were joined felt so amazingly good that he wanted it to go on forever.

He could only hold out for so long, though, and when pleasure burst through him as he convulsed inside of Everett, everything felt exactly right with the world.

"I love you," he panted, relaxing atop Everett as Everett curled his body around Patrick's. "More than I ever thought possible."

"And I love you," Everett sighed, affection warm in his voice.

They flopped to their sides, entwined together, mouths meeting for several heady, soul-filling kisses. In his heart, Patrick knew those kisses would never end, no matter what the world threw at the two of them. They'd overcome more than most men would ever face, battled more demons than a human soul should ever see, in order to be together, and nothing would stop the two of them from living their lives together as one for the rest of their days.

EPILOGUE

"The fact that Eastleigh, Castleford, and Chisolm have managed to escape capture, even when we've known exactly where they will be, is a testament to the fact that they knew the ring would eventually be thwarted," Lord Clerkenwell said as he paced the offices of Dandie & Wirth.

"They're clever," David said. It felt like a rock in his stomach to admit as much. "Only clever men could carry on with what they did for so long without getting caught."

Clerkenwell snorted. "The fact that we're still uncovering pockets of kidnapped children and accomplices responsible for stealing and hiding them is proof of that."

"Have most of the children been rescued at this point?" Hope gnawed at David's heart. It would be a crying shame if, after all their effort, even one child slipped through the cracks. And they had yet to find Lily Logan.

Clerkenwell seemed to sense his thoughts. He continued to pace with a grave expression. "It pains me to say that at least some of the children will never be found. Some were shipped abroad, for one. I'm doing the best I can in connection with the foreign office, but those poor souls will be the hardest to recover of all."

David hummed, wishing there were more he could do. A stray thought hit him, and he asked, "What about the lion?"

"The one Castleford kept in a pit on his estate?" Clerkenwell paused and shrugged. "As I understand it, a zoologist in York was called in to assess the animal. The verdict was that the poor thing was too enfeebled to be returned to Africa and too mistreated to be trusted at a public zoo. But the man seemed to know of an eccentric Scotsman with a personal menagerie who was willing to take him."

David scowled. "That's hardly a fitting end for a once-noble beast."

"It's the best we could hope for. At least the lion will be fed and looked after by the Scotsman."

"Which is more than some of those poor children can say," David finished with a sigh.

He stood from where he had been leaning against Lionel's desk and crossed to where the papers and files Clerkenwell had brought him were resting on one of the side tables next to the office's two sofas. Before he could form his next line of questions, the office door opened and Lionel walked in.

Twin feelings of longing and fury pulsed through David. Lionel looked as though he hadn't slept the night before. He had the same sort of haunted look that he'd worn when the two of them had first met several years ago, when John Dandie had hired him. That alone was enough to set David's nerves on edge.

The moment Lionel realized David wasn't alone, his entire countenance changed from pale and closed-off to cheery and amiable. "Lord Clerkenwell," he said, shrugging out of his cloak, hanging it on the rack by the door, then greeting Clerkenwell with an outstretched hand. "To what do we owe the pleasure?" The way he emphasized the word "pleasure" set David's teeth on edge. That would be at the forefront of Lionel's mind.

Clerkenwell laughed as he shook Lionel's hand. "While I appreciate your charm, Mr. Mercer, I believe my lovely wife wouldn't."

Lionel's smile was too good-humored for David's liking, as if the only reason Lionel was flirting with a man they both knew adored his wife and family was to irritate him. "The handsomest ones are always taken," Lionel sighed.

"Lord Clerkenwell came here to ask our assistance in closing the last bits of the investigation into the kidnapping ring," David said, knowing full well his jealousy was on display.

Lionel stared at him with one eyebrow arched,

tension bristling between them as it had been since the confrontation at The Chameleon Club over Everett Jewel. He turned deliberately back to Clerkenwell with movements worthy of a dancer. "What can we do for you, my lord?" he asked, still flirting.

Clerkenwell's grin was amused, though David wasn't sure it was wise to encourage Lionel. "As I'm sure you know, Eastleigh, Castleford, and Chisolm are still at large."

"So I've heard." Lionel's expression hardened to business, and he crossed to the stove in the corner of the room to see about tea—a sure sign his mind was working.

"The fact is, they've managed to evade capture at every turn these last two weeks," Clerkenwell went on. "As I was just explaining to your partner—"

"He's not my partner," Lionel cut him off, sharp and curt.

David fought with everything he had not to take offense, not to let his heart break over Lionel's coldness.

Clerkenwell cleared his throat. "Yes, well, the point is, Scotland Yard can only do so much. We are forced to go through proper channels in our search for the men. But if someone who wasn't bound by procedure—or the law, even—were to take up the search for the three noblemen, perhaps they could be caught and brought to justice after all."

"Are you asking us to use whatever channels we have available to hunt Eastleigh, Castleford, and Chisolm down?" David asked. "Even if they are less than legal?"

"I am not at liberty to make any sort of statement," Clerkenwell said, his expression telling another story. "But I can say that if a few eggs were broken in the process of hunting the men, all the king's horses and all the king's men might be willing to look the other way."

"Delicious," Lionel said, pouring water from the pitcher David had filled earlier into the teapot to heat.

"Do you have any idea where any of the three of them are?" David asked.

Clerkenwell nodded. "We believe that Eastleigh is trying to leave the country through Liverpool or some other port on the west coast. Chisolm may be trying to head to his holdings in the Caribbean, though he must know we have agents there as well. And Castleford has headed north, to Scotland."

"That doesn't sound like much of a challenge," Lionel said, leaving the stove to join the discussion. "I'd wager we could have all three of them rounded up and incarcerated within a month."

Clerkenwell sent him an appraising look. "You think you're that good?"

"My lord, I am the best," Lionel said with a look that sent a chill down David's spine.

Unfortunately for him, that chill settled in an entirely uncomfortable and inconvenient spot, making David's blood heat. He held himself doubly stiff because of it. Three weeks ago, he might have used that burst of energy to tease and tempt Lionel, but not now. After the way he'd thrown himself at Jewel, the way he'd made it clear to everyone who had been in that dining room at The Chameleon Club, Lionel didn't deserve the sort of interest David had considered showing him for so long.

But damned if he could convince his own body—not to mention his heart—of that fact.

"We'll do it," he said, taking charge as best he could. "We'll hunt the three down for you. Rest assured that they will answer for their crimes."

Lionel eyed him as though resentful that David had been the one to formally take up the charge. Then again, Lionel had been nothing but resentful of David since David had started rebuffing his advances after that horrible afternoon.

"Those men will be made to answer for their crimes," Lionel added in the sort of tone he used when he wanted to prove he was more than just a pretty face. "Particularly Chisolm."

David frowned. Was Lionel's resentment of Chisolm due to the horrors the man had perpetrated on Jewel? Or was there another reason? He could ask, but he didn't want to give Lionel the satisfaction of letting on how much he cared. He would have to pry the truth out of Lionel some other way.

"I put my trust in you, gentlemen," Clerkenwell said, nodding at them both with a grim smile. "This investigation is in your hands now. I'm relying on you to destroy this kidnapping ring and the men behind it once and for all."

JUST A LITTLE DANGER

I hope you've enjoyed Everett and Patrick's story! They were a really fun couple to write. I've enjoyed coming up with ways for my heroes to be together in spite of society in general's disapproval of LGBTQ people and lifestyles. Historically, it wasn't as hard to create an excuse for two men to be living together as you might think. Especially in the world of theater. I have an extensive background in theater myself (yay Villanova University's Theater Master's Program, class of '02!), and theater people have always been incredibly accepting of alternative lifestyles. Historically, actors have always had a scandalous reputation, and part of the reason why was their acceptance and inclusion of all sorts of people, even <gasp> women! So I am quite confident that Everett and Patrick would be able to live a long and happy life together without fear of judgement from their closest friends. The public, however.... Well, let's just say it's a smart idea to set Patrick up as Everett's bodyguard.

What about David and Lionel, you ask? What are the deep, emotional currents running between them? And what secrets has Lionel been keeping from David? What things has David been keeping from Lionel, particularly where the mysterious John Dandie is concerned? How will the two of them track down Eastleigh, Castleford, and Chisolm and bring them to justice when there is so much tension between the two of them that they might destroy each other before seeing that justice is served? And will they be able to locate and rescue Lily Logan in the process? Find out all of this and more in book four of The Brotherhood, *Just a Little Seduction*. Keep clicking to read a bit of Chapter One!

ALSO, IF YOU'RE INTERESTED IN LEARNING MORE about Jack Craig, Lord Clerkenwell, and how he ended up married to the wild and feisty Lady Bianca Marlowe—not to mention the story of how he rose so high in the ranks of Scotland Yard so fast—be sure to check out the book *It's Only a Scandal if You're Caught*, part of my May Flowers series.

IF YOU ENJOYED THIS BOOK AND WOULD LIKE TO HEAR more from me, please sign up for my newsletter! When you sign up, you'll get a free, full-length novella, A Passionate Deception. Victorian identity theft has never been so exciting in this story of hope, tricks, and starting over. Part of my West Meets East series, A Passionate Deception can be read as a stand-alone. Pick up your free copy today by signing up to receive my newsletter (which I only send out when I have a new release)!

Sign up here: http://eepurl.com/cbaVMH

. . .

Are you on social media? I am! Come and join the fun on Facebook: http://www.facebook.com/merryfarmerreaders

I'm also a huge fan of Instagram and post lots of original content there: https://www.instagram.com/merryfarmer/

AND NOW, GET STARTED ON JUST A LITTLE SEDUCTION…

London – June, 1890

Whenever there was a vital task to be done, David Wirth was the one who did it. It had been true from David's earliest childhood, when his hardworking parents handed him the responsibility of keeping his younger siblings out of harm in their rough-and-tumble, working-class neighborhood. It stayed true when his father had earned enough to move them onto a quieter, middle-class square in Belgravia. It had been true all through university as David paid his own way by tutoring his higher-born classmates. And it had been true when he and John Dandie banded together after leaving university to form the law offices of Dandie & Wirth. David was always the man people could count on to make even the most impossible tasks possible. He was a man with something to prove.

That had never been truer than as he walked from table to table in the dining room of Stephen Siddel and Max Hillsboro's newly-established orphanage in Earl's Court, interviewing the recently rescued children who had been victims of a kidnapping ring.

"Your name is Jimmy Hollis?" he asked the frightened boy of six who sat on the lap of Annie Ross, a woman who had worked side-by-side with Stephen at the orphanage in its old location and who had relocated, along with her mother, to the new site.

The boy nodded, his eyes wide with fright.

"And you were taken off the street in Limehouse?" David asked on, making his voice as soft as he could and smiling, in spite of the seriousness of his questions.

Again, Jimmy nodded.

"Do you have a mama or papa who is looking for you?"

Jimmy shook his head.

David's heart squeezed in his chest, and he met Annie's eyes. "Another orphan?"

"He must be," Annie said with a sigh. "Or, if not an orphan, his family must be bad enough that he doesn't want to go back."

David had heard the same story too many times in the last few days. He and Lionel had been working to reunite the rescued children with their families, but more often than not, the poor things either didn't have any or didn't want to go back.

A swell of determination filled David. "We'll find a place for you, lad." He rose, ruffling Jimmy's already messy hair as he did. He had to prove that he was competent and capable of so much more than people assumed a boy from his background, a boy just like Jimmy, was capable of. "Mr. Siddel's orphanage is for girls, but Sister Constance is willing to take in any boys."

"And Lord Hillsboro has been pressing Mr. Siddel to start an orphanage for boys across the square," Annie added.

"That's a good idea." David smiled and stepped away, heading to the next table and the next group of rescued children.

The child kidnapping ring had been broken, thanks to the efforts of actor Everett Jewel and Officer Patrick Wrexham, not to mention the weeks of work David himself, and his business partner, Lionel Mercer, had put into tracking down the ringleaders. The work wasn't over yet, though. Not only were there dozens of children to return to their families or to find homes for, the ringleaders—all three of them noblemen of high rank—had disappeared when the police raided Castleford Estate in Yorkshire. Enough evidence had been secured to arrest Lord Castleford, Lord Eastleigh, and Lord Chisolm for their crimes, but the men were still on the loose. Rage rolled through David's gut every time he thought about how easily the nobs had gotten away. The same nobs who looked down on men like him simply because of where they were born. They wouldn't get away entirely, though. Not if he had anything to say about it.

A chorus of light laughter broke the gloom of David's thoughts, and he turned toward a table of slightly older girls at the other end of the room. Lionel sat among them, reading from a leather-bound book, a pair of spectacles balanced on his nose. His expression was as grave as a minister's, but the girls all beamed at him as though he were a clown performing magic tricks on a stage.

A hitch formed in David's chest as he watched Lionel. The man was dressed impeccably, as usual, in a dove grey suit with a lavender cravat. Not a hair on his head was out of place. His pale face was splashed with just enough color to make him seem lively. The way his lips moved as he read to the girls hinted at humor, even though David was too far away to hear what he was saying. The gentleness of Lionel's face was in direct contrast to the broad lines of his shoulders and the decidedly masculine, though slender, set of his body. Lionel was an erotic blend of masculine and feminine that never failed to leave David breathless. Which was inconvenient in a room filled with children.

He sucked in a breath, forcing himself to stop watching Lionel and get on with his business. But the second he resumed walking to the next table, Lionel darted a covert look at him. He managed it without moving a single muscle, only his eyes, and the effect had David breaking out in prickles down his back. It was no surprise to him that Lionel was aware of him staring. Lionel always knew when David was watching him. Possibly because David was always watching him.

David cleared his throat and sank into a free chair at a table with three boys who looked to be between nine and eleven. "Hello," he said, holding out his hand as though they were adults. "I'm Mr. David Wirth. Has Mr. Siddel explained who I am?"

"You're the man trying to find people's families," the boy with ginger hair said.

"That's correct. Can you tell me anything that might help us search?"

"Fred here cries for his mama in his sleep." The ginger boy stuck his thumb out at the mousey boy sitting next to him.

"What's her name, lad, and where are you from? I'm sure we can find her and reunite the two of you," David said.

"She's dead, sir," Fred confessed, lowering his head. "Trampled by a horse two years ago. I got no other family."

David let out a sympathetic breath and reached out to pat the boy's hand. He'd been hearing the same story over and over from the remaining children. Everyone who had a family they could be reunited with had already been taken home. The ones who were left had no homes to go to.

The sensation that thought brought with it was oddly familiar, tender, aching, and emotional. David glanced across the room to Lionel, feeling it acutely in his chest. Lionel was still reading and the girls around him continued to giggle, but there was a distinct tension in the air, tension in the distance between him and Lionel, a barrier keeping them apart in spite of the pulse of emotion that throbbed between them.

David let out a breath and leaned back in his chair, rubbing a hand over his face.

"You all right, guv'nor?" the ginger boy asked.

David lowered his hands and sent the boy a lopsided smile. "I honestly have no idea."

And he didn't. In the last few weeks, his life had gone from business as usual to a jungle of intense and conflicting emotions, and all because of Lionel. He didn't try to hide the way he stared at his partner and thorn in his side. He'd never hidden the way he felt about Lionel from himself. Lionel captivated him. He had almost from the moment John had hired him four years before, right before he left for Manchester and a new life. Lionel was brilliant, powerful, and beautiful. It was impossible not to want him in every way. And for a while there, David had been convinced he was on the verge of having him at last.

Until Everett Jewel had blasted into the picture, like a cannonball tearing down a wall.

No, that wasn't fair. Jewel wasn't interested in Lionel and hadn't been for years. Besides which, Jewel was happy as a clam with Patrick Wrexham now. But Jewel was also under Lionel's skin somehow, as evidenced by the very public argument they'd had at The Chameleon

Club a fortnight ago. An argument that had proven to David that there was no place for him in Lionel's heart as long as he still carried a torch for Jewel.

Nothing destroyed a man's pride faster than being hopelessly in love with a man who loved someone else.

But there was something else, something David couldn't put his finger on. He couldn't shake how uncharacteristically upset Lionel had become during the argument with Jewel or some of the vague things Lionel had said. There was something Lionel wasn't telling him, something important.

"Oy!" The ginger boy snapped his fingers at David, startling him back to attention. "You gonna stare at the girls all day or you gonna try and find my folks?"

David burst into a smile in spite of himself. "You're a cheeky one, aren't you?" He sat straighter, sending Lionel one last look before focusing on the boy. "What's your name and where are you from?"

"Mick Lang," the ginger boy said. "And I'm from Poplar."

"Alright, Mick." David nodded, charmed by the scamp. "Who are your parents and where can we find them?"

"My dad's Prime Minister Gladstone and mum's the washerwoman," Mick said, then burst into laughter. The two other boys laughed raucously with him.

David smirked, figuring Mick was just as much of an orphan as every other child in the room, but one with a wicked sense of humor. "Well then, Mr. Gladstone," he laughed. "We'll see what we can do about getting you settled."

He leaned in, ready to ask more questions, but a commotion in the doorway snagged everyone's attention. As Jack Craig, Lord Clerkenwell, Assistant Commissioner of Scotland Yard, strode into the orphanage's dining room, every adult who knew who he was rose in respect, David along with them. The urge to prove himself to someone he admired flared so potently in David that he almost laughed at himself. Lionel stood as well, passing the book he'd been reading to one of the girls and stepping away from his table.

"Excuse me, lads," David murmured, doing the same.

By the time David reached the dining room doorway, Stephen and Max had also left their work with the orphans to converge on Lord Clerkenwell, along with Lionel.

"It's an honor to welcome you to our establishment, my lord," Stephen greeted the man with a firm handshake.

"Mr. Siddel." Lord Clerkenwell nodded and smiled as he shook Stephen's hand, then moved on to Max, and then David. "Gentlemen. I've come to see how much progress you've made in settling the children."

When Lord Clerkenwell reached for Lionel's hand, rather than offering his, Lionel bowed. "They are perfect darlings, as you can see," Lionel said with a smile over his shoulder for the girls, who continued to beam at him and giggle.

Lord Clerkenwell chuckled, then turned to Stephen. "I take it the ones who remain are in need of new homes?"

"Correct, my lord." Stephen nodded. "But we're doing our best to accommodate them."

"Good," Lord Clerkenwell said. "And in the meantime, we can move on to the more pressing matter of tracking down the men responsible for their sad state and bringing them to justice."

"As I mentioned the other day, my lord, Lionel and I are at your disposal and would relish the chance to hunt the men down," David said, bristling with the energy to show Lord Clerkenwell what he could accomplish.

Lionel glared sideways at him. "You're speaking for me now, are you?"

David flinched, gut filling with indignation. "I'm speaking on behalf of Dandie & Wirth."

"Oh, of course." Lionel rolled his eyes dramatically. "Because you always speak on behalf of *Dandie & Wirth*."

David turned more fully toward him, crossing his arms. "What in blazes is that supposed to mean?"

"Only that you seem to have elected yourself spokesman for the both of us without consulting me first." Lionel's back was ramrod straight, and his usual aura of calm power crackled with irritation.

David gaped at him. "What has gotten into you these last few weeks?" he asked, too startled by the bitterness of

Lionel's attitude to remember that any argument they fell into would be public.

"Nothing," Lionel said in a hoarse and haunted voice. "Nothing has gotten into me in quite some time, as you well know."

David snapped his lips shut, clenching his jaw, no idea whether Lionel was trying to make a joke about his self-imposed celibacy or drive home the point that they were not lovers, in spite of knowing how David felt about the possibility. Beyond that, the feeling that Lionel was holding something back from him twisted David's gut. He'd never kept secrets before. As badly as David wanted to prove to Lord Clerkenwell that he was competent, he wanted to prove to Lionel that he adored him and could be trusted with his heart even more.

WANT TO READ MORE?
PICK UP JUST A LITTLE SEDUCTION TODAY!

Click here for a complete list of other works by Merry Farmer.

ABOUT THE AUTHOR

I hope you have enjoyed *Just a Little Danger*. If you'd like to be the first to learn about when new books in the series come out and more, please sign up for my newsletter here: http://eepurl.com/cbaVMH And remember, Read it, Review it, Share it! For a complete list of works by Merry Farmer with links, please visit http://wp.me/P5ttjb-14F.

Merry Farmer is an award-winning novelist who lives in suburban Philadelphia with her cats, Torpedo, her grumpy old man, and Justine, her hyperactive new baby. She has been writing since she was ten years old and realized one day that she didn't have to wait for the teacher to assign a creative writing project to write something. It was the best day of her life. She then went on to earn not one but two degrees in History so that she would always have something to write about. Her books have reached the Top 100 at Amazon, iBooks, and Barnes & Noble, and have been named finalists in the prestigious RONE and Rom Com Reader's Crown awards.

ACKNOWLEDGMENTS

I owe a huge debt of gratitude to my awesome beta-readers, Caroline Lee and Jolene Stewart, for their suggestions and advice. And double thanks to Julie Tague, for being a truly excellent editor and assistant!

Click here for a complete list of other works by Merry Farmer.

Printed in Great Britain
by Amazon